STACKING THE DECK

DISCOVERING US SERIES
BOOK ONE

C.L. COLLIER

Cover Design by Amy Queau, Q Designs

Editing by Jenny Sims, Editing4Indies

❀ Created with Vellum

I dedicate this book to Jackie,
simply because you told me to.

Seriously, though, thanks for being a great friend!

PROLOGUE

"She's beautiful," Scott says to me, kissing me on the forehead and looking down at our baby in my arms. "Just like you."

My husband is always saying sweet things like that. I'm a lucky woman.

"What time do you get off tonight?" I ask him as he gathers his gear for work and walks toward the door.

"Late. Probably not until two a.m."

"Be careful. Love you!"

"Love you too," he says as he leaves for work.

I look down at Ellie in my arms. She's fast asleep, and I can't believe she's already three months old. Time has gone by so fast, and I want it to slow down. She's growing so much; I wish I could freeze time to keep her this little a bit longer. I absolutely love being a mom. Scott has been an amazing dad and supportive husband. We waited several years to have a baby, and this new phase in our life has been surreal.

Scott and I decided it would be best for me to be a stay-at-home mom, so instead of going on maternity leave after I had her, I quit my job. I am so thankful for the opportunity to raise her. Now I'm a full-time stay-at-home mom while Scott works his ass off to support us. I'm used to him working long shifts, though, so it's nothing new. Being married to a police sergeant, this is our reality. Hell, I was used to working long shifts myself as an ER nurse before I quit. Now, he's just committing to more overtime since we're a one-income household.

I'll admit, it's hard being home alone with a newborn, but I'm also very grateful for what he's doing for our family. He took a couple of weeks off right after Ellie was born, but now that he's back at work, we only see each other a few hours a day.

Ellie soon falls asleep, and I decide to take advantage of my time. I carefully put her into her bassinet and go about my chores. Who knew a baby could produce so much dirty laundry! She has been the easiest baby so far, though. She sleeps well and is easy to soothe when she's upset, so I consider myself lucky.

As I clean up a pile of mail on the kitchen counter, I find a couple of envelopes that look important. Across the tops of them the words *Final Notice* are written in bold red letters. *What the hell is this?* Maybe it's just junk mail, trying to entice the unsuspecting recipients to open it and look at the contents before tossing it in the garbage. Scott hasn't opened them yet, but my curiosity gets the better of me, so I take a look.

I scan over the first letter I open, and my stomach drops. It's not junk mail. It's real. And it's scary.

I read it three times before I set the paper down on the counter and feel my blood pressure rising. *Holy fuck!* There must be some mistake! How can our house be going into foreclosure? The letter says if we don't make four months' worth of mortgage payments by next month, they will start the foreclosure process?!?

There's no way we can afford to pay that much all at once.

Then I realize, it's November. Does this mean our house is going into foreclosure by Christmas? *This can't be happening to us!*

I feel a lump in my throat as I slowly pick up the other envelope and tear it open. What can be worse than losing the house? One of our cars? Questions are racing through my mind. Why hasn't Scott been making the mortgage payments? Where has all our money been going? This must be a mistake!

The second letter is from a credit card company. It says they will start garnishing Scott's wages next month for the payments. They haven't received a payment in over a year, and they apparently have already gone through the process of suing him for his debt.

What the fuck is happening?

I drop the paper onto the counter and cover my face with my hands. Scott has always been the one in charge of paying our bills. We have a joint bank account, and I often go online to check our balance, but it's always been pretty typical, so I assumed he was making all our payments like normal.

I also know he makes enough money to cover all our bills even without my paycheck. So where the hell is all our money going? *Fuck!* This started way before I even quit my job.

Entering the living room, I go to my phone and quickly pull up our bank app. I log on and decide to scroll through the withdrawals to see what they have been for, which is something I *don't* usually do. As I scroll, I'm shocked at what I see. There have been several ATM withdrawals for hundreds at a time. *What the hell?*

I try to calm my nerves and not overreact. Surely, there *must be* some sort of explanation for all this! This *must be* a mistake! Scott wouldn't let our house go into foreclosure or get this far behind on credit card payments. I want to call him and clear all of this up, but I know he's busy at work and won't have time to discuss this right now. I'll have to wait until he gets home later.

I'm sitting in the living room nursing Ellie at two thirty a.m., one of her usual feeding times, when Scott comes home from work.

"Hey, honey," he says as he walks in and sees us on the recliner. He sets his phone on the table next to my chair, then leans down and kisses the top of my head. He reaches his hand out and cups the back of Ellie's head. "How was her day?" he asks.

"It was good," I reply. I'm dying to ask him about the debt we apparently owe, so I don't waste any time. I take a deep breath, then dive right into it. "Can you tell me why we got a letter in the mail saying our house is going into foreclosure if we don't cough up nine thousand dollars in the next month?"

Scott stands up straight, looking down at me in my chair with a blank look on his face. Ellie pulls away from my breast and starts fussing a bit. That's my cue to switch sides, so I move Ellie to my other side, all the while waiting for a response from my husband.

After I have her situated, I look back up at him. "Well?"

Scott takes a deep breath and rubs the back of his neck with his hand. "Fuck," is all he says, turning his gaze from me to stare at the fireplace.

This is not good. He's not denying it. He's not saying this is a mistake. *This is really happening!* We're going to lose the house!

I need an explanation from him. "Tell me, Scott," I demand, the mixture of anger and worry evident in my tone.

He doesn't look at me as he answers quietly. "I fucked up."

"Well, no shit!" I exclaim, raising my voice. Ellie squirms in my arms, and I'm reminded I need to stay calm for her sake, though I'm feeling anything but calm right now. "Tell me what happened to all our money."

Scott finally turns around to face me again. He crosses his arms across his chest, and I can see the shame written all over his face. I've never seen him look this way, and it's scaring me to death because I know whatever he's about to say to me right now *won't* be good.

"I've been gambling," he says, his voice almost a whisper. "I, um, lost it all."

My stomach drops. I knew he liked to play the occasional poker game with his buddies, but I had *no* clue he was gambling to *this* extent! "What do you mean? Explain it to me," I say, needing to know more.

He sits on the couch and rests his elbows on his knees, placing his head in his hands. "It started with the small games I played every once in a while with the guys at work," he starts, then moves his head up and looks at me. "Then I found out about some other games going on where players would pay big bucks to join but also win big, too."

"Are you kidding me?" I ask him, feeling ashamed that the man I've loved for a decade, a man who I thought was a responsible, confident caretaker of his wife and baby, has thrown everything we've worked hard for down the drain over some poker games.

I feel sick.

Scott shakes his head and looks down. He can't look me in the eye. He knows he fucked up. "I'm sorry," he says as he starts to cry.

"What are we going to do? We'll be out of a house soon! Oh, and your credit card payments are so overdue they're going to start garnishing your wages," I say as I try not to cry again, waiting to hear his response.

Scott just looks at me with tears in his eyes. "I don't know, Brooke."

Ellie has finished feeding and fallen asleep. I carefully adjust her and fix my bra and shirt. I don't want to wake her up now, so I have to continue to talk quietly even though all I want to do is yell and scream at my husband!

"Well, we need to come up with a plan, and you need to stop gambling."

Scott looks at me, but doesn't say a word. I'd really like to know what he's

thinking right now.

"Say something," I prompt.

He shakes his head, and replies, "I have an idea. You might not like it—"

"Don't even tell me if you don't think I'll like it," I interrupt before he can finish. "And it'd better not involve any more gambling!"

"There's a game this weekend," he continues, ignoring what I've just said. "I could win a lot of money that can help us with this debt!"

I'm dumbfounded. How the hell can he even consider this right now? He's lost thousands of dollars already, so how can he possibly think he can win it all back in just one game?

I'm so angry and shocked that I feel completely frozen to my seat. I don't know what to do. I realize I'm shivering, but I'm not cold. My heart is pounding, I'm shaking, and I'm not thinking rationally at the moment.

Refusing to look at Scott any longer, I look down at my precious baby's face. She's asleep in my arms, and I don't want to disturb her. Looking down at her innocence, I realize some things. *My husband has been lying to me for months. We're going to be homeless. Nothing will be the same again.*

What am I going to do? How will Scott and I get through this? I never imagined this happening to *us!*

"I'm sorry," he says as he kneels on the floor in front of me and places his hands on my arm. "Please forgive me. I'll fix this."

Up until now, I've held myself together and not cried. But hearing him discuss it, knowing that this is *not* a misunderstanding and it really is happening, causes the floodgates to open and my tears start to flow.

My life is changed forever.

FOUR MONTHS LATER

I can't breathe. Waking up in the middle of another panic attack, I sit up in bed and reach over to turn on the light on my bedside table. *Just breathe. Relax. Count to ten. Breathe.* I pull my knees up to my chest and rest my forehead on them as I hug my legs. This is the third night in a row a panic attack has caused me to wake. These past few months have been rough, but with everything going on this week, they started to spike again.

I decide to get out of bed and go to the kitchen for a glass of water. I tiptoe past Ellie's room so I don't wake her. At seven months old, she is finally sleeping through the night. I, however, at the ripe young age of thirty-two, can no longer get a good night's sleep. *Funny how things work.*

I get a glass of water and sit down at the kitchen table to drink it. I'm wide-awake now, so I might as well stay up for a bit. At least the panic attack subsided quickly this time. My therapist taught me techniques to get them under control, and I'm so grateful for that. When I first started having them, I thought I was having a heart attack and dying, which only made me freak out even more. Now when I get one, I can recognize it and immediately start calming myself down. It usually works pretty quickly. Sleep, on the other hand, is not so easy to come by nowadays.

I filed for divorce about a month ago. I should feel relieved not to be attached to the man who gambled all our money away, kept our debt a secret from me, then continued to gamble even after I found out about it. Instead, I just feel like a failure. We tried marriage counseling, but it was pointless. Scott has an addiction and chose to put gambling before his wife and daughter. I couldn't take it anymore, so I told him I wanted a divorce.

Scott doesn't want a divorce, but he knows he betrayed me. He knows I can't trust him anymore and that he has to let me go. Luckily, he's not fighting me on anything I'm asking for. He agreed to our parenting plan, which basically gives me sole custody. I've agreed to let him see her when he wants as long as it's scheduled ahead of time. He also has to either drive all the way to Seattle, or at least meet me halfway in Olympia to see her. He's going to pay me child support and spousal support every month, but it won't be a lot. He still has a lot of debt to pay.

He didn't fight me on moving so far away with Ellie, either. He knows he fucked up. Not only that, but he's probably also relieved I won't be around to beg him to stop his nasty habit anymore.

I don't even want to know how much he gambles away every month. It makes me sick to think about it.

After the night I confronted Scott about his gambling, things went downhill for us quickly. He continued to gamble, and he continued to lose. We couldn't make the house payment, so a month later, it went into foreclosure. The credit card company also started garnishing wages from Scott's paychecks. Not only that, but we got *another* letter from *another* credit card company the next month telling us they were going to do the same thing. So now, he has two credit card payments being withdrawn directly out of his paychecks.

I guess I should just be glad he continued to make our car payments so we didn't have those repossessed, too. Luckily, both our car payments are automatically withdrawn from our account, so he didn't have that option. In hindsight, I wish we'd done that with our mortgage.

With a newborn at home, I couldn't just go back to work to help pay off our debt. Affordable daycare for a newborn is practically impossible to come by. My entire paycheck would basically pay for daycare, so it would have been completely pointless for me to work in the first place.

Not only that, but I can't imagine having to go back to work after everything I've been through these past few months with our debt and divorce, plus becoming a single mom. To say I've been stressed would be an understatement. I would have lost my mind if I had to go back to work. Being an ER nurse, or really *any* type of nurse, is stressful enough.

As I look out my kitchen window, which faces the front of the house, I can see the headlights of a car coming down our street. I watch as it pulls into the driveway across the street from us. It's Amber, coming home from work. She's an ER nurse who works odd hours. I don't miss those work schedules. We used to work together. In fact, she was the one who told me about this house when Scott and I started looking five years ago. She was always a great colleague and an even better neighbor and friend. I'll miss her when I move.

I glance at the clock on the oven and notice it's three thirty a.m. *Great.* Only about three hours until Ellie wakes up. Four if I'm lucky. She never sleeps past seven thirty in the morning, although she's prone to waking up sooner than that.

Tomorrow, or rather today, is moving day for us. I'm sad to be moving out of our home, but this will be for the best. We were allowed to stay in the house while the foreclosure process started, but now we have to go.

Scott already moved out and is staying with his buddy from

work. I kicked him out when I told him I wanted a divorce. I couldn't stay married to someone who continued to lie to me. He refuses to admit he has a real gambling problem even though he continues to play! I can't depend on him anymore, and it makes me sad. He's not the same man I fell in love with and married. I still love him in the sense that I care for him and his well-being—not to mention he's the father of my child—but he's let me down so much that I'm not able to be *in* love with him any longer.

He seems to be in love with gambling now anyway.

Even though I love this house and have some good memories here, it also holds sad memories I'd like to forget. Losing it to foreclosure has been devastating. I've always pictured us raising Ellie here together, but that dream has been ripped away.

I wipe my hands down my face, hoping it will somehow help me feel tired again. I have so much to do today, and I could really use more sleep. We have a three-hour drive ahead of us after we load the U-Haul with all our stuff, then a lot of unpacking and settling to do at our new home. It's not the most ideal situation, but when my parents offered to let Ellie and me move in with them, I decided to take them up on it. Actually, I don't have much of a choice since I'm unemployed and being forced out of our house.

My parents are more than happy to have us move in with them, especially since they'll get to see their only grandchild grow up before their very eyes. I'm hoping that it works out as well as we all think it will. I haven't lived at home full time with my parents since I was eighteen years old, so I know there's going to be some adjustment. Plus, I'm moving back to my home-town, nearly two hundred miles away from where I've lived for the past ten years. I've become used to this town, a suburb of Portland, Oregon, and I have many friends here who I'll miss. However, I am looking forward to leaving my ex behind as well as all the recent bad memories. Being back in the Seattle area, closer to my family and my best friend, Sarah, is just what I need right now.

Although we're living in his hometown now, Scott doesn't have any family left here. His parents retired and moved to Florida a couple of years ago, and his sister moved to Idaho with her husband and kids. The rest of his family—aunts, uncles, and cousins—are spread out all over the country. So when I told him I was moving to Seattle, where I could have the support of my parents to raise Ellie, there was no reason for him to fight me on it.

Scott and I have been together since our junior year of college. He proposed to me when we graduated, and we moved to his hometown where he got a job as a cop, and I got hired at a hospital. We were happy, loved to travel together, and I thought we had the perfect marriage. We waited to have kids until we were in our thirties, simply because we enjoyed traveling so much and wanted to see the world together. Our annual trips hold so many wonderful memories that, unfortunately, now leave a sour taste in my mouth. This was obviously before he developed his bad habit since we could still afford to take such trips.

When we turned thirty, we were ready to add a child to our family. It took several months for us to conceive, which was a little frustrating, but we had a lot of fun trying. When we found out I was pregnant, we were ecstatic. I would've never guessed he would betray me by gambling.

Since that fateful night, I've found out more about his deceit. On some of the nights when he said he was working overtime, he was actually at poker games. So not only was he not making the overtime money like he said, but he was losing money as well.

Sure, he won big sometimes, or that's what he's told me anyway. But those winnings were often lost in the next game.

Looking at the clock again, I decide to try going back to bed. Maybe if I lie down, I'll fall asleep. As I pass Ellie's room, I decide to sneak in to peek at her. She has been my touchstone, the one thing really holding me together. I must stay strong for her.

Ellie is peacefully sleeping in her crib in her nearly empty bedroom. Everything is packed up and ready to go in a few hours. I can't wait to set up her new bedroom at my parents' house, which was my sister's room when we were growing up. I'll be in my old room, and it hits me just how bizarre living with my parents again might be. I have a great relationship with them, but I can't believe I'm moving back into my childhood home. I never thought my life would take this turn.

I tiptoe back to my bedroom as quietly as I can. My parents are asleep in the room next to Ellie's. They drove down a couple of days ago to spend the weekend helping me pack up the house. My dad is going to drive the small U-Haul I rented to Seattle for me. I'm so thankful for all my parents' support.

I crawl back into bed and will myself back to sleep.

BROOKE

6:47 a.m. is the time on the clock when my Ellie alarm goes off, but I am too tired to get up. I don't know what time I finally fell back to sleep, but I know I didn't get enough of it. Just as I'm about to drag myself out of bed to go get her, I hear my mom with her. "Oh, Ellie girl, let's let your momma sleep, shall we?"

I love my mom.

* * *

The sound of someone knocking on my bedroom door wakes me up. I turn and look at the clock and see it's nearly nine o'clock. I got to sleep for two more hours! "Come in," I say as I sit up and wipe my eyes.

"Good morning," my mom says as she walks in with Ellie in her arms. Ellie smiles at me and puts her arms out, wanting me to take her. She babbles and says, "Mamamama!"

"Good morning," I reply as my mom walks over to me and hands me my baby girl. I take her and give her a kiss on her forehead.

"She's already had her morning bottle, so she shouldn't be hungry yet," Mom says. She sits on the edge of my bed next to me.

Ellie wants to stand, so I let her stand on my legs as I hold her hands to keep her from falling over. She bounces herself and smiles at me, giggling and babbling away. I feel so fortunate to have her, but it makes me sad that Scott and I won't be raising her together.

"Thanks, Mom. Is Dad awake yet?"

"Oh yes. In fact, he's already loading the U-Haul."

"I should get up and help him," I reply, feeling guilty that he's doing all the work. I hold Ellie in my arms again and turn to get out of bed. My mom puts her hand on my knee.

"Are you all right, Brooke?" she asks, looking concerned.

I look at Ellie's adorable face to keep myself from breaking down. I'm tired and vulnerable, and I don't want to have a breakdown today. "I'm fine," I tell her.

"I heard you get up last night at around three a.m.," she says, trying to get me to look at her. "Did you get enough sleep?"

I glance at her, then back at Ellie. I smile and kiss my seven-month-old on the nose, then look back at my mom as I say, "Yeah, I'm fine now. I just woke up and was thirsty." I stand and hand Ellie back to my mom. "Can you watch her for a minute while I use the bathroom?"

She takes her granddaughter back into her arms and stands up. "Maybe you'll sleep better once you're settled back at home tonight."

"I'm sure I will," I say as I head into my bathroom. My mom walks out of my room with Ellie.

I hate not being truthful with my mom. I could've just told her a panic attack woke me up, but I don't want her to worry about me any more than she already is. I know I'm fine. Moving is a big stress, so I'm sure that's what triggered it. I'll be okay once we're settled in at their house. I'm sure of it.

By noon, everything is loaded and ready to go. I'm not taking all the furniture, so the house isn't completely empty. Scott gets to deal with the extra furniture neither of us wants anymore. I told him to store what he wants to keep somewhere or just sell it. He agreed to give me half of what he makes from selling the furniture, but I don't have my hopes set high on that. Knowing him, he'll probably gamble it all away.

As I go outside to put the last of my things in my car, Amber walks over from across the street to talk. "Is today moving day?" she asks as she approaches me in the front yard.

"It is," I reply, giving her a hug.

She puts her arms around me and pats my back. "Keep in touch with me, okay? I'm going to miss you!"

We pull apart from each other, and I cross my arms in front of me. I knew it would be hard to say goodbye to this place, and Amber is one of the few people I know I'll miss. "I will, don't worry," I assure her. "Besides, we're friends on Facebook, so that'll make it easy."

She smiles and nods her head, then adds, "I still can't believe you're moving away. After everything that's happened ..." She doesn't finish her sentence. She just looks away from me, shaking her head. I confided in Amber, telling her what Scott did and how he has a gambling addiction. She was a good friend to talk to and offered her support by just being there for me. We've shared many bottles of wine over the past few months as I vented all my stresses to her.

"I know," I say as I look down at the ground, trying to hold back the tears threatening my eyes. I promised myself I would *not* cry today.

"Well," she says in a more chipper voice, pulling my attention back to her, "just remember all the fun times we've had together in the neighborhood and at work. And feel free to use me as a reference when you end up looking for a job in Seattle!"

"Thanks," I say to her, smiling. "I really appreciate that."

She embraces me one more time. "Good luck and have a safe drive. Please, keep in touch, okay?"

"Thank you. I will," I reply, hugging her tighter. Then she pulls back, smiles, and walks back home.

Mom walks out of my house, holding Ellie. "She's got a fresh diaper on, she's had her lunch, and she's ready to go!"

I walk up to the porch to meet her, then take my daughter in my arms. "We better get going then!"

* * *

We have a caravan of three cars heading up to Seattle. I'm in front, driving Ellie in my car, then my dad is behind us in the U-Haul, and my mom is following him in their car. We figured it was best for me to be in front in case I needed to stop to feed or change Ellie along the way. Then they can follow me off the freeway and help me out if needed.

Ellie ends up being a great traveler. After being on the road for about twenty minutes, she falls asleep and doesn't wake up until we're practically home.

Our new home.

My old home.

Just home now.

It only takes a couple of hours to unload all our things into the house. The U-Haul may be empty, but Mom and Dad's house is in disarray. The basement is anyway. That's where Ellie's and my bedrooms are, as well as the family room we can use as our own living space. Of course, we're welcome upstairs with my parents anytime, but our belongings will be downstairs.

My parents return the U-Haul truck, leaving Ellie and me left to start sorting through our boxes. Not that Ellie is any help with this task. Luckily, I know exactly where I'd packed some of her favorite toys, so I get those out and lay them on the family room floor. "Here you go, Ellie Bell," I say, using her nickname as she squeals and grabs for her most coveted toys. She'll be happy for a while, which gives me time to start unpacking.

Some of the things I packed will actually stay in boxes and be stored. I won't need any of my favorite kitchen gadgets since Mom has her own for me to use while I'm here. Nor do I want to take out and display old photos of Scott and me that I couldn't bear to throw away. No, those boxes will stay packed and put away in the storage area of my parents' large basement. I'm really glad they have the space so I don't have to rent a storage unit.

I spend the rest of the evening moving boxes into the storage area and unpacking Ellie's things. I figure we'll need her stuff before I'll need my own. Diapers, her clothing, and toys to keep her happy and busy are much more important than putting my things away right now. Though I'm determined to get settled in sooner rather than later. My parents help by keeping Ellie occupied and unpacking the necessities they know I will need.

By nine o'clock, Ellie is tired. Luckily, my dad already set her crib up in her room, so it's ready for her. I change her diaper and put her into pajamas, then gently lay her in her crib. To my surprise, she doesn't fuss at all. I think she's so worn out from all the activity from today and is more than ready to go to sleep. I kiss her good night and then return to unpacking my bedroom.

Mom and Dad stay up with me for about an hour after Ellie goes to bed. They help me unpack a few more boxes, then they go upstairs. Their bedroom is on the main floor of the house, and they both have to get up early for work in the morning.

Mom is a fifth-grade teacher, and Dad teaches high school math. They're getting closer to retirement, but they still have a few more years. One of the perks of me moving in with them and being a stay-at-home mom with Ellie is that I'll be here to cook dinner for them every night. I also plan to help Mom with all the household chores. It's the least I can do for them after all they're doing to help me.

As I look around at the mess of clothes I've unpacked and still need to put away, I realize how strange it is to be living in my old bedroom again. Hanging my clothes up in the same closet and tucking them into the same set of drawers I used while I was growing up is a bit surreal. After all the times I stayed in this room as a guest when I visited my parents, I never imagined I'd actually ever live here again.

Not much has changed since my sister, Becca, and I shared this basement space years ago. Her bedroom, now Ellie's, is just across the hall from mine. Becca is two years younger than I am. She lives in New York City and works in the fashion industry. She's single and loves it, with no intentions of settling down or having kids anytime soon. She comes home every year at Christmas, so it's only been a few months since we last saw each other. We were pretty close growing up, and we still are although we hardly get to see each other in person anymore. We text, call, email, and FaceTime as often as possible. She says she will try to get time off in the spring or summer to come out for another visit.

Before I know it, it's after midnight. I'm almost done unpacking, but my body is calling for bed. Hopefully, I will get an uninterrupted night of sleep.

BROOKE

I can't believe it! Ellie and I both slept soundly our first night in our "new" home. I wake up to the sound of my parents' footsteps above me as they get ready for work. I glance at my alarm clock to see the time. It's 6:50, and Ellie is still asleep. I have a feeling that won't last very much longer, though, so I get out of bed and head to the bathroom. I can hear Ellie moving around in her crib as I close the bathroom door.

When I'm done, I walk into Ellie's room and find her happily lying in her crib, grabbing her feet with her hands and babbling away to herself. She smiles at me as I take her out of her crib and kiss her, thanking her for letting me sleep all night. I was afraid she might wake up in the middle of the night since she was in a new space. She has slept here a couple of times when we visited my parents, but that was long before she was sleeping through the night on a regular basis. I had no idea how she would do in our new environment, so I'm pleased our first night went smoothly.

I change her diaper, then head upstairs with my happy girl. Mom is in the kitchen, pouring coffee into a travel mug. "Good morning," she says as we enter the kitchen.

"Good morning," I reply, and Ellie waves her hands and babbles at her.

"Your dad just left for work, but I don't have to leave for a few more minutes."

"What time do you think you'll be home tonight?" I ask her as I sit down at the kitchen table, setting Ellie on my lap.

"Oh, your dad usually gets home at about four o'clock," she says as she continues moving around the kitchen to pack herself a lunch. "I usually get home between four thirty and five."

"I'm thinking about making tacos for dinner tonight. Does that sound good?" I ask her.

"That would be great, Brooke. Anything you want to make will be wonderful."

I bounce Ellie on my knees as she babbles away. Mom finishes packing her lunch, then walks over to us, giving both Ellie and me a kiss on our cheeks.

"I love you both," she says. "Have a good day. I'll see you this evening!"

"Bye, Mom," I reply as she grabs her lunch and turns to leave. Ellie waves goodbye to her as she walks out the door for work, then looks at me and gives me her hungry face. "Are you hungry, girl?" I ask her as I get up to make her a bottle.

After I mix her formula into a bottle, I walk us into the living room where I plop down on the comfy couch to feed her. I had to quit nursing because she was always really fussy after eating, and after taking her to the doctor, we discovered she had bad reflux. Her doctor recommended a special kind of formula, and switching to that has helped immensely.

Glancing at my phone sitting on the coffee table in front of me, I realize I was so busy yesterday that I haven't looked at it since we got here. I pick it up and notice I have a few text messages. One of them is from Amber, just saying she hopes we made it to Seattle safely and telling me again to stay in touch. I send her a quick reply, letting her know we made it here in one piece and that I will definitely keep in touch with her.

The next text I read is from my sister.

Are you at Mom and Dad's yet? Call me when you can. Miss and love you! XOXO

I reply to her as well, saying that I'll call her later tonight. I know she's at work right now and can't talk anyway.

The next one I read is from my best friend, Sarah. She lives here in Seattle, and she's one of the reasons I'm happy to move back. We've been friends since junior high, which is about twenty years. We've stayed in touch all this time, and I consider her a sister. We were each other's maids of honor, and we've always been there for each other.

I read her text.

Brookie! Have you moved yet? I can't wait to have you close again! Text me when you get a chance. We need to get together!

I text her back as well. She's also a stay-at-home mom, but with three kids of her own, she might be too busy to reply right away.

Finally, I check the last text I have. It's from Scott.

Drive carefully to Seattle. I already miss you and Ellie. I will never stop saying sorry to you even though I know you won't forgive me. I don't know why I did what I did. Text me back to let me know you arrived safely.

. . .

It's nice of him to be concerned about our long drive to Seattle. It's also nice that he misses us, but it still hurts like hell when he says such sweet things to me. I know he's truly sorry for what he's done, but he hasn't proved he's willing to do anything to *stop* it! What hurts the most is that he doesn't love us enough to admit he has a gambling problem and needs to get help with his addiction. We are over. I need to move on with my life and accept the fact that Scott is not the same man I married. *That* man wouldn't have lost our house or run our credit cards into so much debt. *That* man would still want to be here to raise his daughter instead of caring about the next poker game he can play.

I take a deep breath and then text him back.

We made it safely to Seattle. Let me know when you'd like to see Ellie.

To my surprise, he texts me back right away.

I have next Sunday off. Can we meet at the children's museum in Olympia for the day?

I roll my eyes. I know he's her father and has every right to see her, and I know this is what we agreed to in our parenting plan, but this fucking sucks. He hurt me in a way I didn't know was possible. I reluctantly send him a reply.

Me: *Yes, that works. Let me know what time you want to meet.*

. . .

Scott: *Let's meet at 11:00. I'll buy you lunch, too.*

I roll my eyes at his offer. Lunch? I don't want to sit down for a meal with him, but I also don't want to fight about it right now. I send him a short text, not mentioning his lunch invitation.

See you there at 11.

Ellie finishes her bottle, and I burp her. I hear my phone buzz with another text message coming through. I look down at the screen, and I'm happy to see it's from Sarah, not Scott. She's asking how I am, and if I'm all moved in yet. I reply, letting her know how things are going. Then she invites Ellie and me over for lunch tomorrow. Of course, I accept. I can't wait to see her.

I spend the rest of the day making the basement more of a home for Ellie and me. I decorate my bedroom and the family room, hanging up a few pictures and setting out some personal pieces to make it cozy. The entire basement has been drab and undecorated since Becca and I moved out years ago. It used to be the place where we hung out with our friends when they came over, but Mom and Dad never came down here after we moved out since they have all they need upstairs.

Throughout the day, I take breaks to play with Ellie. When she gets fussy, I give her a change of scenery by giving her different toys to play with or moving her to the baby swing or jumper. At one point, I even turn on the TV to some baby cartoons to keep her occupied so I can continue working. When my dad comes home from work, I take Ellie upstairs to greet him.

"How was your day?" I ask Dad when I find him sinking into the recliner in the living room with a beer in his hand.

He tips the beer bottle to me, then takes a swig. "I'm having a beer. What does that tell you?" He winks at me and chuckles. "I love my job, but I have some challenging kids in my classes this semester." Growing up, I always knew that if Dad had a beer after work, he'd had a stressful day.

"Sorry to hear that." I sit on the couch and set Ellie next to me. She's gnawing on one of her teething toys.

"How was your day?" he asks me.

"Good! I've unpacked everything now. I hope you and Mom don't mind, but I've hung up some pictures and decorated a bit."

"Of course not. We've told you to make it yours. It *is* your home, for crying out loud. Feel free to decorate and update that old basement." Dad chuckles and takes another sip of his beer.

I smile at my dad's kind words. I really feel lucky because I have the best parents in the world. I know they love Ellie and me, but I also know it's not easy having us live here. Ellie's only seven months old. Having a baby living in their home must be a big adjustment since they've been empty nesters for the better part of a decade. I'm more than grateful that my parents are willing to make that sacrifice for us.

"I'm going to visit Sarah tomorrow afternoon," I decide to tell my dad.

"Good! How is she doing?"

"She's doing well. I'm looking forward to finally having time to talk with her tomorrow. I didn't get a chance to see her at Christmas."

"I'm glad you still have Sarah in your life. She's always been a good friend to you," Dad says.

"I know, I'm lucky." I look down at Ellie and think about her growing up. I can only hope she'll make friends that will last a lifetime.

Sarah and I have always been there for each other. We met on the first day of seventh grade, having several of the same classes together, and clicked right away. To say we've been through a lot together would be an understatement. We've been side by side through the awkward teen years, and although we went to different colleges, we remained close. We've been there for one another through our weddings, careers, kids, and now my divorce.

I notice the clock on the wall and realize I should start making dinner within the next half hour or so. "Do tacos sound good for dinner?" I ask Dad as he takes another sip of his beer.

"That sounds delicious. Having you move in will sure have a lot of perks," he says, winking at me.

I chuckle. "I know, the only reason you offered to let me live here was so you'd have a live-in maid."

"Oh, you figured us out," Dad jokes, putting his beer bottle down on the table next to him. Then he turns to me again. "Seriously, though, Brooke, you're not obligated to do all the cooking and cleaning while you're here. We're just happy to help you and Ellie out."

I smile at him. "Thanks, Dad. I know, but I think I can handle cooking for you guys and helping out around the house since you both work full time, and I'm here all day."

"Do you ever think about going back to work someday?" His question catches me off guard at first. Sure, I've thought about it, but I just know it's not a reasonable thing for me to do until Ellie gets a little older. Daycare's just too expensive.

I look at my dad and smile before giving him my honest answer. "I do want to go back to work eventually. I love being a nurse. I just don't think it's realistic right now, with Ellie being so young. My schedule would be crazy. If I work at a hospital, I'd most likely have to work the night shift, which would make me exhausted during the day with Ellie. I'd never sleep. If I got hired at a clinic, I'd have a more manageable schedule, but I'd have to pay for daycare since you and Mom work during the day, too. I think I'll be a stay-at-home mom for a little while longer, but someday I *would* like to go back to work."

Just then, we hear the front door unlock. We both turn our heads to see Mom walk in the house. "Hi!" she says as she enters the living room and sets her school bag and purse down.

"Hi, Mom," I reply. Then I pick Ellie up and hold her on my lap. "I was just about to start tacos for dinner."

"You are a lifesaver," she says, sounding relieved not to have to cook dinner. "What a day it's been! Is it a full moon this week? Because I swear my students are losing their minds."

Dad chuckles and picks his beer up off the table, tipping it to her. "I see we had a similar day, dear."

Mom lies down on the couch, kicking her feet up and resting her back against a pillow propped up on the arm. "It's definitely a Monday," she mumbles as she tries to get comfortable.

I silently laugh at them, then stand and walk into the kitchen to get to work. Not much has changed since I've left. Seeing what my parents had to deal with as teachers made me *not* want to go into the profession. They have the toughest job. I don't know how they do it.

I set Ellie in her high chair and give her one of her sensory books to play with while I cook.

* * *

After dinner, Mom walks downstairs with me to see what I've done with the place so far. She looks at the pictures I've hung up as well as some of the knickknacks I've put out on the shelves and tables. Then she turns to me and smiles. "It looks like a home," she says.

"I also decorated my room a bit," I tell her. We walk in there so she can see that room as well.

"Very nice," she says as she looks around the room. "Have you decorated Ellie's room yet?"

"No, but I plan to start on that soon."

"I hope you don't mind that we kept the spare twin bed in there. There's still enough room for her crib, changing table, and dresser, though."

"That's fine." Of course, I didn't expect my parents to pack up and move all their furniture out for us. I hardly moved any furniture here for that exact reason. "One nice thing about these bedrooms is that they're big. There's plenty of space in there."

Mom smiles, and we walk back out to the family room. "Do you need help with anything?" she asks me.

I shake my head. "No, I have it covered." Knowing my mom had a stressful day, I want her to relax.

"I'm really glad to have you and Ellie living here." Mom hugs me, and I fight back the tears that threaten my eyes. I don't know why I suddenly get so emotional, but I do. I love my mom so much.

"Thanks, Mom," I say, my voice cracking just a bit. I manage to hold myself together.

"I have some papers to correct upstairs," she says as she breaks our embrace. "So I'll just be working up there if you need me."

We walk upstairs together and find Dad playing with Ellie on the living room floor. He's such a good grandpa to her. They're playing peek-a-boo.

"Well, well, are you having fun down there?" Mom asks him as she stands over the two of them.

"Of course, we are!" Dad exclaims as he continues to play. Ellie is giggling at him. I love seeing her have so much fun and hearing her laugh. It's the best sound in the world.

"Do you want me to take her downstairs with me?" I offer, not wanting her to be a distraction since Mom is going to be working.

He looks up at me. "Are you crazy? We're in the middle of some serious business here!" Then he turns his attention back to his granddaughter and makes her giggle again.

"You two have fun. I'll be in the office, grading papers," Mom says to him as she grabs her school bag off the floor and starts to walk down the hall.

I smile and tell Dad I'll be downstairs if he needs me. Then I turn and head back down to work on Ellie's room.

BROOKE

I wake up the next day feeling refreshed. I slept another
night free of panic attacks, and Ellie slept through the
night again, too. So far, moving here seems to be working out
perfectly.

I finished decorating Ellie's room before I went to bed last
night. She fell asleep in her swing in the family room, so I left her
there while I worked in her room. When I finished, I carefully
moved her to her crib before going to bed myself.

I hear Ellie stirring in her crib when I get out of bed. After
changing her diaper, we go upstairs and say hi to my mom before
she leaves for work. Then I feed Ellie. Maybe this will become
our morning routine. We need to settle into a routine now that
we're living here.

After she finishes her bottle, I go into the kitchen, put Ellie in
her high chair with her book, and make myself coffee and cereal.
Ellie starts fussing, watching me eat my breakfast, and I know I'll
have to feed her a jar of baby food when I'm done.

I quickly finish my cereal, then find a jar of pureed pears in
the cupboard for Ellie to eat. Her favorite. I feed her, then we go

back down to the family room. I put Ellie on the floor with some of her toys, then I decide to check my phone.

I was so busy again yesterday that I didn't check it much, but this time, there aren't any new texts. I scroll through Facebook to see what my friends are up to. Then I decide to write a post saying how good it feels to be living in Seattle again. My friends know I'm getting divorced, but I haven't said anything about moving yet. I change my current city from Portland to Seattle. It feels liberating.

I look at Ellie, and she looks adorable, so I snap a picture of her. I decide to text the picture to Scott. He is her father, after all, and he sacrificed a lot by not fighting me when I decided to move. He could have fought to keep us living closer to him so he could see her more often, so I'm grateful he let us go. Although I'm still furious with him, I know I can't keep his daughter from him. That wouldn't be right.

He texts me back right away.

She's beautiful. Like her momma. Thank you.

I don't reply.

* * *

At noon, I pull into Sarah's driveway. After I get Ellie out of the car, I grab her diaper bag and walk up to the front door. Sarah opens it before I can even knock. "Brookie!" she exclaims while extending one arm for a hug. She's holding her one-year-old daughter, Riley, in her other arm, so I hug her with my free arm. "Come in," she says as she steps back so I can enter her house.

We set Riley and Ellie on the floor with their toys in the play-room, adjacent to her kitchen. Her oldest, Nathan, is at school.

He's in first grade. Madison is four years old and plays alongside the babies.

Sarah and I go into the kitchen to prepare lunch. We can still see the girls while we talk and get the food ready. It's cute to watch them play on the carpet together. Ellie and Riley each play with their own toys separately while Madison tries to socialize with them with little success. All three girls seem content, though, and that's all that matters.

"Okay, now that we don't have any distractions, let's *really* talk."

I chuckle.

"Tell me what's going on with Asshole now. We haven't had enough time to talk in person the past few months."

Sarah now refers to Scott as *Asshole.* She can't believe what he did to our finances and that he basically chose gambling over Ellie and me. I think back to the last time Sarah and I had the chance to really discuss it all. It was shortly after I filed for divorce, so she really knows everything already. Nothing new has happened since then. "There's really not a lot to tell you that you don't already know," I tell her.

Sarah shakes her head. "I still can't believe what you've been through! You guys seemed like you had the best marriage!"

"I felt like we did, too." I look down at my glass of water on the table and run my fingers around the rim. "I guess I just never really knew my husband."

"I guess not. It's just sad," she adds. "I mean, how could he bankrupt his family by gambling away thousands of dollars like that ...?" She looks at me sympathetically and shakes her head. "It makes me so angry that you had to go through that."

I smile sadly at her. "I know. Believe me. I'm so mad at myself for not seeing the signs, though. I mean, I should have paid more attention to our bank account. I just trusted that Scott was taking care of all the bills and there was nothing to worry about."

"Asshole," Sarah mutters, lifting her glass to take another drink.

"I have to take Ellie down to Olympia on Sunday for his visitation." I scowl at her.

"Where are you meeting him?" she asks.

"The children's museum."

"Oh, we went there once! It's a great place for kids," Sarah tells me. "They have an area for babies to crawl around and play in, so that's a good meeting place for you."

"I really don't want to see him, but I know I can't avoid him. He has every right to see his daughter."

"I don't blame you," she replies. "Why would you *want* to see him? You don't actually have to hang out with them the whole time, do you?"

I shake my head. "No, thank God."

"So what are you going to do while they're visiting?"

"I don't know," I reply. I actually hadn't even thought about this yet. "Is there a cafe I can sit in and read or something?"

Sarah looks as though she's trying to remember. Then she replies, "Yes, I think there is! Not a huge place, but they serve coffee and some food, if I remember correctly."

I feel a little relieved knowing I'll have something to do while Scott visits with Ellie. That'll be perfect.

"Hey, maybe if you meet him there again sometime, the kids and I can tag along with you, then you'll have some company. I can't go this Sunday, though. We already have lunch plans with Joe's parents."

"That would be great," I say to her. I'd love to have someone go with me. Maybe I'll ask Mom to go with me on Sunday.

I take another drink of my water, wanting to change the subject. I'm tired of talking about Scott. I want to move on with my life. As I set my glass back down on the table, I look at my friend and notice that Sarah looks like she has lost weight since the last time I saw her. She looks more fit and healthy, now that I'm really taking a closer look. "Have you lost weight?" I ask her.

Sarah straightens up in her chair and smiles. "Why, yes, I have!"

"Look at you, hot momma! How'd you do it?" Sarah was never really fat, but she had gained some weight after having each of her kids. I guess I'd been too distracted with the kids earlier to really notice Sarah looks more like she did before she had Nathan seven years ago.

"I joined a gym and work out as often as I can," Sarah explains. "I also started eating healthier, but I swear I owe most of it just to exercise. You should come with me sometime!"

I give her a dirty look to give her a hard time. "Do I look like I *need* to lose weight?"

She rolls her eyes at me. "I'm not saying you're fat, but ..."

"You bitch!" I playfully hit her arm, and we laugh together. "Seriously, though, I know I'm not in the best shape of my life, so I'd love to go work out with you sometime."

Sarah shakes her head. "You know I was totally kidding. You look great. I was just teasing."

The truth is, I have lost a lot of weight over the past few months. I don't have the appetite I used to, and I chalk it up to stress. I'm thinner than I was before I got pregnant with Ellie. However, I wouldn't say I'm healthy at all. My eating habits aren't the best, and my muscle tone is practically nonexistent. I used to be pretty fit, and I'd love to get back in shape.

"I know I look skinny, but you should see me naked," I tell her. "I'm all skin and bones. I need to get some muscle back and start eating healthier."

Sarah leans in. "Has anyone seen you naked lately?" she asks, digging for dirt.

I actually laugh out loud at her question. *As if!* "Only you can ask me that without it being intrusive! No, no one's seen me naked in a *very* long time. Scott was the last one, besides my OB/GYN, and I'm pretty sure she doesn't count."

Sarah sits back in her chair and crosses her arms. "We need to get you back out there."

I'm caught off guard by her comment. "Get me back out there? As in *dating*? I don't think so," I reply, and I mean it. Dating? It seems too soon. Plus, I have a baby. Ellie is my priority.

"Yes, as in dating," Sarah retorts. "You could use a fun night out with a hot guy."

I roll my eyes at her and copy her stance, sitting back in my chair and crossing my arms. "You're funny."

"You were with Scott for a long time. He lied and betrayed you. You're entitled to move on, and you deserve to have some fun!"

I look at Sarah as though she's crazy. "I have a baby, and I'm living in my parents' basement. I think I'll concentrate on getting my life back on track before pursuing a love life."

Sarah shakes her head. "I'm just saying, it's okay to go out and have fun. Have some good sex. It'll help you de-stress."

I laugh at her. "I don't need a man for that. I can *de-stress* on my own," I say with a hint of sarcasm.

Sarah laughs. "True, you can take care of business on your own ... but there's just something about having a guy do it for you." She winks at me.

"Again, you're the only person I can have this conversation with," I say, shaking my head and laughing some more.

"Have I told you how happy I am to have you local again? I've missed you," Sarah says, changing the subject.

"Well, I'm happy, too. And I'm so thankful for our friendship." I smile at her, and she smiles back.

Ellie and I spend a couple of more hours at Sarah's house before heading home. Sarah invites me to go to the gym with her tomorrow night. She usually goes Monday and Wednesday nights, and early Saturday mornings. She works out at home on the other days. I told her I'd be more than happy to join her.

I decide to make spaghetti for dinner. As we're eating together around the kitchen table, Mom asks how my visit with Sarah went. I tell her how she and her family are doing, and how great it was to spend time with her. Then I ask if they would mind watching Ellie tomorrow night while I go to the gym with Sarah.

"Of course, we don't mind," Dad replies. "That's what we're here for, to help with Ellie."

"What gym are you going to?" Mom asks.

"It's a new one over by the mall. I forget the name. Sarah said it just opened a few months ago."

"Oh yes, I know which one you mean," Mom says. "I've heard it's a nice gym."

"Well, I'll see how nice it is tomorrow night. I need to start exercising again. I haven't done anything since I got pregnant. I'd love to start running 5k races again someday."

I think about how fit I used to be and how exercising always seemed to help my mood. I always felt more positive and confident when I worked out on a regular basis. I think this is exactly what I need right now.

BROOKE

I meet Sarah in the gym's parking lot at six thirty the next night, and we walk in together. It's a state-of-the-art facility, and I'm immediately impressed. We walk up to the front desk so she can scan her membership card and sign me in as her guest. She gets to bring one free guest with her as part of her membership deal.

"What do you usually do here?" I ask her.

"I usually start with thirty minutes on the elliptical, then do about thirty minutes of various strength training exercises."

"Sounds great," I say as we walk toward the elliptical machines. The place is pretty busy, but we find two ellipticals right next to each other and claim them.

We spend the next hour working out, and it feels great. I haven't exercised in so long, and even though it's hard on my body, it feels amazing. I know I'm going to get back in great shape.

As we're walking back to our cars, Sarah asks me, "Are you going to be my new workout partner?"

"Of course! This was great. Thanks for letting me tag along."

"Any time! It's more fun to have you here."

* * *

On Saturday, I drag myself out of bed at six a.m. so I can meet Sarah at the gym again. It's difficult to get out of bed so early, but once I'm up and ready to go, I'm glad I make myself do it. I feel bad for going so early, but Mom said just to bring the baby monitor into their bedroom when I leave so they can hear when Ellie wakes up. Ellie's been sleeping in until about seven o'clock all week, so I'm hoping she lets my mom sleep in a while after I leave.

When we get to the gym, Sarah and I do the elliptical machines again, followed by some work on our arms. Even after just a few times, I can feel myself getting stronger. Not just physically but mentally, too. I'm so glad to have Sarah in my life.

I spend the rest of the day playing with Ellie. It's a nice day out—not a typical gloomy March day in Seattle—so I walk Ellie to the park down the street in her stroller. It's nice to get some fresh air and enjoy the day with my girl. I push her around the park along a walking trail, and I watch as toddlers and older kids play on the playground. I can't wait for Ellie to get to the stage when I can run around and play with her like that. However, I also feel a little sadness as I see a mom who has two little girls playing together.

It hurts me that Ellie won't ever have a full sibling. Sure, it's possible she could have step-brothers or sisters in the future or maybe even a half sibling if Scott or I ever end up having more kids with someone else, but she'll never have a *full* brother or sister. I remember Scott and I used to discuss having two or three kids together. We both have one sister each, and we agreed to have more than one child so Ellie wouldn't be alone. Now that will never happen. I didn't realize how sad this would make me until now.

. . .

The next day is Sunday, and I have to drive down to Olympia for Ellie's visit with Scott. I'm grateful my mom agreed to ride along with me. I really didn't want to spend the whole afternoon with Scott, so I figured I could sit in the cafe or something while he takes Ellie around the children's museum. With my mom going, I'll have someone to keep me company.

We get to the museum a little before eleven o'clock, and I text Scott to let him know we're here. He replies, telling me he's waiting for us inside. I put Ellie in her stroller, and we walk in to meet him.

Watching Ellie light up when she sees him melts my heart. I want her to have a good relationship with her dad. At first, Scott tries to talk my mom and me into walking through the museum with him and Ellie, but I tell him no, this is *his* time with her. I let him know that my mom and I will be in the museum's cafe if he needs us for anything.

Mom and I get coffee and sit at a small table. We make small talk, then we both read the books we brought with us. We knew this might get a little boring, so we came prepared.

A couple of hours later, Scott returns with Ellie. "Can I buy you lunch?" he asks me.

"No, I don't think that's a good idea," I reply. I really don't want to spend time with him. He hurt me, and I'm still not completely over it. How can I sit and eat with the man I used to love and built a life with before he crushed everything we had?

"Why not? It's just lunch," he pleads.

I take a deep breath. I want to be firm with him so he understands where I stand. Our marriage is over, and I don't plan on having lunch with him whenever he visits Ellie. "Because we have nothing to discuss, Scott. It'll be awkward. If you'd like to spend more time with Ellie, feel free. We can go somewhere else if you don't want to stay here."

He looks down, then back up at me. He looks sincerely regretful. "This sucks, Brooke."

I swear he's about to cry. *What the hell?* Does he actually regret his choices now? Is he ready to admit he has a gambling problem? Even if he did, I don't think it would change how I feel, though. Yes, I loved him for a long time, but he betrayed my trust, and I can't love someone I don't trust.

My mom stays silent in her seat next to me. Scott looks down at Ellie in the stroller, and she's asleep. He bends down and gently kisses her on the forehead. "I guess I should just go home then. She's going to sleep for a while, and I don't want to take up your whole afternoon."

I stand and look him in the eye. I want him to know I care about his relationship with Ellie. "Scott, I have no intention of keeping her out of your life. I want her to have a good relationship with you."

He tries to smile at me, and I can tell he's choking back tears. His eyes are watery. "Thank you. I know I don't deserve it."

"Just text me and let me know when you want to meet again," I say to him.

"I will," he says.

I take the stroller handles and start pushing her out to the car. Scott walks with me, and my mom follows behind us. *This is awkward.* When we get to my car, he waits as I buckle Ellie in, then load her diaper bag and the stroller. My mom leaves us alone and gets into the car, so I'm left standing there with my ex.

"Well, I guess I'll see you later then," I say, trying to figure out how to end this visit.

"Yeah, I'll text you about meeting again next weekend. I might have to work," he says.

I nod my head, tell him goodbye, and then get in the car. He turns and walks away.

"You're a good woman," my mom says to me as I start the car. "I wanted to claw his eyes out for what he did to you, and you're so calm and nice to him. Ellie deserves that."

"It's hard," I reply. "I want to claw his eyes out, too, but what good would it do? It took a lot of hours of therapy for me to realize I can't control what he does, but I *can* control how I react to it. He needs to have a relationship with his daughter whether I like it or not. I can be civil and make reasonable accommodations for the two of them to spend time together, or I can be a terrible mom and possibly ruin my daughter's life by keeping her father away from her. I'm not going to do that."

"I'm proud of you," my mom says. "You're a great mom."

"I learned from the best," I say to her and smile.

BROOKE

*A*fter a month of living at my parents' house, I still haven't felt the need to make an appointment with a therapist here. I'm sleeping well. I haven't had any panic attacks. Ellie and I are doing really well here. We've established a routine, and I'm even continuing to work out with Sarah regularly.

Another early Saturday morning rolls around and I drag myself out of bed again at six o'clock to meet Sarah at the gym. Once inside, we start on the elliptical machines as we usually do. The gym isn't nearly as crowded at this time of day, which is a bonus to being here early.

The lack of people also makes it easy to notice a guy who appears to be watching us. He doesn't seem creepy or anything, but I've caught him looking in our direction more than once. His baseball cap makes it hard to see exactly who, or what, he's looking at. I ask Sarah if she's noticed. Maybe it's just in my head.

"He looks hot," Sarah replies when she sees him and nudges my arm.

"Oh, stop it," I say to her. "He's probably a douchebag weightlifter who's full of himself. I swear he's been watching us, though."

"I haven't noticed, but maybe there's a reason you have," she says. "Besides, being a weightlifter does *not* make him a douchebag."

I roll my eyes at her. "Besides, I told you I'm not looking to date anyone right now."

"Don't 'whatever' me. Admit it, he's hot."

Just as she says that, I glance his way and see that he's looking at us, or at least in our direction once more. Thankfully, he's far enough away he can't hear us talking. He's lifting weights, and yeah, Sarah's right, he is attractive. With his hat, I can't see his facial features, but his body is absolutely perfect. Maybe it's that I've always found guys in baseball caps sexy, but there's just something about this guy.

"Should we go lift weights with him?" Sarah asks me, jokingly.

"Ha-ha, very funny," I reply.

We finish our elliptical workout, and the hot guy is gone by the time we finish. Sarah and I move on to some arm exercises. I don't see the guy again until we're finished and walking toward the exit. He's behind the counter. Apparently, he works here.

"Brooke Miller?" I hear my name—my maiden name—and notice it's the hot guy who's called it out. *How the hell does he know me?*

Sarah and I stop in front of the counter to get a better look at him. His baseball cap's pulled a little low, so it's hard to see his eyes. He must notice that we don't know who he is, so he takes his hat off to give us a better view.

Holy. Shit.

My heart actually skips a beat the second I recognize my ex-boyfriend, leaving me speechless.

"Ryan?" Sarah asks before I can remember how to talk. She sounds as surprised as I feel.

"It's me," he says, smiling at us. He walks around the counter, and before I know it, he's hugging Sarah. Then he gives me a hug, too. It feels better than it should to have his strong, warm arms wrap around me. I hug him in return, patting him on the back, and he lets go of me way too soon. I'm still shocked that it's him.

"You work here?" Sarah asks.

"You could say that," Ryan replies. "My brother and I actually own the place."

My mind is spinning. My high school sweetheart owns this gym? *What? How?*

I have to say something. I feel like a total idiot just standing here, staring at him. I can't believe Ryan Hall is right in front of me, and I didn't even recognize him. Now that I know who he is, it's obvious to me that it's him. He's just older and much more fit than the teenager I knew. He has the same friendly brown eyes and brown hair, although it's a little longer than the buzz cut I last saw him with. In fact, he looks absolutely adorable since he took off his hat, and his hair is in disarray.

I want to reach out and run my fingers through it.

Wait, what am I thinking?

"I thought you moved away from Seattle," he says to me.

Finally, I make words come out of my mouth. "I just moved back."

"Funny, so did I," he replies with a kind smile. I swear I see his eyes look down at my hand. Is he searching for a wedding ring? It makes me look at his—subtly, of course—searching for the same. *He's not wearing one.*

"I can't believe it's you," Sarah says to him. "The last I heard, you were stationed out of the country."

"I was, but I'm out of the Marines now. It's good to be back home."

"Well, it's good to see you," I manage to say. "I guess we'll probably see you here again." I start to move toward the exit, and Sarah follows my lead. I feel like if I don't leave soon, I might collapse from a combination of the shock I'm feeling and the extreme attraction I'm having toward him.

"Definitely. It's good to see you both after all these years,"

Ryan says as we turn and walk toward the door. Sarah and I both smile and wave as we leave.

"It's good to see you, too," Sarah says to him before the door shuts behind us.

How many times can we say *it's good to see you?* I guess we were all thrown a little off guard. Who would've thought we'd see Ryan Hall today? Or ever again, for that matter?

Once we're out of view of the gym's front windows by my car, Sarah finally says something. "I can't believe your old boyfriend owns this place! And I can't believe you stormed out like your ass was on fire!"

I look at her and roll my eyes. "He was my boyfriend a *very* long time ago. And I can't believe it, either. I didn't even recognize him! How messed up is that?"

"Oh, don't beat yourself up. I didn't recognize him at first. He's bulked up a lot since high school! The Marines did him good."

I'm still in shock. Ryan was my first serious boyfriend. We were friends for a long time through junior high and high school before we became more than friends in the middle of our junior year. After I moved away for college and he joined the Marines, a long-distance relationship became too difficult, and we decided the best thing to do was break up.

"When's the last time you saw him?" I ask Sarah. Sarah stayed close to home and attended the University of Washington while I went away to college. I remember her calling me to say she ran into him at a bar in Seattle a couple of years after I had lost touch with him.

"It was my third or fourth year of college because I was old enough to be in a bar. He was home on leave. But you were dating Scott by then and didn't seem too interested in knowing about him."

I was actually *very* interested, but I'd convinced myself I shouldn't care and that it didn't really matter. Somehow, I'd been successful. Ryan and I didn't break up because we stopped loving each other or because one of us did something to hurt the other one. We broke up because of distance. I was in college, and he was in the Marines, and it seemed impossible for us to stay together. It was the early 2000s, and technology wasn't like it is now. It took me a long time to get over him.

"He asked about you that night," she reminds me.

"I remember you saying that before," I reply, remembering when she told me how Ryan asked how I was, if I was enjoying school, and if I was single. Of course, I was in love with Scott by then, but the second she mentioned running into Ryan that night, I didn't stop thinking about him for a while. Eventually I did, though, and went on with my life with Scott.

Neither of us says anything for a moment. I'm still in shock from running into Ryan because I haven't thought about him in years. I moved on with my life and was happy for a long time. Of course, every time I heard news about a Marine from Washington State getting killed overseas, I'd hold my breath until I knew it wasn't him. And, sure, I've sometimes wondered in the back of my mind how he's doing now, how his life had turned out, and where in the world he was living. But I've never thought about him and had my heart beat this fast in a very, very long time.

"So are we still on for working out Monday night?" I ask Sarah, changing the subject.

"Of course!" She gives me a quick hug, and we say our goodbyes.

* * *

I try not to think about Ryan, but he keeps popping up in my mind throughout the day. When I go to bed that night, he's still in my thoughts. It's difficult not to think of him as I lie in the same bedroom that he used to sneak into when we were teenagers. He used to come over in the middle of the night, and we'd spend countless hours making out. Luckily, we never got caught.

God, Ellie better not ever try to do anything like that when she gets older!

After dating for almost a year, Ryan and I lost our virginities together right here in this room. It's been so long since I've thought about it, but it was a really special night.

Our last time together was the night before I left for college. The next day, he came over to say goodbye, and that was the last time we saw each other until this morning. We kept in touch for a while by writing to each other and calling when we could, but then we both decided it was too difficult, so we broke up. The last I'd heard, he was still in the Marines, living somewhere overseas. I did not expect to run into him today.

I wonder if he is married? Some guys just don't wear their wedding rings. What brought him back to the Seattle area? He said he just moved back a few months ago. Where did he live before?

My mind wanders back to when we were teenagers.

Ryan was always a nice guy. He took me out on special dates and surprised me at school with flowers just because. I remember other girls telling me how much they wished they had a boyfriend like Ryan. It made me feel special.

Ryan was even nice to my parents. My parents liked him nearly as much as I did. His parents liked me, too. I wonder how his parents are doing now? I spent a lot of time at their house back in high school, and it makes me wonder if they even live in the same house?

Ryan snuck over here in the middle of the night countless times. We shared a lot of firsts together. He was the first boy to see me naked. The first to kiss me in other places besides my mouth. The first to have oral sex with. The first to give me an orgasm. And I was his first for those things too.

Thinking about it now, we had an amazing connection back then. Even though we were both inexperienced, we figured things out together, and it was *good*. I didn't know how good we'd had it until I met my rebound boyfriend, Jordan, and I was sadly disappointed.

I refer to Jordan as my "rebound boyfriend" because that's pretty much what he ended up being. He helped me have fun and move on. I dated him for a while and eventually forgot how amazing Ryan and I had been together. What other choice did I have? I was a freshman in college, lived a few hundred miles away from my family and closest friends at the time, and my ex-boyfriend was now in the Marine Corp, unreachable and doing who knows what. I literally had to force myself to move on, and Jordan was easy to do that with. He was kind, good looking, and fun to hang out with. What else could a girl ask for?

Chemistry, for one.

Maybe love, for two.

I met Scott a few months after Jordan and I broke up, and we hit it off better than Jordan and I had. We definitely had more chemistry, and then the love followed. Sex with him was better than it had ever been with Jordan although, subconsciously, I knew it still didn't compare to how Ryan and I were together. But, again, there was nothing I could do about that.

When Sarah told me she had ran into him at a bar, my heart practically leaped out of my chest. My first instinct was to drive home and find him, but Scott was literally sitting right next to me when she told me over the phone, and I convinced myself that would be a stupid idea. My relationship with Scott was going well, and it would've been illogical to drive five hours home just to see someone who I didn't even know wanted a relationship anymore. Scott was safe and easy for me. Ryan would've been complicated. I already had to get over him once, and I didn't want to subject myself to that kind of heartbreak again. So I stayed with Scott.

My last thoughts before I fall asleep are of Ryan and me together, a happy, young couple in love before life got in the way.

BROOKE

The next day, I take Ellie down to Olympia, and my mom tags along again. I enjoy having the time alone with her. We don't usually get time to talk at home without Ellie interrupting. We eat lunch, talk, and then read our books.

Scott actually gives me cash for some of the furniture he finally sold. I was sure he had already gambled it all away since I had moved out over a month ago, but I'm grateful for the extra three hundred dollars he hands me. I decide to put it into my savings account.

Monday evening, I'm getting ready to go work out with Sarah again, and I find myself primping in front of the mirror a little more than I did last week. If I'm going to see my old boyfriend again, I at least want to look good.

I'm surprised when I feel a little let down that we don't see Ryan at the gym. I'm also surprised I'm looking for him. Of course, Sarah notices.

"Looking for someone?" she asks.

"What?" I try to act nonchalant.

"I know you're looking for Ryan."

I look at her and roll my eyes. "Whatever." I deny it.

"You can't fool me," she says with a smirk on her face. I don't reply.

After our workout, I want to kill Sarah for what she does on our way out. She walks right up to the front desk and asks if Ryan is working tonight. The young employee behind the counter tells her that he doesn't work on Mondays. She asks him when Ryan works, and he tells her he now works Tuesday through Friday nights, and Saturday mornings. She smiles and thanks him, then turns and smiles at me.

Of course, when Wednesday's workout comes around, I find myself primping again. As Sarah and I walk into the gym, my heart rate speeds up when I see him behind the front counter. He's wearing the same baseball cap again. His head is down as he reads something. As much as I wanted to see him, now I just want to sneak past him and go work out. I'm nervous. But, of course, Sarah walks right up to him. I suddenly feel very shy.

"Howdy, stranger," she says. He looks up, and my mouth goes dry. He really is *very* good looking. He always was when we were younger, but he has improved with age.

"Hey, ladies. It's good to see you again," he replies. He looks at me and smiles. "Hi, Brooke."

I manage to smile back at him. "Hi, Ryan."

"How come I've never noticed you here before?" Sarah asks him. "I've been working out here for a few months now."

Ryan pulls his gaze away from mine and looks back at Sarah. I take a deep breath. *I hadn't realized I stopped breathing.*

Then he answers. "I used to work different hours. I'd always open the gym and get off in the early afternoon. My brother and I recently switched our schedules around, so I'm closing Tuesdays through Fridays now, and I open on Saturdays. It gives him more time with his family."

"Well, what about you? Don't you have a family?" Sarah asks, and I know it's for my benefit. *I'm going to kill her.*

Or kiss her. I'm not sure which.

He chuckles. "No, no, I don't. I'm single." He glances at me, then looks back at Sarah. I feel frozen in place. I want to move away from this situation and just go work out. And maybe do a cartwheel or two in celebration that he's single.

"I see," Sarah replies. She starts to step away from the counter. Yes, good, let's go, Sarah …

"Is there anything I can do for you ladies?" Ryan asks. "Are you interested in having a personal trainer?"

Sarah looks at me, then back at Ryan. "Who would that personal trainer be?"

He smiles. "We have a few to choose from, but I'm the only one here tonight."

Sarah looks at me again and smirks. "I don't know. Brooke, do you need a personal trainer today?"

I'm really going to kill her.

"No, I think we're good," I manage to say.

"Well, if you ever change your mind, let me know," Ryan says. He smiles at me again.

"Thanks," Sarah replies. "We'll definitely let you know if we need you."

Oh. My. God.

Sarah and I walk away and head over to the elliptical machines.

"What the hell was that?" I ask her when I'm sure Ryan can't hear us.

Sarah laughs. "I'm trying to help you out!"

I shake my head. "Really? Could you be any more obvious? *We'll let you know if we need you. Sarah!?!*"

She laughs again. "Well, at least I talked to him. You were practically a statue standing there. Nervous much?"

I can feel my face blushing. Did I look that uncomfortable with him?

"Look," she starts, now sounding more serious, "you have a history with him. A good history. I used to wish I had a boyfriend like yours when we were in high school. Maybe fate brought you two back together. What are the chances that you both move home within months of each other, you're both single, and you work out at the gym he owns? You can't ignore this."

I don't say anything. I just start moving on the elliptical, and Sarah follows suit. I really don't know what to say, actually, because she could be right. But this is too soon for me. I'm not even officially divorced yet. I have a baby. I can't start dating anybody right now.

"Are you going to say anything?" Sarah asks a few minutes later.

"I can't right now."

"Are you that out of breath already?"

"No," I reply, rolling my eyes at her. "I mean, I can't pursue anyone right now. It's too soon. And what kind of single, hot guy like Ryan is going to want to date a woman with a baby? It's just not in the cards right now."

"Awww, so you admit he's hot," Sarah says. I roll my eyes again. He's obviously very attractive. No one would deny that. "First of all," Sarah starts again, "it's really not too soon. You and Asshole have been separated for what? Five months now? He royally screwed you over. Why aren't you allowed to be happy? Second of all, how do you know a hot guy like Ryan wouldn't want to date you? Being a mom doesn't make you undesirable. He loved you in high school. You two were *in love* with each other! Have you forgotten that?"

Again, I don't reply. I just keep moving on the elliptical. She's got a point, though. We *were* in love. We have a pretty important history together. If he hadn't joined the Marines, who knows what would've happened between us.

Sarah and I don't talk the rest of the time we're on the ellipticals. Afterward, we work out our legs. She doesn't mention Ryan again.

On our way out of the gym, Ryan is still at the front counter.

"Did you have a good workout?" he asks us as we walk by, so we stop at the counter in front of him. I'm nervous again, but I try not to let it show.

"Of course," Sarah replies.

"Good to hear. I want to make sure our customers are happy." He looks at me and smiles. "You're welcome to keep coming as a guest with Sarah, but do you think you'd like to have your own membership, Brooke?"

Jeez, I hadn't even considered that. Sarah was being so kind and letting me tag along for free, but maybe I should sign up on my own. Then I won't just be a freeloader.

"Don't be silly, you can always be my guest," Sarah says before I can answer.

I believe Sarah, but I suddenly feel a little guilty for getting all my workouts for free. "How much is a membership?" I ask Ryan.

"Thirty dollars a month. It includes all the amenities: the sauna, various fitness classes, and if you show your membership card at the juice bar next door, you'll get a discount. Plus, if you find another friend you'd like to bring along, you could bring her as a guest." He winks at me. *Why is he so cute?*

Not wanting to be a tagalong anymore, I decide I want my own membership. "Sure, I'll sign up," I reply. I can handle paying thirty dollars a month. I might not have a lot of income now, but I also don't have many monthly expenses either since Scott is paying off all the debt he created.

Sarah smiles at me. All of a sudden, she looks at the watch on her wrist and says, "Well, I should get going. I need to get home to put the kids to bed. I'll see you both later!" Then she waves and walks away, leaving me there with Ryan. I hadn't anticipated her leaving me! *Crap!*

Ryan looks at me. He looks absolutely adorable with a sexy smirk on his face as if he knows that Sarah's plan was to leave us alone together just now. "Do you want to sign up now, or the next time you come in? I didn't mean to put you on the spot." *He's giving me an out.*

"Let's just do it now," I reply as I shrug my shoulders, trying with all my might not to stumble on my words as I talk. *Why am I so nervous around him?* But I might as well get this over with.

"Great," he says. He moves to the end of the counter where there's a lower desk with a computer and two chairs. He motions for me to sit down. He sits down across from me in front of the computer and types something, then asks me, "Is your last name still Miller?"

I swallow. Here goes nothing. "No. It's Ford."

"Brooke Ford," he says, testing out my name. Honestly, hearing my married name out loud now makes me cringe, but I'm not going to change my last name back to Miller. It's too complicated, especially with a kid. I think it'll be easier to bear the same name as Ellie. Plus, it takes so much time and paperwork to change it back. I honestly just don't want to deal with it right now.

Ryan types on the keyboard, then asks, "Address?"

"4458 South 160th," I recite to him. He types it in, then looks at me as if he just realized he knows that address.

"Your parents' house?" he asks, his curiosity evident.

I just nod my head.

"When did you move back there?" he asks, sounding genuinely interested.

"Just over a month ago, actually."

"Oh? What brought you back home?"

I nervously pick at my fingers in my lap, feeling fidgety as I sit across from my high school sweetheart. I might as well just tell him the truth. "I'm getting divorced."

I swear I see a fleeting look of relief before he gives the same look of sympathy everyone else gives me when they hear the news. "I'm sorry to hear that," he says.

"Thanks," I reply with a shrug, trying to play it off like it's no big deal because I honestly don't want to discuss my divorce with him right now.

Ryan nods his head, seeming to understand I want to change the subject, and turns his attention back to the computer. "Phone number?"

Why do I feel a little excited to give him my number? I rattle it off to him, and he types it in.

"Birthdate? Wait–don't tell me," he says. He types something, then turns the computer screen so I can see what he typed. He points at the place where he typed my

birthdate in, and he got it right. He remembered.

"You have a good memory," I say to him, smiling. The fact that he still remembers my birthday sparks something inside me, and I vaguely wonder when I last felt like this. When was the last time someone besides Ellie genuinely made me smile?

"Of course, I remember," he says, smiling back at me. We hold each other's gaze for a moment before I force myself to look away. I swear he's trying to tell me he remembers more than just birthdays. "And I should wish you a belated birthday," he adds. My birthday was just a couple of months ago. He turns the computer screen back toward him. "Any health problems I should be aware of? Anything that could flare up while you're exercising?"

I shake my head.

"Okay, then. All I need now is your payment info, and we'll be done."

I dig my debit card out of my phone case, and he types in everything he needs.

"There you go. You're now an official member of our gym! Congratulations," he says as he extends his hand for me to shake. When I touch his hand with mine, I swear there's a spark, followed by an electrical current pulsing steadily between us. I think he feels it, too.

"Thanks," I say as I pull my hand away, suddenly missing his touch. *Why do I have the overwhelming need to touch him again?* I stand and so does he, handing me my new membership card.

"Will I see you here tomorrow night?" he asks, almost sounding hopeful.

"Probably not," I reply. "Sarah and I will be back on Saturday morning."

I swear he looks a little let down, but that can't be possible. "You know," he says as his mouth turns up in a crooked smile, "you can come whenever you want now and not just when Sarah works out."

I hadn't even considered that as a possibility yet. "You're right," I say, nervously smiling at him. "Maybe you'll see me before Saturday."

I start to walk toward the exit, and he walks around the desk to follow me. He catches up to me, and says, "Brooke, wait."

"What?" I ask as I turn around to face him, surprised he's standing as close as he is to me now. I could reach out and touch him again just as I wanted to do a minute ago. But I don't.

He looks down at his hands, then back at me, and answers, "It's really good to see you again."

I smile. "It's good to see you, too."

We stand there, just looking at each other for a couple of seconds, although it feels like minutes. I swear my heart is pounding loud enough for him to hear it. He seems to be nervous too, though. I don't think I'm the only one feeling this way. Finally, he moves and pushes the door open for me. "I'll see you next time you come in."

I walk out, and say, "Yes, you will."

RYAN

*H*oly shit. I can't believe Brooke is really back in Seattle! And out of all the gyms she could possibly go to around here, I can't believe she goes to my gym. I also can't believe I just spent time talking with her alone. It's been fourteen years since I saw her last, and she's even prettier than I remember.

I couldn't believe my eyes when I first saw her here last week. I thought I was seeing things. Not only was Brooke Miller here, but she was with Sarah Knight, her best friend from high school. It was surreal, to say the least. The last I heard, Brooke was living in Portland. I never expected to see her again even though I've always had this fantasy of running into her someday.

I'm not ashamed to admit that I was a pussy-whipped teenager in love. She took my breath away back then, and I considered myself lucky to have her as my girlfriend. I honestly thought we would end up getting married someday, but when I followed my dream of joining the Marines, and she followed hers by going to college, we realized how difficult it would be to stay together. More like impossible. And I didn't want her to be tied down to me while I was away. If I was killed in combat, I didn't want Brooke to suffer and be left alone. I guess you could say I loved her enough to let her go.

Now, though, I'm out of the Marines, and she's apparently getting divorced. What are the chances that we'd both move back to Seattle, our old stomping grounds, and run into each other like this? I can't help but wonder if fate is stepping in.

I've thought about Brooke countless times over the years, always wondering how she was doing, if she was married, and if she was happy. When I ran into a classmate of ours a few months ago, she told me she was friends with Brooke on Facebook and filled me in on what she knew. That's how I knew she was living in Portland, and I figured I'd never have a chance to reconnect with her. I accepted that as a fact and let it go. But now, I can't stop thinking about her.

She seemed kind of nervous talking to me tonight. Actually, she's seemed nervous *every* time we've talked since we ran into each other. I wonder why that is? We have a lot of history together, going all the way back to junior high. We were friends for a long time before I got up the nerve to finally ask her out. I'd had a crush on her since the first day I met her. She just took my breath away. She was smart, funny, athletic, and beautiful. I had to hide my first boner at school because of her, then several more after that. When we finally became a couple in high school, I wasn't going to let her go after I'd wanted her for so many years.

But then I did. Because I felt like it was the best thing to do.

Fuck. I really want to take her out on a date. Talking with her tonight was nice, but it was mostly just business. I'd like to take her out and really get a chance to reconnect. I wonder if she would be up for that, though? She did say she was getting divorced, and she's living at her parents' house now. Maybe she's not ready to start dating yet? I hope that's not the case. I'll be her friend for as long as I need to be and just chat with her here at the gym, but I want the chance to get to know her again. Hopefully, she doesn't shoot me down when I finally get the balls to ask her.

BROOKE

When I walk in the front door of my parents' house, I find them sitting on the living room floor playing with Ellie. It warms my heart to see her so happy, surrounded by her grandparents who love her so much.

"Hi there," Mom says, looking up at me.

"Hi," I reply. I put my keys and phone down on an end table and sit down on the floor with them. Ellie crawls over to me, and I pick her up, giving her a kiss and setting her back down between my legs. She crawls to my dad, who has one of her toys in his hands.

"You're a little later tonight than usual," my mom says.

"Oh, sorry," I start to explain. "I decided to sign up for my own gym membership, so that took a little extra time."

"No need to be sorry," Mom replies. "I was just wondering what kept you later. You must really like the place if you signed yourself up."

"I do. It's a great place to work out."

"Does it have anything to do with Ryan working there?" Dad asks.

My head pops up. "What?" *How do they know about Ryan?*

"We know he co-owns the place with his brother," Dad replies with a smirk on his face.

Shit! Have my parents known all this time and assumed I was only going there to see Ryan?!? I suddenly feel like I need to defend myself, but my parents keep talking before I can say anything.

"We didn't want to say anything at first because we weren't sure if you knew he worked there or not. We knew you'd figure it out sooner or later," Mom says. Her explanation makes me feel a little better. At least, they weren't thinking I was acting like a lovestruck teenager going to hang out with her crush.

"Have you seen him yet?" Dad asks.

I'm shocked that my parents kept this a secret from me. *What the hell?* "Yes, I've seen him. He seems to be doing just fine. I didn't recognize him at first, though. He looks a lot different than he did in high school."

"He was such a nice boy," Mom reminisces. "When I read the article in the newspaper a few months back about his brother and him opening the gym, I'd wondered how he was doing now."

"I can't believe you didn't say anything to me about it."

"Well, we weren't sure how you would take it," Dad says. "We didn't want to spoil your plans to work out with Sarah. We never knew if you and Ryan ended things on good terms or not."

"Well, okay," I reply. That's true, I guess. I didn't exactly tell my parents all about my relationship problems back then. Actually, I didn't want to talk to anyone about my breakup with Ryan. I kept my feelings to myself. Occasionally, I'd talk to my college roommate about it, but mostly, I wanted to forget about him so I could move on with my life. My parents knew we broke up, but they never knew the story of *why.* I'm just surprised they've kept this information about him owning the gym from me for the past month.

Looking at the clock, I see it's Ellie's bedtime and use that as the perfect excuse to change the subject. "I need to get Ellie ready for bed now."

Ellie is lying on the floor, winding down, and I can tell she's getting tired. I go to the kitchen to make her a bottle, then go back to the living room to pick her up. My parents say good night to us, then I take her downstairs with me.

Ellie falls asleep in my arms as I feed her. I rock her in the rocking chair a little longer before I get up and put her to bed in her crib. Then I go upstairs to retrieve my phone. Mom and Dad have already gone to bed, but I see I have a text message from Sarah:

Sarah: *Did you sign up for a gym membership?*

Me: *Yes. Thanks a lot for leaving me there.*

Sarah: *I really did have to get home to put the kids to bed. Sorry, though. Did you survive being alone with Ryan? ;-)*

I roll my eyes at her text. Then I remember how sexy he looked tonight. And how he remembered my birthday after all these years. I pause to wonder if I remember his? Of course, I do. July 20th.

I text her back just a short and sweet *yes*.

She responds with a smiley face. Then our texts end. I decide to watch a little TV before going to bed.

* * *

My parents don't mention Ryan the rest of the week. I'm glad because I really don't want to discuss him. I'm having a hard enough time not thinking about him on my own. I don't need to have an actual *conversation* about the guy.

By the time Saturday morning rolls around, I'm anxious to see Ryan again. I can't stop thinking about him. I couldn't resist any longer, so I dug my old high school yearbooks out of storage last night. Oh, the memories that came flooding back! We had so many good times together, and he really was one of the most important people in my life growing up—even before we were a couple. It's funny how life took us in such different directions, and we lost touch after all we had been through together. Now, I just want to see him again.

He's at the front counter when Sarah and I walk in. He's reading something, and his baseball cap is low, so he doesn't notice us right away. He really looks irresistible. His T-shirt is taut across his chest, and the short sleeves look like they might rip if he flexes his arm muscles. I have butterflies in my stomach as we scan our membership cards in front of him. The beep it makes catches his attention, and he looks up. He instantly smiles when he sees us. "Good morning, ladies," he says. I try not to swoon, but the combination of his deep voice and how attractive he looks this morning has me feeling all hot and bothered.

"Good morning," Sarah and I both say, almost in unison.

"Enjoy your workout," he says, then he goes back to whatever he's reading. Why do I feel a little upset that he didn't spend more time talking to us this time?

Ugh, I'm being ridiculous.

Sarah and I finish our workout, then head back out. Ryan isn't at the counter anymore. *Where is he?* I think to myself. We walk out of the gym, and Sarah says, "Are you sad you couldn't say goodbye to your boyfriend?"

I snap my head toward her, and reply, "He's *not* my boyfriend."

Even if I *am* upset I didn't see him, I'm not ready to admit my feelings even to Sarah. Not yet.

"He *was*," she shoots back. "Plus, I saw you looking for him. You can't hide your feelings from me. I know you."

I don't want to admit I'm having feelings for Ryan because I don't feel as if I've given myself enough time since separating from Scott. As much as I keep thinking of him, I know I need to act logically. *It's too soon for me.* I just want to keep my feelings to myself and admire him from time to time.

"I can't date anyone right now, Sarah," I tell her as we stand next to her minivan.

Sarah rolls her eyes at me. "Yes, you can."

"I need more time. I'm not even divorced yet."

Sarah puts her hands on my shoulders and looks me in the eyes. "Brooke," she says, "you are my best friend, so I feel obligated to tell you this. It doesn't take a genius to see that you think about him. You didn't make yourself look so cute when we came to the gym until we ran into Ryan. Yeah, I've noticed your hair is pulled up a little neater, and you have a little makeup on. The way he looks at you when we're here makes it obvious he's interested, too. Don't deny what could possibly be the best thing for you right now."

I look at my friend and take a deep breath. I don't know what to say except, "I'm not cute." I crack a smile and try not to laugh.

Sarah rolls her eyes at me and chuckles. "You're right. You're not cute; you're hot and single!" I can't help but laugh with her. "Now, go home, enjoy Easter tomorrow with Ellie, and I'll see you here on Monday night, hot momma," Sarah says with a wink. Then she kisses me on the cheek and pats me on my back to send me on my way.

"Thanks for the pep talk," I say to her as I start walking toward my car.

"Hey," she calls to me. "Text or call me if you want to talk!"

I smile and wave at her, then go to my car and drive home, all the while thinking about what she said. Maybe it's not too soon for me to date? Sarah's right; she *does* know me, and she hasn't missed the fact that I'm interested in Ryan. It's exciting that she thinks he's interested in me, too. I guess I can just go with the flow and see if anything happens with him. If he ever asks me out, maybe I'll say yes.

Oh, who the hell am I kidding? If he asked me out, I'd definitely say yes!

BROOKE

*I*t's Ellie's first Easter. I've never done this before. She's too young to really get into all the fun traditions like egg decorating, but my mom and I do it anyway. I also got her an Easter basket, which I filled with baby food and toys.

On Sunday morning, my parents, Ellie, and I go to church. We're not regular church-goers, but we try to go on Christmas and Easter at least. After church, we just enjoy a quiet day at home together. Mom and I cook a ham and all the fixings for dinner. Ellie enjoys her Easter basket goodies. All in all, it's a nice day.

Scott calls to wish us a Happy Easter, and he talks to Ellie for a minute. He just wants her to hear his voice since he can't meet us this week. She babbles at him. He's at work, but he makes the time to call anyway.

My sister calls, too. It's so good to hear her voice and talk to her. We text each other regularly, usually about random stuff to make each other laugh, but it's not the same as talking. After I put her on speaker so Mom and Dad can also talk to her, I take my phone downstairs so I can speak with her privately.

"What's up?" she asks, obviously wondering what I want to say to her that I can't say in front of our parents.

"I saw Ryan," I tell her. After the talk with Sarah yesterday, I decide I need another person's perspective on things.

"Ryan, as in your high school boyfriend, Ryan?"

"Yes. He owns the gym I've been going to with Sarah," I tell her.

"*And ...?*" Becca says, waiting for me to say more.

"And he's gorgeous. I can't stop thinking about him." There. I said the words out loud and admitted it.

"He always was gorgeous," Becca says with a laugh. "Are you going to see him outside the gym?"

"No ... I don't know. I don't even know if he's really interested although Sarah thinks he is. I just don't know if it's the right time for me."

"Why not? Your divorce is almost final. Go have fun!"

For some reason, her comment makes me smile. "That's what Sarah told me, too."

"See? It's good advice, then," Becca replies. "I know you, Brooke, and you're probably trying to do the responsible thing. You think it's too soon for you to date, right?"

"Isn't it?" I ask her.

"For God's sake, girl," she says, "you are under no obligation to wait a certain amount of time before moving on. It's already been months since you filed for divorce, so it's not like it happened last week. If you want to date Ryan, go for it! You guys were the cutest couple back in high school! In fact, you kind of ruined me. I thought all boys treated their girlfriends the way Ryan treated you. Boy, was I mistaken."

Becca and I both laugh. She's right; he was the best boyfriend. "Well, I'm sorry that I messed up your perception of teenage relationships."

"Not just teenage relationships. Adult ones, too. Seriously, though, Brooke, if he's as interested as you are, you should definitely go out with him. Have some fun!"

I appreciate my sister's honesty on the situation. I know I can always trust her to tell me how it is. I thank her for her advice, and she promises to come visit soon before we say goodbye and hang up.

That night as I lie in bed, I consider what Becca said to me on the phone. She basically said the same things as Sarah. Maybe they're right, then? Scott and I separated months ago. It's not as if I planned on running into Ryan and having all these feelings come back. It just happened. There's no rule saying how long I have to wait to start dating again.

The only question is, does Ryan even want to date me?

* * *

On Wednesday night, Sarah and I work out again as we always do. Ryan's there, but he's busy doing a personal training session with some guy. He waves to us, but he's too busy to talk. I try to hide my disappointment. Sarah doesn't mention anything, and I'm grateful.

On Friday afternoon, I walk Ellie to the park. I get a text from Scott.

I have to work on Sunday, but I can meet you and Ellie on Monday. Does that work?

I text him back and tell him Monday works, and we agree to meet at eleven o'clock again.

I wonder what Ryan would think of Scott and vice versa? I'm finding it harder and harder to get Ryan out of my head.

Not that I really *want* to get him out of my head, but I feel like a silly teenager thinking about him all the time.

Later that evening, I feel restless and decide to go work out. Sarah won't be there, but that's okay. I just feel the need to run. Besides, maybe if I see Ryan, it will somehow help me stop thinking about him.

Or something like that.

When I walk into the gym, I don't see Ryan at the counter. I feel a little let down but also a little relieved. I don't know why I always get so nervous around him.

Instead of doing the elliptical today, I hop on the treadmill. I used to love running, but I haven't gone for a run since I found out I was pregnant. I had terrible morning sickness that lasted practically all day long, so that ruined my daily jog, and I just never got back into the routine.

The gym isn't very crowded, but a few people are here. It is Friday night, after all. Most people probably want to go out on a Friday night rather than exercise.

I set my pace and start to jog, keeping myself focused. I also scan the area periodically to see if Ryan is around. When I finally see him, about ten minutes later, he's with a woman, and it looks like he's doing a training session with her. She looks about our age, blonde, beautiful, and she's bench pressing what looks like a ton of weight. She's strong. I immediately feel like a silly little girl.

Jealousy. That's what this feeling is.

I don't stare, but I look over at them frequently. I see them laughing. I see him touch her. Okay, so it looks like it's all part of the job of training her, but I can't help the surge of jealousy. *What is wrong with me?*

They move out of my view, so I can't see them anymore. *Dammit!*

After my thirty-minute jog, I decide I've worn myself out enough and stop. I step off the treadmill, turn around, and Ryan is right in front of me. He's alone. "Hi," he says, a grin spreading across his face.

"Oh, hi," I say, trying to sound as casual as I can. Inside, my heart is racing, and it's not because I was just running on the treadmill. How long has he been standing there?

"I wasn't stalking you," he says as if he can read my mind. "I just happened to be walking by here and saw you were done, so I thought I'd say hi. I didn't think I'd see you again until tomorrow morning."

"Well, I felt the need to run tonight, so I decided to come here on my own," I explain to him.

He smiles at me again. I can't help but smile back. *He's so good looking.* He's not wearing his baseball cap tonight, so I can see his whole face unobstructed. His hair is a little messed up, and he looks adorable.

Hot.

Sexy.

"Are you done working out? Or are you going to do something else? I won't keep you," he says, pulling me out of my lust-filled daze.

God, I hope he didn't notice how I was just admiring him.

"I was just going to leave," I tell him. "I'll do more tomorrow morning with my workout partner."

He cocks his head a bit. "Are you sure? I'm free if you'd like a training session. On the house, of course." The thought of him training me scares the hell out of me for some reason. I'm already nervous around him. How would I manage to *exercise* in front of him while he just watched and critiqued me?

On the other hand, it would give him an excuse to touch me, too ...

"No, thanks," I reply. "I just wanted to run a bit tonight."

I start to walk toward the exit, and he walks beside me. When we're almost to the door, he stops and touches my arm to get my attention. It takes me by surprise, and his touch sends a tingle down my arm. "Okay, I'm just going to come out and say it," he says. "I want to spend some time with you."

I don't know what to say. I'm surprised, flattered, excited, and speechless.

"I have to close the gym tonight, so I'm stuck here until ten o'clock. Do you want to meet up somewhere then?"

Did he just ask me out?

"Well?" he asks, sounding hopeful. I realize then that I actually need to speak.

"I don't know," I answer him, and his face starts to fall as though he feels rejected. I need to be honest with him, so I just come right out and say it. "Ryan, I have a daughter. I don't know if my parents will be okay with watching her that late tonight."

His face lifts into a smile again. "You have a daughter?"

"Yes." At least he's smiling. Maybe the fact I have a kid won't freak him out after all.

"I had no idea. That's awesome, Brooke."

I suddenly don't want to leave. I want to spend more time with him, too.

Before I can say anything else to him, he starts to talk again. "Well, how about now then? Can you stay here a little bit longer and hang out with me? We can just sit behind the counter and talk. You don't have to stay late."

I smile, and reply, "I can do that."

He turns, and I follow him. He offers me a seat on a stool behind the counter, and he sits next to me. "Friday nights aren't busy at all. Hopefully, no one will need me for anything," he says. He seems a little nervous, which makes me feel better, because I'm nervous as hell.

"So when did you move back to Seattle?" I ask him. I've been wondering how long he's been living here.

"In October, when I got out of the Marines. I had been stationed in California for the past year, and Dan and I started

70

our plan to open this place while I was down there. I moved up a week before we opened."

"Wow, that's great," I say to him. "And business has been good?"

He nods. "Business has been great since we opened. We're really pleased. It's exciting for us."

"How's your brother, by the way?" I ask. His brother, Dan, is three years older than us. He joined the Marines when he graduated high school, so he wasn't around at all when Ryan and I were dating. I just vaguely remember him.

"He's doing great. He's married and has two boys. His wife is a nurse, so her work schedule is a little crazy. That's why I traded shifts with him, so he can be home more when he needs to be."

"Where is she a nurse?" I ask, finding it interesting that we share the same career.

"Overlake Hospital in Bellevue. She works in the ER."

What are the chances? I chuckle, and reply, "What a coincidence. I used to be a nurse in an ER. I quit working when I had Ellie."

He raises his eyebrows in surprise. "Really? So you didn't become a physical therapist like you wanted to in high school?"

I shake my head. "No, I had a change of heart and switched my major. I'm glad I did because I loved being a nurse."

"I can see you being great at that. You were always good at taking care of people," he says. The unexpected compliment catches me off guard a bit.

We're interrupted by a customer who has a question about something, so Ryan excuses himself. I sit and wait, thinking about what I can discuss with him next. We haven't talked in nearly fourteen years, so there's a lot we could say. He's back before I have finished gathering all my thoughts.

"So," he says as he sits back down on his stool, "tell me about your daughter."

Of course, mentioning my daughter automatically makes me

smile. "Ellie is perfect," I begin. "She's eight months old, and she is such a good baby. Here, let me show you a picture." I open my phone and search through my photos. I show him one of the hundreds I have saved of her.

Ryan looks at the photo. "She's beautiful," he says. "And she's only eight months? When did you get divorced?"

Here we go. I knew I'd have to discuss this with him eventually, but I just never imagined how the talk about my failed marriage to my ex-boyfriend would go. I close my phone and start to talk, but Ryan interrupts me before I can get a word out.

"I'm sorry, I hope that didn't sound rude. I just meant..."

"No, it's okay." I honestly don't blame him for asking. "My divorce isn't quite finalized yet. My lawyer says it just takes time on the court's end, but it should be soon. When Ellie was three months old, I found out my husband had been gambling all our money away. We were in a ton of debt and lost our house. He refused to admit he had a problem and get help, so he basically chose gambling over Ellie and me."

He looks surprised. And sympathetic. And upset. "Are you serious? What kind of guy does that to his wife and baby? I'm so sorry, Brooke."

"It's okay," I say to him, looking down at my hands. "I thought we had a great marriage, but apparently, we didn't."

"Wow," he says, and I look back up at him. He looks genuinely sympathetic as he shakes his head in disbelief. "How long were you two married?"

"Nine years," I reply. Neither of us says anything for a moment. I pick up my phone and start absentmindedly fidgeting with it. I don't really know what to say next. I'm sure he doesn't want to hear all about my ex-husband.

Then I think of something to ask him that will get the focus off me. I look at him again, and ask, "How about you? Have you ever been married? Any kids?"

He shakes his head and kind of chuckles. "No. I've been the

single military guy. I had a couple of relationships here and there, but they never got serious."

Huh, that's interesting. I wonder why none of his relationships ever got serious? I can't just come right out and ask him that, though, so I decide to ask him a more appropriate question. "Tell me about being in the Marines."

"I loved it," he says without hesitation. "It was obviously hard work, both physically and mentally, but it was exciting. I got to travel the world and see things I never thought I would see in my life."

"Where in the world did you go?" I ask. I wonder if we've been to any of the same places. Scott and I had traveled to several different countries over the years.

"Outside the US, I was in Japan, Thailand, several countries in Europe, and obviously the Middle East."

I don't want to think about him fighting in war. It was a fear I had when we were younger and he told me he was joining the Marines. It still makes my heart clench to hear him say he's been to the Middle East. I don't know why, since he obviously survived all his tours of duty and is doing just fine now. I decide not to dwell on that and focus on my original thought of finding out if we've traveled to any of the same places. "I've been to Japan and all over Europe, too," I tell him.

He raises his eyebrows and looks surprised again. "Really?"

"Yup. Scott, my ex, and I traveled a lot before we decided to have a baby. That's why we waited to have kids. We wanted to see the world first. We took one big trip each year."

"What was your favorite country to visit?"

I think about that for a moment. Every country we visited had something I loved. "I don't know," I reply. "That's a hard question to answer. But I absolutely *loved* Croatia. The sea organ in Zadar is amazing. Have you ever been there?"

"No, Croatia is one country I haven't been to," he says.

"Well, you should go someday. It's amazing." Then I ask him the same question. "What was your favorite country?"

He thinks about his answer. Then he replies, "Alaska."

I laugh out loud.

"What?" he asks, holding his hands out to his sides.

"You do realize that Alaska is *in* the United States, right?"

"You didn't say it had to be a *different* country. I loved Alaska. And honestly, it almost felt like another country. I would move there someday if I could."

"What did you love about it?" I'm curious what he found so fascinating about the state.

"It's calming there. So low key. I love the outdoors. And the mountains ..." He looks thoughtful as if he's remembering something truly wonderful. Then he looks back at me. "Have you ever been to Alaska?"

"I have, actually. We took a cruise there."

"So you know," he says. "You know how beautiful it is up there."

I do remember how beautiful Alaska is. That was actually the last vacation Scott and I took because I got pregnant with Ellie a month later.

Thinking about that trip now, I suddenly remember how preoccupied Scott seemed on that trip. He also spent a lot of time in the ship's casino.

Holy crap! Looking back on it now, maybe he started his gambling habits sooner than I realized? After all, our credit card debt had really gotten out of control, almost as if he started racking up charges years ago to cover payments for things we needed to buy. He must have started all this much sooner than he let me believe. Wow, I feel stupid all of a sudden for not realizing this before!

"Hey, are you okay?" Ryan asks me.

I realize I must look the way I feel. "I'm fine. I just remembered something about that trip that I didn't think about before."

"What's that?"

Do I really talk to him about this? I'm sure he doesn't want to hear all about my ex. "It's nothing, really."

He looks at me for a moment, unsure, then says, "Okay. Well, I'm all ears if you change your mind and want to talk about it."

I smile at him. He really hasn't changed much since high school. He was always a great listener when we were younger. I could talk to him about anything. "Thanks, but I'm all right."

He changes the subject then. "So tell me more. What else have you been up to for the past fourteen years?"

Where do I even start to answer that question? I decide short and to the point is best. "Well, first there was college, then I got my job as a nurse, then Ellie was born, and now here I am."

"That's the edited version," he says, deadpan.

"You could say that." I laugh a little, and he gives me his crooked smile. He looks adorable. I always loved that look. "What about you?" I ask him.

"Well, first there was the Marines, then the Marines, then more time in the Marines, and now I'm here." He answers just as I did, only the Marines has been his whole life until now. "I can give the edited version, too." He winks at me.

I laugh. "Okay, okay. I get it."

"So are you going to tell me the unedited version?" he asks.

I look down at my hands, then back up into his beautiful brown eyes. "I'm not
sure if you'd really like to hear it all."

"Of course, I do," he says sincerely, looking into my eyes. The butterflies return to
my stomach in full force, and I feel myself blushing.

We're interrupted by another customer, and the moment is over. He
has to go help him with something.

While he's away, I decide to call my parents and let them

know why I'm running late. My mom answers the phone. "Hi, Brooke."

"Hi, Mom. I just wanted to check in and let you know I'm running a little later tonight. Is everything okay with Ellie?"

"Of course," she replies, sounding curious. "What's causing you to run late, dear?"

"Oh … I'm just chatting with Ryan. He wanted to talk." I try to sound nonchalant and pray she doesn't make this a bigger deal than it is.

"Oh?" My mom actually sounds excited. Jeez.

"I won't be too late. I can leave now if you need me to come home."

"No, no," Mom says almost a little too quickly. "Stay out as late as you want. Ellie is fine here!"

I see Ryan walking back, so I tell her I have to go and end the call.

"I was just talking to my mom," I tell him as he sits down on the stool. "I wanted to check on Ellie."

"Is everything okay?"

"Yeah, she's fine."

"Does your mom need you to come home soon or something?"

I chuckle as I reply. "No, actually, she told me to stay out as late as I want."

Ryan smiles and looks at his watch. "Well then," he says. "Maybe I'm pressing my luck here, but it's only eight thirty. Why don't you go home, see Ellie, put her to bed, and I'll pick you up after I close here? We can go grab a drink somewhere and talk some more."

I smile. I really want to spend more time with him, so how can I say no to this? "That sounds like a great idea."

We both smile. I feel like the luckiest girl in the world, getting to spend more time with this handsome man in front of me. I can't wait for him to pick me up later.

BROOKE

*W*hen I walk in the front door, Mom looks surprised to see me. "I didn't expect to see you so soon!"

She's giving Ellie her bedtime bottle. When Ellie looks up and sees me, she immediately starts reaching for me to take her. I walk over, and my mom hands her to me, so I sit down and let her finish her bottle. "Ryan is going to come pick me up when he gets off work. I hope you don't mind if I go out for a bit?"

Mom smiles at me. "Of course not. Go have fun! Ellie will be asleep soon, so just bring her baby monitor up to me."

"Thanks," I say to her. I look down at Ellie, who is peacefully sucking down her formula. Her eyes are heavy, so she'll be asleep soon.

"How is Ryan doing?" Mom asks.

"He's good," I reply.

"When did he get out of the Marines?" Mom is fishing for more.

"Just before he moved back up here. He was stationed in California last, but he's been all over the world."

"Has he ever married? Does he have kids?"

"No and no," I reply.

"Where is he going to take you tonight?"

"I don't know," I say. "He just said we could go somewhere to get a drink and talk. I'm not sure if he has a place in mind or not."

"And he's picking you up here? What time?"

"He closes the gym at ten, so sometime after that."

Just then, Dad walks into the room. "Did I hear you say you have a date tonight?"

My parents seem just a bit too happy about me dating already. And I can't believe I'm going out.

After I put Ellie to bed, I decide to take a shower. I was a mess after my workout, and if we're going out, I want to look nice. I don't get too dressed up, though, because I know Ryan will still be in his work clothes. I settle on a pair of jeans and a nice blouse. Casual-dressy.

At about ten twenty, there's a knock on the front door. My parents went to bed already, luckily, so they're not around. They seemed just a bit too anxious for me to be going out with Ryan, and I don't want them to say something embarrassing.

Wow, I sound like a teenager.

I open the front door, and there he is. Just the way he looks at me makes my heart race. He may just be wearing track pants and a hoodie, but he still looks sexy. My fingers suddenly tingle with the urge to touch him.

"Hi," he says, his eyes raking my body up and down. "You look beautiful. Are you ready to go?"

"Sure," I reply. Inside, I'm glowing at his compliment. *He thinks I look beautiful.* I grab my purse and keys, then walk out and lock the door behind me. "Where are we going?" I ask as we head toward his truck.

"There's a place just up the road that has a nice atmosphere. It's not too crazy loud, so we can talk."

"Sounds good," I say as I get in his truck. It's nice. It looks new and seems to be fully loaded with leather seats. It's much different from the old truck he used to drive in high school.

When he starts the engine, loud music immediately blares out the sound system. He quickly turns the volume down. I see on the screen that he's listening to Linkin Park. He still has the same taste in music. So do I.

"Sorry about that," he says.

"I don't mind," I say.

"Well, I know you *used* to like this kind of music," he replies, "but I wasn't sure if that was still the case. You *are* a mom now." I can tell he's joking with me.

"What's that supposed to mean?" I try to sound offended.

"You know, moms listen to boring, quiet music."

I laugh. "Well, not *this* mom. Some things never change," I say to him. After I say it, I realize how that could mean a lot of things right now.

"Well, in that case then …" Ryan turns the music back up, and we drive to the bar, which is not very far away.

When we get there, we find a booth in the corner and take a seat. The place is busy, but as Ryan said, it's not too crazy. It has a fun and casual atmosphere. We sit across from each other and look at the drink menu on the table.

"What do you like to drink?" he asks me.

"It depends on my mood," I reply. "Sometimes, I like fruity mixed drinks, sometimes, I like a good glass of wine, and sometimes, I just want a beer."

"What are you in the mood for tonight?"

"I don't know yet," I reply as I look at the menu. "What do you like to drink?"

"I'm a beer guy," he says.

This is definitely new territory for us. We never really drank in high school. Ryan was an athlete and played every season— football, basketball, and baseball—and I was a cheerleader. Sure, we went to parties where there was drinking, and we occasionally indulged with our friends, but neither of us ever got too crazy drunk because we didn't want to get suspended from our teams.

The waitress comes over to take our order. I decide to get a beer as well.

"So you're a nurse?" Ryan starts talking first. "Are you going to be looking for a job now that you're living up here?"

I shake my head. "No, it's just not feasible right now. I would either have to work terrible hours, or I'd have to pay for daycare. My parents aren't charging me rent, and my ex pays alimony and child support, so I can afford to be a stay-at-home mom for a while."

"That's nice," he says.

"It really is," I reply.

"So when you do decide to get a job again, will you go back to the ER? Or would you prefer to be a nurse in a different setting?"

"I don't know. I love the fast pace and excitement the ER brings, but if I work in a clinic somewhere, I can have normal hours. I guess I'll see when the time comes."

"Cari, Dan's wife, loves her job. I think you two would get along really well."

I smile at him and think about all those questions I had thought of and wanted to ask him. "So how are your parents? Do they still live here?"

"They're doing great, and yes, they still live in the same house."

I remember his parents were a little older than mine. His dad was a retired Marine and worked for Boeing, and his mom was a housewife. They were very nice people and always made me feel welcome at their house.

"Where are *you* living?" I ask him.

"I'm actually living at Dan and Cari's house right now. They have an extra room, like an in-law quarters, above the garage, and they're letting me stay there for a while. It's just a bedroom and bathroom, but it has its own entrance with a back deck. It's perfect for now anyway. I can save up some money and buy my own place in a few months. The market here is crazy, plus I'm still not exactly sure what part of town I want to buy in. This gives me time to figure that out."

"That sounds familiar," I say. "I'm hoping to save up money so I can buy my own place someday, too. I won't be able to afford it for a couple of years or more, but that's my goal."

The waitress brings our beers and sets them on the table. Ryan picks his up and holds it up to toast. "To reuniting with old friends."

I smile and lift my bottle to his, clanking them together. Then we both take a sip while keeping our eyes on each other as we drink.

"What made you and Dan want to open the gym?" I ask him. I've been wondering about this since he never mentioned wanting to work at a gym when we were younger.

"Dan has always wanted to do it. He's talked about it for years. He talked me into being his partner, and I figured it would be a good job to start with coming right out of the Marines. I earned my personal trainer certification through an online program, and here we are. I don't know how long I'll be an active owner, though. I might become more of a silent partner in a few years and pursue another career."

That comment surprises me. "Really? What do you want to do?" The only thing Ryan had ever talked about doing for his career when we were in high school was joining the Marines.

"I've thought about being a police officer."

I practically choke on my sip of beer.

"You don't think that's a good idea?" he asks me, obviously noticing my reaction.

I clear my throat. "No, you'd probably be great at it," I say, contemplating in my head whether I should tell him that Scott is a police officer, too. I quickly make the decision to just be forth-coming. "It's just that my ex is a cop."

"Oh," he says, surprised. "So you're probably turned off by all cops now?" He gives me his crooked smile that I find so hard to resist.

I shake my head. "No, not at all. Just him."

Neither of us says anything for a moment. I'm trying to think of something else to talk about. Discussing my ex is not exactly the best topic of conversation.

"Did you go to our high school reunion?" he asks, changing the subject.

"No, I was actually on vacation in Japan when they had it."

"That's funny." Ryan chuckles. "I was stationed in Japan at that time."

My eyebrows shoot up in surprise. We both missed our reunion because we were in the same country at that time. "What a coincidence! Where were you stationed?"

"Okinawa."

"I was in Tokyo," I tell him.

"Well, it's funny we were in the same country at the same time. So close yet so far," he says, then takes a sip of his beer. "Have you kept in contact with anyone else from high school besides Sarah?"

I shake my head. "Not really. I connected with some people on Facebook, but Sarah is the only one I've stayed in contact with in person. How about you?"

He also shakes his head. "Nope, I pretty much lost contact with everyone. I never joined Facebook. Maybe if I did, I would find some of the old guys I used to hang with."

"I'm sure you would," I say, knowing I had seen some of his old friends on there. I never "friended" any of them, though. Deep down, even when I was still happily married, I knew the only reason was to avoid having contact with anyone close to Ryan. I wanted to avoid any chance of getting back in contact with him. I'm beginning to realize that maybe it was because subconsciously I knew being their friend would lead me down a road of feelings I didn't want to get mixed up in.

Now, I think I'm ready to go down that road.

"I haven't thought about high school as much as I have the past couple of weeks," Ryan says, bringing me back to reality. "Ever since I ran into you and Sarah, I started thinking about all the fun times we had back then."

I smile at him, happy he's been thinking about the old days together as well. "Oh, yeah? What fun times have you remembered?" I ask, curious what he has been thinking about.

Ryan shrugs. "Just various stuff. Parties people had, school dances, state championships I went to ... and us."

I feel myself blushing again. "Oh?" I can't think of what else to say.

"I have to be honest with you," Ryan says. My heart rate picks up, anticipating what he's going to say next. He leans in closer to me with both his arms on the table, his hands interlocked. "When I first moved back here, I was really hoping I'd run into you again. I ran into Dawn Winters from high school, and she said she heard you moved down to Portland or someplace, so I thought it would never happen. But then I saw you at my gym, and I was so thankful. I've thought about you a lot over the years, Brooke. Probably more than I should admit."

I'm speechless. What do I say to that? He's being completely honest with me right now. Do I tell him I haven't been able to stop thinking about him, too? Yes, I think I should. Am I brave enough to do that, though? I take a deep breath to steady my nerves. Now's the time to say it if I'm ever going to. "Ryan," I start, my voice a little shaky, "I haven't been able to stop thinking about you since we ran into each other."

He smiles and reaches across the table for my hand. I love the feeling of his hand holding mine. It's strong and comforting. It feels familiar yet different at the same time.

We finish our beers, order another, and discuss various things for the next hour. It's so easy to talk to him, like over a decade hasn't passed since the last time we've talked. He also keeps at least one of his hands on mine the entire time. I love that he wants to touch me in this small way while we talk. It makes me feel comforted and cared for, and I haven't felt this way in so long.

As the night goes on, I realize it must be getting late because I'm getting tired. I can't help the yawn that escapes my mouth. Then I remember he has to get up early to open the gym tomorrow morning. "What time is it?" I ask him.

He looks at his watch, and says, "A quarter to twelve."

"Don't you have to get up early in the morning for work?"

He smiles. "Don't you have to get up early to meet Sarah for your workout?"

I chuckle. "Yes, but you have to be there earlier. What time do you open, anyway?"

"Six a.m. I usually get there by five thirty."

As much as I enjoy spending time with him, I realize it's probably not the best idea to keep him out much longer. "Should we get going then? You're going to be tired in the morning."

He shakes his head, chuckles, and says, "Always the responsible one."

"What do you mean?" I ask, surprised by his comment.

"You always kept my head on straight. It's a good thing."

I guess I was responsible back in high school. I always reminded him about assignments he had to finish or chores his mom wanted him to do.

As if our waitress could read our minds, she approaches our table with our bill. Ryan pays and then we leave. I'm surprised when he actually holds my hand all the way out to his truck. I can't remember the last time Scott and I held hands. We just stopped showing any PDA when we went out. I guess it's just because we had been together for so long, but it still makes me wonder. It doesn't matter now, though, because I am enjoying the way Ryan's strong hand is linked with mine. It makes me feel safe, secure, and ... *his*.

When we get back to my house, he walks me the short distance from the driveway to the front porch. We don't hold hands this time, but that might be because I'm fumbling around in my purse for my house key. I find myself craving to touch him again, though. Maybe I'll get a good night kiss? *I can only hope!*

"I guess I'll see you in the morning," he says as we approach the front door.

"I guess you will," I reply, smiling at him. I start to put my key into the door lock, but he stops me by placing his hand over mine. *Yes! Touch me again!* I feel an instant spark between us. I look up at him, wondering if he feels it, too. He steps closer to me.

"Can I kiss you good night?" he asks, lowering his head closer to my level. His hands rest lightly on my hips, his touch sending an electric current up my back. I shiver slightly even though I'm not cold. In fact, standing this close to Ryan warms me up. His brown eyes look into mine, and I can't tear mine away. I'm drawn to Ryan just as I was many years ago as a teenager.

I have never wanted to be kissed as badly as I do right now. I don't answer his question; I just move closer and kiss him myself. The second our lips touch, I feel at home. This is *Ryan!* It starts as a slow kiss, tender and sweet, but then it becomes more. It's like Deja vu. The feeling of his lips on mine takes me back fourteen years and reminds me of what we had back then. I snake my hands around his waist, and at the same time he pulls me closer to him. I melt against his body. I can't get over how strong he is now. His body definitely feels different than it did at eighteen.

His tongue volleys with mine, and we find the perfect rhythm. I don't remember kissing anyone else quite like this. Except Ryan. But even this kiss is better than what I remember from our teenage years together. I don't want this kiss to end, but all too soon, he pulls his lips away. He looks at me, and I feel dazed. *Just from one kiss.* His eyes search mine, seeming to look deep into my soul. The connection I feel with Ryan is unreal. *Why did we break up?*

"Thank you for moving back here and going out with me tonight," he says with a smirk on his face.

I laugh a little. "You're welcome."

He kisses me again, but this time, it's just a quick peck on the lips. When he pulls away, he takes a step back as if he's going to leave, and I instantly miss his touch.

"I'll see you in a few hours," he says to me.

"Okay." I accept the fact he has to leave, so I turn and unlock the front door. Before I can actually open it, though, I feel his hands grip my waist again. I gasp as he takes me by surprise and hauls my body against his.

"Just one more kiss," he says before crashing his lips to mine once more.

Yes! I'm suddenly remembering how great a pastime kissing Ryan was. One that I hope I'll get to do again and again from now on. I could kiss him all night long.

"I'm really going to leave now," he says between kisses, but he doesn't back away. We continue kissing, his hands gliding up my back, my hands wedged between us, resting on his chest. I wish I could just invite him in, but I don't think that would be a smart thing to do. I live with my parents, and my baby is asleep across the hall from my room. Not only that, but this is only our first date. Well, our first date in fourteen years, anyway.

My lips are left feeling used and swollen when he ends our kiss and pulls away.

"I have to go. I had a great time tonight, Brooke," he says to me as he takes a step back.

"I did, too. Thanks again for taking me out tonight," I say as he starts walking down the porch steps.

Ryan looks back at me and smiles. "I'll see you in a few hours. Sleep good."

"You too," I tell him as he smiles at me again. *God, I love his smile!*

He turns and walks back to his truck. I go inside the house and feel as if I've died and gone to heaven.

RYAN

*a*s I drive home from Brooke's house, all my thoughts are of her. My lips are still buzzing from our kisses, and I can still smell her in my truck. Whatever perfume she wears is fucking sexy, and I'm drawn to it. Just like I'm drawn to her. Tonight felt like a dream come true, and I hope I'll get more chances to take Brooke out.

She's still the same sweet girl I remember, although something about her is different. I can't explain what it is, and it's not a bad thing. She's obviously not the eighteen-year-old girl I used to know, yet she still is in a lot of ways. She's been through a lot in her life since we broke up, and those experiences have shaped the person she is today. I hope I get to know the new Brooke a lot better.

As I ponder all this, I wonder what she really thinks of me after all these years. I know I look a lot different. Hell, she didn't even recognize me when she first saw me at the gym. I've also been through a lot in the past fourteen years, especially after being a Marine. I know I'm different than I used to be, but deep down, I'd like to think I'm basically the same Ryan I've always been.

One thing that was definitely still the same about Brooke was her sexy as fuck mouth and ability to kiss me like no other woman ever has. The second our lips touched, I remembered how much I loved kissing her. We would make out for hours when we were horny teenagers. There's just something special about our connection, and I hope she felt it tonight like I did.

When I get home, I walk around back to my private entrance. My room is directly above the garage. I can also access it from the main part of the house, but I don't want to disturb my brother or his family this late. They're probably all asleep.

I immediately get ready for bed because I have to get up in less than five hours. I can't seem to fall asleep, though. All things Brooke keep going through my mind. And then I remember the one thing that could potentially cause a problem in our relationship. She has a baby, and she's not even officially divorced yet.

Now, don't get me wrong. I have no problem with the fact Brooke has a child. I'm totally fine with that. It's just the fact that *she* might have a problem with dating me. It's possible she's not ready to pursue a new relationship so soon after separating from her husband. What if she decides she's not ready to introduce a new man into her daughter's life? I've never dated a woman with kids before, but I've heard that it can throw a wrench in relationships.

I've always wanted to have kids, though. I *want* to get married and have kids someday. Living here with Dan and Cari and watching them with their two boys has sealed the deal for me. I grew up in a loving household and always looked up to my parents' marriage. I may have had a lot of fun while I was in the Marines, but I'm ready to settle down now.

On the other hand, I don't want to rush into anything. I may have loved Brooke in high school, but I don't know if things will work out between us now. We've been on one date, so I can't rush this. And the fact she's not divorced yet could mean she's not looking for a relationship. I may have missed my chance with

Brooke fourteen years ago, but I can only hope that's not the case now.

breath on my skin tickles and makes me wish Sarah wasn't here right now. And that we weren't in his gym.

God, I want him!

"A little," I whisper back.

He leans in a little closer to me and whispers in my ear, "So was I."

Ryan pulls back and looks at me. I smile at him. Knowing that he was also nervous makes me like him even more. *If that's even possible.*

He gives me one last quick peck on the lips.

"I'll see you when you're done," he says as he releases me so I can join my friend.

I walk with Sarah, heading to the ellipticals. "What the hell, Brooke?" she says as we choose our machines. She's clearly not mad, just surprised.

As we start exercising, I explain to her how I decided to work out last night, how Ryan asked me to stay and talk with him afterward, and then how he asked me to go out after he got off work.

"And you left me out of the loop?" she asks, trying to sound offended even though I know she's really not. "This is the sort of thing you at least send a text to tell me about!"

"I know, I know," I say, chuckling. "Honestly, I was freaking out a little and not thinking straight!"

"Okay, so now spill," Sarah says. "What did you two discuss? Are you guys a couple now? Did you ...?" She looks at me and wiggles her eyebrows.

"No! We just kissed." I shake my head at her and laugh again. "Okay, so we talked about a lot of stuff. We basically filled each other in on our lives now. Lots of small talk to get to know each other better, you know? But then he admitted that he was hoping to run into me again after he moved back, and he's thought about me a lot over the years. When he took me home, he kissed me good night."

I look at Sarah, and she looks at me, smiling. "It's fate, I tell you."

"Maybe," I admit. "It just feels right. Is that weird?"

"I don't think so," Sarah says. "It's not like you two just met. You were friends for several years, which then evolved into a serious relationship. I used to think you two would still somehow end up together. That is, until you got married."

The thought of my marriage reminds me of something I wanted to ask her. "Oh, that reminds me," I start. "I'm meeting Scott at the children's museum again on Monday. Want to go?"

"Sorry, but weekdays don't work very well since Nathan has school. Let me know the next time you go on a weekend, though!"

"I understand," I say. "I'll definitely let you know next time."

* * *

We finish our workout about an hour later and head toward the exit. Why am I so giddy to see Ryan again? I have butterflies in my stomach just with the anticipation of seeing him in a moment, and it's so silly. When we get to the counter, he's talking to a customer and doesn't notice us approaching. Sarah and I stand to the side, waiting for him.

"Why does this feel like high school all over again?" I say to her.

"What do you mean?"

"We're standing here together, waiting for Ryan to finish talking to a customer. It's like how you used to wait outside the locker room with me for him to come out after practice."

Sarah laughs. "You're funny."

Just then, the customer leaves, and Ryan notices us standing off to the side. "Hey there," he says, smiling at us. We walk over to talk to him. "What are you two up to today?" he asks.

"I've got three kids. I'm spending the day at home playing

with them and cleaning up messes while also doing about a gazillion loads of laundry. Don't be jealous," Sarah says in a sarcastic tone.

"Same with me, only I guess I have it easier with just one kid," I say, chuckling.

"Wow, you two know how to party," Ryan says.

"Just wait until you have kids one day," Sarah says to him. "You'll see how much fun you've been missing out on."

Ryan's eyebrows shoot up at Sarah's comment, but he doesn't say anything. I wonder what he thinks of having kids? Does he want kids someday? He knows I have a daughter, so he knows if he's with me, it's a package deal. I'm curious if having a family was ever in his plans.

I decide to change the subject, though.

"How late do you have to work?" I ask him.

"I get off at two thirty," he replies. "Why? Do you want to see me later?" He gives me his irresistible crooked smile.

I quirk an eyebrow and smirk at him. "Maybe." *Actually, my answer is hell yes!*

"Well, I think I'm going to head home now," Sarah interrupts, clearly wanting to give us some time alone. She starts walking toward the exit. "Call me later, Brookie, okay?"

"Okay," I promise her before she walks out the door. I look back at Ryan, and continue, "What do you have in mind for later?"

He leans on the counter to get closer to me. "I don't know. Can you go out for dinner?"

The fact he wants to spend more time with me and take me out on another date excites me. I have to think rationally, though. I can't just leave Ellie with my parents without asking them first. "I'll have to ask my parents if they can watch Ellie. Can I call or text you?"

"No, absolutely not," he says, shaking his head. Then he chuckles and his mouth curves into a smile. His good looks momentarily distract me as I stare at his talented lips. "Of course, you can call me."

I snap out of my lust-filled haze, and reply, "Well, I need your number in order to do that."

Ryan chuckles. "I guess you're right. I forgot we haven't exchanged that information yet."

I take out my phone so I can add his number, then I immediately text him so he has my number, too.

"I'll let you know what my mom says," I say to him, realizing that this, too, is like high school all over again. I haven't had to ask permission to go on a date since the last time I was dating Ryan.

"Okay, good. I'd really like to take you out again," he says to me.

I smile, enjoying this time with him even if we are just having a casual conversation inside his gym. I realize that I haven't felt this happy in a long time. It's nice to have Ryan back in my life. The past few months have been so depressing and stressful, so it's nice to have this positive relationship in my life again. Sure, I've had my friends, parents, and Ellie in my life, but this is different. It's nice to feel wanted and have an attraction to each other.

Thinking of Ellie and my parents makes me realize I should probably get back home, though. "I need to get going," I say, giving Ryan an apologetic look.

"I understand," he replies. "You have to get home to that baby of yours."

Ryan comes around the counter to walk me to the door. When he takes my hand in his, I just want to melt into him. We stop by the door, and he wraps his arms around my waist. My hands glide up his sculpted arms and wrap around his neck. He leans in and kisses me softly on the lips. It's brief but sweet. "Bye," he says.

"Bye," I reply as we release one another. As much as I don't want to let go of him, I have to leave.

I feel as if I'm floating, high on Ryan, as I walk out to my car.

When I get home, Mom is drinking her morning coffee at the kitchen table with Ellie sitting in her high chair next to her, eating Cheerios. "Good morning," I say as I walk in the room.

"Good morning," Mom replies. "How was your date last night?"

I kiss Ellie on her forehead, then sit down at the table. I can't help but smile at Mom's question. "It was good."

"And?" she prompts for more information.

My smile widens a fraction more. "And he wants to take me out again tonight. I told him I wasn't sure, though. I mean, you watched Ellie for me last night, so I feel kind of funny asking you again so soon."

Mom reaches out and puts her hand on top of mine. "Brooke. Last night, Ellie was asleep the whole time you were out. I really don't mind watching her again tonight for you. You deserve to go out and have fun after what you've been through these past several months."

I feel like the luckiest daughter with the most understanding mom in the world. "Thanks, Mom."

"You're welcome. Now, tell me about Ryan."

"What do you want to know?" I ask. "You kind of already know him."

"I know an eighteen-year-old kid. Tell me about the adult Ryan."

"Well ..." I try to decide what to tell her first. It's true he has changed a lot in the past fourteen years; however, in some ways, he hasn't. "He's still kind and thoughtful; he's living at his brother's house right now so he can save up to buy a house, and his sister-in-law is an ER nurse. Funny, huh?"

"What a coincidence," Mom says. "Do his parents still live around here?"

"Yes. In the same house, in fact."

"They were nice people," Mom replies. "And they raised a nice boy. I hope you have fun tonight."

"Thanks," I say as I look at Ellie again. She's happily chewing on her dry cereal.

"She already had her bottle," Mom tells me.

"Thank you. I think I'll take her downstairs for a bit."

"Okay."

I pick Ellie up and walk downstairs to the family room with her. I set her on the floor with some of her toys and sit down to play with her for a bit. After several minutes of playing with me, she becomes mesmerized with a toy and starts doing her own thing. I decide to text Ryan, letting him know I can go out tonight.

Instead of texting me, he calls me back.

"Hi," I answer, unable to stop myself from smiling.

"Hi," he replies. His deep voice sounds sexy over the phone. "So you can go out tonight?"

"Yes. What time are you picking me up?"

"I'll come get you at five thirty. We can go to dinner, then maybe see a movie afterward. How does that sound?"

"Perfect," I tell him.

"Good. I'm looking forward to it."

"Me, too."

"Good."

"Good."

I don't want to get off the phone with him yet.

"How's work?" I decide to ask him to hang on the phone a little longer.

He lets out a sigh. "It's slow here today."

"I'm sorry."

"That's okay. I can talk to you," he says, and I can hear the smile in his voice.

Ellie crawls over to me and crawls onto my lap. She tries to grab the phone and does her babbly talk.

"Is that your daughter?" Ryan asks me.

"Yes," I say as I try to distract her with another toy. It works, but she keeps babbling loud enough for Ryan to hear her.

"I can't believe you're a mom," he says. "She sounds adorable."

"Sometimes, I can't believe I'm a mom, either," I say to him. And it's true. Sometimes I look at her and it's so surreal. It's hard to believe that this miracle belongs to me.

"Dan's kids are eight and ten," Ryan continues. "I wasn't around when they were babies, so I missed that stage of their lives. It's cool living at their house now because I get to see them every day. They remind me of Dan and me."

I like that he enjoys being an uncle. It means he likes kids. I'm reminded of my thoughts earlier when I wondered if Ryan wants a family someday. I'll have to find this out somehow although I don't know how I'll ever ask him. Now is not the time. "That's great," I say, referring to how he feels about his nephews. "I think my parents love having Ellie and me here. They love her so much, and this way they get to be around her all the time."

"And they don't mind babysitting for you, so that's a bonus," he adds.

"Very true," I reply.

I hear someone talking in the background on Ryan's end. Then he says, "Sorry, Brooke, I have to go. I'll see you at five thirty tonight."

"Okay, sounds good. I can't wait," I reply.

"Neither can I," Ryan says. "Bye, Brooke."

"Bye," I reply, then end the call.

I turn my attention back to Ellie. Ryan seems to be fine with the fact that I have a baby, so that's good. I don't know what I'd do if he *did* have an issue. She's my life, and I can't date anyone who has a problem with that.

The day seems to drag on. It always seems to do that when I'm anticipating something fun later. I text Sarah and let her know

I'm going out with Ryan again tonight. She texts back a couple of minutes later.

Sarah: *Thanks for telling me this time. ;-) Have fun tonight!*

Me: *I'm sure I will! Thanks!*

A little later in the afternoon, I get a text from Ryan.

Ryan: *Is it 5:30 yet?*

I laugh.

Me: *I wish.*

An hour later, he texts me again.

Ryan: *Is it time yet?*

I love that he's just as excited as I am about our date tonight.

Me: *Closer.*

. . .

At five o'clock, he texts me a third time.

Ryan: *Close enough?*

I can't get over how cute he is, and I don't want to wait any longer to see him. I text him back.

Me: *YES!*

Ryan: *I'll leave right this second if you're ready. I can be there in less than ten minutes.*

I'm in the bathroom, just finishing my makeup. Ellie is upstairs with my parents. I can definitely be ready in ten minutes.

Me: *Okay. Can't wait to see you. :-)*

I go upstairs and tell my mom that Ryan's on his way over already. She's in the kitchen cooking dinner.

"He couldn't wait until five thirty?" she asks and winks at me.

"I guess not," I say nonchalantly, although I'm buzzing with excitement.

I walk into the living room and find Ellie sitting on my dad's lap. Ellie is looking at her sensory book, happy as can be.

"You look nice," Dad says to me as I walk in.

"Thanks," I say. I decided to go for dressy-casual again and wore another nice blouse and jeans along with some high-heel booties.

I sit down on the couch next to my dad. Ellie looks at me and reaches her arms out, so I pick her up and place her on my lap.

"Where is he taking you?" Dad asks.

"I don't know," I tell him. "Dinner and a movie, but I don't know where."

"Well, we won't wait up for you," he says with a wink.

I laugh. "Okay, Dad."

It's at this moment I realize how strange all this is. I live with my parents. I'm going on a date. I'm not divorced yet. I have a baby. A year ago, my life was so different. I was happy, yet blissfully unaware that my husband was ruining our lives. I never would have guessed that I'd find myself where I am now.

I try not to have a mini panic attack and focus on all the good in what I just thought of. Yes, I live with my parents. *I'm lucky to have their support.* Yes, I'm going on a date. *With Ryan, who is an amazing man.* No, I'm not divorced yet. *But the paperwork is filed.* Yes, I have a baby. *And Ryan seems to be okay with that.*

Ellie looks at me, offering me the book in her hand. I smile at her and feel myself relaxing. *Everything is going to be fine.*

A few minutes later, I hear Ryan's truck pull into the driveway. Mom must have heard it too because she pokes her head in from the kitchen. "Is he here?"

I smile and stand with Ellie in my arms and walk toward the front door. He knocks just as I get to it. I take a deep breath and open the door.

BROOKE

"Hi," Ryan says as I open the door.

I didn't think it was possible for Ryan to look any more attractive, but he does. This is the first time I've seen him outside of his gym, or like last night, right after he left his gym. He's not wearing his usual workout attire. Instead, he's wearing jeans that fit him perfectly and are faded in all the right places, along with a maroon three-quarter-sleeve Henley. I can see he was also going for the dressy-casual look, and boy can he pull it off well. He's also not wearing a hat, and his soft brown hair is just begging me to rake my fingers through it.

He smiles at me, then turns his attention to Ellie. "Hello there," he says as he bends down slightly to her level in my arms and smiles at her. He's just adorable.

Ellie smiles at him and claps her hands together.

"She must like you," I say to him. "Come on in for a second."

We walk into the living room and find both of my parents standing there, just waiting to see Ryan. He walks right up to my dad and shakes his hand as they re-introduce themselves. My mom gives him a hug.

"It's so good to see you again," she says to him.

"It's good to see you both, too," he replies.

"Where are you taking Brooke tonight?" my dad asks. *What am I? A teenager?*

Ryan is polite and answers my dad right away as if it's *not* abnormal to be grilled by a date's parents at the age of thirty-two. "We'll go to dinner first, and then we'll see a movie somewhere. It depends on what Brooke wants to see."

"Sounds like fun," Mom says.

I give Ellie a hug and kiss her a couple of times, then hand her over to my parents. My dad takes her again. "Thank you for watching her," I say to them.

"It's no problem. Have fun," Mom says.

Ryan and I head toward the door, saying goodbye to my parents and telling them he hopes to see them again soon. I grab my purse, and we leave.

Ryan takes me to an Italian restaurant nearby called Vince's. We went there a few times in high school. It's a good restaurant, and I'm happy to go there since I haven't been in years. We have a delicious dinner and talk the whole time. We don't seem to run out of anything to say. He tells me more about being in the Marines. I tell him about my old job and Ellie while trying to avoid bringing my ex into the conversation. We reminisce about people we were friends with in high school, and if I'm friends with them on Facebook, I fill him in on what they're doing now. Before we leave the restaurant, he looks up movie times on his phone. We decide on one we both want to see, then we head to the theater.

Once we're there, I'm still stuffed from dinner, but he buys a box of candy and a Coke for us to share. I inwardly laugh because this is exactly what he used to do in high school. "It's our dessert," he says, jokingly, although I know he's basically serious. He's so cute.

"Do you always do this on dates, or just when you take me to the movies?" I ask as he pays for the snacks.

He smiles, and replies, "Honestly, I haven't taken very many dates to the movies. You're one of the few. And, yes, I always get my candy and a Coke."

I smile back at him and love that, although he has experienced a lot in his life over the past fourteen years, he still likes the same snacks at the movies.

And he hasn't taken very many women on dates to the movies. *Interesting.*

When we sit down in the theater, Ryan asks, "Do you remember any of the movies we saw together in high school?"

I try to remember, but I honestly can't. "No, but I remember going to movies with you a lot. Why?"

He chuckles. "I can't either. Maybe that's because we didn't really watch them."

I laugh at that thought, too. "I think you're right! All we ever did was make out in the back! We'd snack until all the previews were over, and when the movie started and the lights dimmed, we'd be all over each other!"

"We could move to the back row now if you'd feel more comfortable back there," he says, smirking at me and looking way too adorable.

I playfully hit him on the arm. "You're funny," I say although I really am considering his proposal.

He laughs. "You know I'm kidding. Although I'd be more than willing to move back there if you want to." He winks at me.

I can't wipe the grin from my face as I shake my head. "No, we're grown adults. Adults don't make out in theaters."

"We could," he teases.

Although his proposition is tempting, I lightly elbow him in the arm instead.

He playfully pouts. "Okay, I get the hint. You don't want to kiss me anymore."

I play along and roll my eyes at him, my grin still plastered across my face at the thought of kissing his delectable lips again. I don't know what comes over me (maybe it was the wine I had at dinner), but I lean in closer to him and whisper in his ear, "That's not true. But I'm a grown woman now, not a silly teenager. So if you behave yourself here at the theater, you might get a kiss or two later."

I look at him again and watch as his sexy crooked smile forms on his lips. He looks so damn hot that I can't help myself. I lean in and kiss him. I just mean for it to be a quick peck on the lips, but his hand quickly wraps around the back of my neck to hold me there. Our kiss goes on, his tongue swiping along my bottom lip, asking for permission to enter. I don't pull away. I can't resist him. I open my mouth, and his skilled tongue finds mine.

Our lips feel as if they were made to fit. I don't even care that we're in a movie theater with other people. I don't want to stop kissing Ryan. I feel the delightful clench in my lower belly, signaling how turned on I am right now. I want more of him. I *need* to have more of Ryan tonight.

The theater lights dim, and Ryan pulls away from me. I immediately miss his lips. He puts his arm around me, and whispers in my ear, "I can't wait for another kiss or two later." Then he kisses my ear, which sends a delightful sensation down that side of my body.

I instantly regret going to a movie. We should have just gone back to his place.

Ryan keeps his hands on me in some way throughout the entire movie. Either his arm is around my shoulders, he's holding my hand, or his hand is resting on my thigh. He also leans over to whisper something to me a couple of times during the movie, too, and feeling the tickle of his breath on my skin just ignites my libido even more. I actually feel how wet I am between my legs. My clit is throbbing, and we haven't even done anything remotely sexual yet. I can't remember the last time I felt this way. It's made it *very* difficult for me to concentrate on the movie. All I want to do is crawl onto Ryan's lap and have my way with him.

When the movie finally ends, Ryan takes my hand as we walk out of the theater. He asks if I'm hungry and want to go get a *real* dessert somewhere. I'm just a tad sexually frustrated, though, so getting food to eat doesn't sound appealing right now. "No, that's okay," I say to him. I don't want to come right out and say I want to go back to his place, so I'm hoping he suggests it.

"Okay, good, because I'm not really hungry either," he replies.

I'm suddenly very nervous as we walk to his truck, but I try to act natural. Where are we going to go now? Is he just going to take me home? Is he going to want to have sex on just our second date? Although it's not *really* our second date, and we *have* had sex before. Not only that, I'm not really sure I'd stop him if he tried.

But as we continue to walk hand in hand, I'm not really sure if I want to jump into bed with him yet. Even though this is Ryan, and I haven't had sex in a very long time, I kind of want to take things slow. Until a few days ago, I didn't even want to date anyone until I got my life back in order. I know I was flirting with him in the theater, so I hope he's not going to be upset. As he said last night, I'm the responsible one.

Ryan stops when we get to his truck. I think he's going to open the passenger side door for me, but he puts his hands around my waist instead. It takes me by surprise, and I like it. He looks me in the eye as he walks us back until I'm pinned between him and his truck. Then he kisses me. It's a slow kiss, full of passion, just like all the other kisses we've shared. I slowly move my hands around his waist and hold him close. His tongue dances with mine, and I'm not even concerned that we're in the middle of a parking lot with other people around.

He definitely wants to sleep with me tonight.

Crap!

When he pulls away, he still holds me close. "I want to take you back to my place," he says.

My heart is pounding. I want that too, but I need him to know where I stand. "Ryan, I—"

He interrupts me. "Wait, let me finish first. I want to take you back to my place, but I just want to hang out with you more. And maybe kiss some more, like you promised me." He smirks at me.

I smile, and ask, "Just hanging out and kissing?"

He nods his head. "I think we should wait to do more than that."

"Oh, thank goodness," I say as I let out a breath. "I'm so glad you said that." *What a relief!*

Ryan kisses my forehead, then continues, "I want to take things slow with you, Brooke. I wouldn't feel right doing more than kissing on only our second date."

I lean in and kiss him again, this time a quick peck on the lips. "Thank you," I tell him.

He smiles, then moves to open the door for me. I climb into his truck, then he shuts the door and walks around to his side.

We just listen to music and make small talk as he drives to his house. I'm surprised to find that Dan lives only a few blocks away from Sarah, which is also in the same general area as both Sarah's parents' and Ryan's parents' houses.

"Dan wanted to stay close to home?" I ask him.

Ryan glances at me and smiles. "It's a great neighborhood. I'd buy a house here, too."

"Sarah actually lives close by, too," I tell him. "And I agree, it's a great neighborhood. I think a few other people we went to school with still live around here."

We get out of his truck, and he waits for me to circle around the front of it. He takes my hand as we start walking to the front door of the gray and white two-story home. Just as we walk up the front steps, he says, "I do have a separate entrance to my room, but let's go in the front door so you can meet my brother and his wife."

"Okay," I say to him, now feeling a little nervous. I didn't expect to meet his brother's family tonight.

We walk in the front door and can hear the TV blaring in the back of the house. Ryan holds my hand, leading me back to the family room where we find his brother and his family all watching a movie. "Sorry to interrupt," Ryan says as we walk in.

Everyone turns and looks at us. His brother grabs the remote and pushes pause, and it's suddenly very quiet. "Hi, Brooke," Dan says as he stands. His wife also stands, and they both walk over to where we're standing.

"It's so nice to meet you. I'm Cari," Dan's wife says as she extends her hand for me to shake.

"It's nice to meet you, too," I say as I shake her hand with my right. Ryan is still holding my left hand in his, which I love. I don't want him to let go.

"I don't know if you remember me, but I'm Dan. It's a pleasure to meet you again after all these years," he says, and I also shake his hand. "These are our boys, Mason and Alex," he adds, pointing at the boys on the couch.

"Hi," both boys say. I wave to them and smile.

"Is she your girlfriend, Uncle Ryan?" one of them asks.

We all chuckle. I feel a little embarrassed. *Am I his girlfriend?* I mean, we are holding hands, and we've just gone on a date together, but I'll wait to see what Ryan says.

"Mason, don't put him on the spot like that," Cari tells her son.

"It's okay," Ryan says with a chuckle. "She was my girlfriend in high school," he answers Mason. Then he looks at me and winks.

"What are you guys up to?" Dan asks us.

Ryan lets go of my hand and walks into the kitchen, which is right next to where we're standing. He opens the fridge and takes out a couple of beers. "We're just going to hang out upstairs for a bit before I take Brooke home." He turns his attention to me then, and asks, "Do you want a beer? Or something else to drink?"

"A beer is fine," I reply. *God, I hope Dan and Cari don't think we only came back here to have sex. How humiliating.*

Ryan closes the refrigerator and walks back to me, handing me a beer, then takes my hand in his again.

"We'll be upstairs if you need us," Ryan says to them.

"It was so nice to meet you," Cari tells me with a smile. "We'll have to get together again sometime and get to know each other better."

"I'd like that," I tell her. She seems friendly. So does his brother. I'm actually surprised he remembers meeting me when we were younger. By the time Ryan and I were actually dating, he was in the Marines. I probably met Dan once or twice in passing when I was just hanging out with a bunch of friends at their house.

Ryan leads me toward the stairs, and we go up to his room. It's a big room, much larger than an average bedroom, with enough space for a queen size bed, dresser, couch, coffee table, and an entertainment unit. I also notice there's an attached bathroom, what looks to be a walk-in closet, and a door that goes out to a deck in the backyard. That must be the private entrance he was talking about.

"Have a seat," he says, pointing at the couch.

I sit, and he sits next to me. He opens both beer bottles and hands me one.

"Thanks," I say, then take a drink. "I had fun tonight, by the way."

"Me, too," he replies, looking at me with a sincere smile. *Swoon.*

"Your brother's family seems great."

"They are. I'm fortunate that they're letting me live here."

"Your nephews look just like your brother."

"I know. It's crazy, isn't it? They're great," he says. Then he adds, "And in case you're wondering, I've never brought a woman here before. My nephews have never seen me with a girl, so that's probably why Mason was curious if you were my girlfriend."

I chuckle. "That was cute," I lie. I take another swig of my beer.

"It was?" Ryan says. "I'd say it was more on the embarrassing side, being put on the spot like that." I look at him, and he winks at me.

"Okay, yes, it was." I smile again and laugh. I haven't smiled this much in a very long time. Ellie has been the only person really able to make me laugh or smile in the past seven months. That is, until I moved back here. Now I have Sarah, my parents, and Ryan who can do that, too. It feels good. I feel human again.

"Hey, I've been meaning to ask you about your sister," Ryan says out of the blue, changing the subject and leaving me wondering where I stand on being his *girlfriend*. "How is Becca doing?"

"She's good," I start, wondering if we'll discuss our relationship status again. "She lives in New York City now, so we don't get to see each other very often. We do text and call when we can, though. She's working in the fashion industry and stays super busy."

"That's great," Ryan replies, looking impressed. "I remember she was really into clothes and fashion, so I can see her doing that for her career."

"She's hoping to come visit this summer. She was just here at Christmas."

We continue to chat as we drink our beers. I love that we feel comfortable enough with each other to discuss pretty much anything. Ryan was always easy to talk to.

Ryan finishes his beer and sets the bottle on the coffee table. "I had a lot of fun with you tonight," he says, his voice sounding a little deeper and little more sensual than when we were talking before.

"Me, too," I reply. The look on his face tells me he wants to do more than just talk now. I take another sip of my beer, and as I'm pulling it away from my mouth, Ryan takes the bottle from me and sets it on the table next to his.

He moves closer to me, his head dipping down to mine, but just as I think he's going to kiss me, he doesn't. He stops with his mouth less than an inch away, and my stomach muscles clench at the anticipation.

"Can I get my kiss or two now?" he asks me. I nod my head, and then his lips connect with mine.

His hands hold my arms gently, but as the kiss intensifies, they glide up and wrap around me, pulling my body closer to his. I need to touch him. I snake my arms around his waist, feeling his stomach over his shirt as I do. My goodness, he's all muscle. I still can't get over how much his body has changed. And I thought he was a fit athlete in high school.

Before I know it, we're lying on the couch. He's next to me, but halfway on top of me. Our kiss goes on and on, only making me want more of him. Tingles run down my body as he brushes one hand through my hair. His other hand grips my hip, pulling me just a little closer to him. I feel his arousal against my leg, and I desperately want him to move so I can feel it where I'm aching for him the most.

I know I told myself I wanted to go slow with Ryan, but this feels too good. I don't want to stop. I just want to feel more of him.

Ryan's hand slowly moves up and down my body, tingles of pleasure racing over my skin. He brushes one of my breasts with his hand, but my arm is in the way. I think he's waiting to see if I give him permission by moving my arm, and I do. His hand cups my breast, and he kneads it, causing a moan to escape my mouth. His touch feels so damn good and makes me want more. It's been way too long since I was intimate with anyone, and this is *Ryan!*

Suddenly, it's like a switch flips, and we're kissing each other desperately. Our teeth clash, and we both moan from the immense pleasure. I can't explain it, but I feel like we're making up for lost time, and fourteen years is a lot of time to make up. I try to shift my body, so I can feel him where I need it most. I'm pulsing with need and soaking wet. I need some relief.

Ryan's mouth glides away from mine, and he trails kisses down my neck. As his mouth keeps moving south to my chest, I can only hope he plans on abandoning his original plan to wait tonight, too. I need this, and I don't think there's any way I can stop now.

Still unsuccessfully trying to shift Ryan to settle between my legs, I'm rewarded when his hand finally starts to work its way under my shirt. The feeling of his hands on my bare skin makes my body scream with desire, and another moan escapes my mouth.

Suddenly, Ryan stops and looks at me. "Is this okay?" he asks, his voice deep and raspy. It's sexy. "We can stop if you want."

The fact that he asked me means everything. I know it would be the responsible thing to stop now before we go much further, but this feels too right. I nod my head. "Don't stop."

Ryan doesn't need to be told twice. He smiles, then continues right where he left off. His lips find my neck once again as his hand slips back under my shirt. My heart is pounding as he pulls the cup of my bra to the side. When his fingers make contact with my bare breast, I moan again. Oh, my God; I don't want him to stop. He rubs and pulls my nipple, and the only thing I want is to feel *more*.

Finally, Ryan shifts his body over mine, settling between my open legs. The moment I feel his erection against my core, I'm in heaven. I moan and grind my hips against him. I need more relief. He gets the hint and starts grinding against me in just the right way. It feels so good; if he keeps this up, I might actually come.

Holy shit. We're dry humping. When was the last time I did this? Probably when I was a teenager or maybe my early twenties. I forgot how good things can feel without actually having sex.

Ryan stops again and looks at me with the sexiest look on his face. "I didn't plan on going this far with you tonight, but you feel so fucking good, Brooke."

"So do you," I tell him before I take his head in my hands and pull it down to kiss me again.

Ryan's hand retreats from under my shirt, surprising me at first and missing his touch. But then he grips the hem of my shirt and begins pulling it up. We break our kiss for a moment to lift it over my head. He tosses it to the floor, then kisses me again with even more fervor than before.

Wanting to feel him skin to skin, I pull at his shirt, too. He helps me take it off, and I throw it down on the floor with mine. Then our lips connect again. Feeling his hot skin against mine spurs me on. *I still need more of him.* Not wanting to wait for him to do it, I reach my hands around my back and unhook my bra. Ryan stops and watches as I slide it down my arms and discard it to the floor with the rest of our clothing.

Ryan lets out an appreciative moan, then he lowers his mouth to my breasts. His tongue licks my nipple gently before he takes it into his mouth, sucking and nibbling lightly. Flashes of pleasure race through my body.

Ryan continues to grind against my center. I can feel my orgasm building. It's been so long since I've felt this good, and Ryan was the first boy to ever do this to me.

Ryan's mouth works it magic, alternating between both my breasts. His cock continues to rub against me, and even over our clothing, it feels amazing. Honestly, I'd forgotten how "gifted" Ryan is in this department. He's much larger than my ex.

I can't believe we're going this far, so soon, but I can't explain this energy between us. It's as if I can't think straight or make myself stop. All I want is him.

Before I know it, Ryan shifts his body again and starts

undoing my pants. Within seconds, his hand slides into my panties, and his finger starts circling my clit. *Holy shit!* If he keeps this up, I'm going to explode! I moan into his mouth, and he doesn't let up. Neither do I. His talented tongue continues to toy with my nipples, his mouth latching onto my breasts, sucking and licking and biting me gently. Between the feeling of him rubbing my core and the attention he's giving my breasts, my orgasm comes out of nowhere. It takes me by surprise because I don't remember anyone ever making me come this quickly before.

I moan, and then his mouth is over mine again, kissing me hard as my body continues to vibrate with pleasure. I haven't had an orgasm like that in so long. We weren't even having sex, and he still made me come. I forgot how good it always was with Ryan. No one ever made me feel as good as he did. *I forgot.* I forgot about the connection we had and how our bodies were made for each other. Not even my ex-husband and I had a connection like this. I can't believe I made myself forget what Ryan and I had all those years ago.

Ryan looks down at me with a look of satisfaction, which is strange since he didn't get a chance to come yet. "Sorry, that was a lot more than just kissing," he says to me.

I try to chuckle, but it's barely audible. "That's okay," I reply, my voice a little shaky. "And I'm sorry because you didn't get to finish." I reach for the waistband of his jeans, but he stops me, grabbing my hand, not letting me touch him.

"That's okay," he says sincerely. "We should stop, though. We already did way more than I intended tonight, and I just wanted to make you feel good."

"Oh?" I'm shocked at his confession. *He just wanted to make me feel good.*

He nods his head, then kisses me again.

"Are you sure?" I ask him. "I feel selfish."

He chuckles. "I'm sure. My intention was to take things slow with you, and that obviously didn't happen just now. I've missed you. I didn't intend on going this far tonight, but I couldn't help myself."

"Me either," I say to him as I run my fingers through his hair. He gives me another quick kiss and then sits up. I notice his tattoos. He has one on the left side of his chest and one on his upper arm.

"Tell me about your tattoos," I say as he reaches down and picks up our clothes. He hands my shirt and bra to me, and I sit up to put them on.

"This is the Marines emblem here," he says, pointing at the one on his chest. "This one is just a cool tribal design I liked," he explains, pointing at the one wrapped around his arm. "And this"—he turns around so I can see his back—"is my Semper Fi tattoo." Semper Fi is printed from one shoulder blade to the other. He turns around to face me again and puts his shirt back on. "Do you have any tattoos?" he asks, curious.

I finish putting my shirt on, and reply, "I have one." I stand, pulling my pants down just a bit so he can see the butterfly tattoo on my lower back. "This is my tramp stamp."

Ryan laughs. "It's cute! Don't call it a tramp stamp. You're not a tramp."

I sit down again next to him. "I got it in college. I thought it was cute at the time, but now, I don't know. I don't regret it or anything, but it's not what I would get now if I were to get another tattoo."

"Do you want to get another tattoo?" he asks.

I consider that question for a moment. I had thought about getting another tattoo a few years ago, but I never did because I couldn't decide what I really wanted. "I don't know," I answer. "I honestly haven't thought about it that much. Do you?"

"Maybe someday. I don't know what I'd get right now, though."

"When did you get yours?" I ask him.

"I got the tribal one first, shortly after I joined the Marines. Then I got the emblem a couple of years later. I got the Semper Fi after my last tour in Afghanistan." Ryan stands up then, extending his hand out for me to take. "Let's go sit outside on my balcony."

"Okay," I reply. It's not a cold night out at all. In fact, it's pretty warm for April. I take his hand as I stand, and we start walking toward the door to the back deck. Ryan picks up his laptop on the way. "What's that for?" I ask him.

"You can help me join Facebook," he says.

I chuckle. "Okay then." We sit on some Adirondack chairs side by side, and Ryan starts his computer. "What made you decide to join Facebook all of a sudden?"

He looks at me and shrugs his shoulders. "I guess now that I'm living in Seattle again, it might be nice to connect with old friends. Also, I'd like to keep in contact with some of the guys I served with. Plus, I want to be your friend." He winks at me and smiles.

"I think that's a done deal," I reply. Honestly, I'm still kind of wondering about the *girlfriend* comment from earlier. Based on what he just did to me, I'd guess I'm in girlfriend territory now, but I don't want to assume. I haven't dated anyone since college. Dating in my thirties is definitely new for me.

He logs onto the internet and pulls up the website. I walk him through the steps of setting up his profile. Not that it's rocket science, but he asked me to help. As he's filling out the information about himself, he gets to "relationship status."

"What should I put here?" he asks me, pointing at the screen.

I smile. Maybe I'll get my answer now. "I don't know. What do you think your relationship status is?" God, I hope he says what I want him to say.

He gives me his crooked smile. "You tell me."

Now, I feel put on the spot. Of course, I want to claim him as mine. "I think you should say you're in a relationship."

"I think that sounds right." He leans over and kisses me

sweetly. I feel butterflies in my stomach. I guess that answers my question! I can officially say I'm his girlfriend.

After he pulls his lips away from mine, he clicks a couple of things on his laptop. Then he says, "It's giving me the option to add who I'm in a relationship with."

Crap. It's not that I don't want people to know we're together, but I'm still friends with some of Scott's family members. Not to mention mutual friends. If he adds me, it will tag me, and my friends will see it. I don't want to stir up drama with them seeing me in a relationship already when our divorce isn't quite final. However, we've been separated for months now, so maybe I'm being silly about this. But still … It just seems too soon. "Can you leave that blank for now?" I ask him, scrunching my nose, hoping he doesn't take offense to my request.

Ryan looks at me curiously. "Too soon?"

I let out a breath. "No … well, yes, even though I guess it's really not. I mean, my ex and I have been separated for a while now, but we're not divorced yet. I just don't want to cause any controversy with my Facebook friends who know him, too. Scott doesn't have an account himself, but I'm still friends with some of his family and friends. Does that make any sense?"

"Yes. It's okay, Brooke. I understand." He places his hand over mine and gives me a sincere look, letting me know he really gets where I'm coming from. After a beat, he moves his hand back to the laptop, clicks past that option on the page, and moves on to the other questions about himself. I feel relieved that he understands.

He finishes setting up his profile, and then he searches for friends. He adds me first, and I accept his friend request on my phone. Then he looks through my list of friends for people he knows, and finally, he searches for more of his friends from the Marines. "This is amazing! I didn't realize I knew so many people on here."

We hang out at his house for a little while longer. I'm enjoying spending time with him. I really don't want to go home, but I know I need to. It's late, and Ellie will wake up early in the morning. When we leave, we leave through his private entrance, which is off the back deck.

"Now you know how to get up to my room without going through the house," he says to me as we walk to his truck, hand in hand. "You can sneak over anytime." He winks at me.

"Oh, you mean like how you used to sneak over to my house in high school?"

"Yup. That's exactly what I mean," he says with a chuckle. He opens the passenger side door for me. After I sit in the seat, he leans in and kisses me briefly, then he closes the door and walks around to his side. He gets in the truck and starts it up.

"You can sneak over to my house anytime too, you know," I say to him with a flirtatious tone. "Relive our old high school days."

"I might have to do that sometime," he says and smirks at me. *He is so cute.*

When he pulls into my driveway, I don't want to get out of the truck. "What are you doing tomorrow?" I ask him.

He looks at me, and replies, "Nothing. I don't have to work, and I don't have any plans. What are you doing?"

"I don't have any plans, either. I need to spend time with Ellie, though. I feel a little guilty for leaving her with my parents the past couple of nights."

"Well, if you and Ellie would like some company, let me know. Like I said, I don't have any plans tomorrow."

I lean in and kiss him. The fact he is willing to hang out with Ellie warms my heart.

When I pull away from him, he instantly pulls me back for another kiss. My lips are going to hurt tomorrow. I haven't done this much kissing in years.

We finally make our way out of the truck a few kisses later.

He walks me to the door where he kisses me again, and then we say goodbye.

After walking in quietly because everyone is asleep, I go downstairs and peek in at Ellie. She's sound asleep in her crib and looks like an angel. I want to pick her up and cuddle her, but I know that would be a big mistake; she would wake up and be difficult to put back to sleep. Instead, I blow her a kiss and tiptoe out of her room.

RYAN

I need a cold shower. Fuck, I had such a good time with Brooke tonight, but I have a serious case of blue balls now. She's worth it, though. I can't believe we've only been out on two dates. It feels like our relationship is already so much more. But I guess that's because it kind of is. We didn't just meet each other; we're reconnecting after many years apart. We can skip the whole *getting to know you* part of dating someone new. We're just playing catch up on what we've missed the past fourteen years as well as picking up where we left off.

I honestly didn't plan on going that far with her tonight. I thought I'd take her out, we'd spend time together, and then I'd hopefully get to kiss her again. That's it. The sexual chemistry between us is just as hot as it was when we were eighteen, though. I couldn't help myself once we started making out on my couch. The way she tried to get me to settle between her legs showed me she was just as eager as I was. I tried to be a gentleman until I couldn't fucking take it anymore. I haven't dry humped a girl since high school. In fact, Brooke was the only girl I've done that with.

When I knew she was close to coming just from grinding

against her–fully clothed, no less–I realized she probably hasn't had an orgasm in a long time. Based on what she's told me, she hasn't dated at all since she separated from her husband. With a baby at home, I doubt she's just hooked up with anyone either, so I wanted nothing more than to make her feel good. Sure, maybe she's pleasured herself (and fuck if that doesn't leave a sexy image in my head), but I wanted to be the first man to make her come since her pathetic excuse for a husband did. She deserved it after everything she's been through.

It was so fucking hard not to undress us both and have my way with her. I was more than ready, and I'm pretty sure she was, too. However, I wanted to stick to my original plan, which was to wait. It'll mean more this way. Sure, we've had sex before–a lot of *really good* sex–but I want to treat our relationship like a new one. One that I'm fucking serious about. I don't want to hop into bed with her like I have with other women in my past.

Sure, I've been with a lot of women since Brooke and I broke up. I've even had a couple of serious relationships. But I'm not lying when I say that Brooke meant more to me than any of them ever did. I've spent the past fourteen years wondering where she was, what she was doing, and regretting ever letting her go. I know it was the right thing to do at the time, but I've always felt as though we belong together.

I also tried to convince myself I was full of shit. No one meets the love of their life so young. But since Brooke and I have reconnected, I can't deny it anymore. We belong together. She's what I've been missing all these years. It may seem like we're moving fast, but it also feels right. I just hope Brooke feels the same.

BROOKE

*E*llie's crying. I open one eye and look at the clock. 6:58. *Kill me now.* I was up late two nights in a row. Of course, it's my own fault. There's no one to blame but myself, and now my baby girl needs me. I need to get up before she wakes my parents.

I drag myself out of bed and walk across the hall to Ellie's room. She's lying in her crib crying, and when she sees me, she puts her arms out toward me. "Oh, Ellie Bell, come here, baby." I pick her up, and she stops crying. "How's my girl? I missed you last night." I change her diaper, then I carry her upstairs and make her a bottle. Neither Mom or Dad are up yet; I don't blame them since they got up early with Ellie yesterday and babysat her last night. They deserve to sleep in.

I carry her back downstairs to the family room and feed her in the rocking chair. She's content now. I feel like I've been away from her for so long. In fact, I've never been away from her for as long as I was last night. It's also the first night I didn't put her to bed myself. I'm not sure if I feel guilty or relieved that we survived this milestone. Of course, I haven't talked to Mom yet, so she may have had a hard time putting Ellie to bed last night. I hope she went to bed easily without me and didn't stress Mom out.

My mind wanders to last night. I had such a fantastic time with Ryan. Dinner, the movie, spending time at his house, deciding that we're officially together, and of course, our make-out session that I benefited greatly from with my happy ending. He was so wonderful to me. I don't remember the last time someone paid so much attention to me and showed how much they cared. I'm also still surprised he wouldn't let me return the favor and get him off. His entire focus was making me feel good.

I'm sure he's still sleeping because he's off today with no plans. I think about how cute he must look when he's asleep. That's something we never experienced together in high school. Obviously, we were never allowed to have sleepovers together back then. Our parents would have thrown a fit. Even though he snuck over a lot, he never fell asleep. That would have been too risky.

Then, for some reason, a not-so-happy thought pops in my head. Just how many women *have* seen him sleep? How many women has he been with? What if he's slept with a lot of women over the years? What if he hasn't? I know it shouldn't matter, but now I'm curious.

Really, what difference does it make, I try to tell myself. I was his first, though, and now—I think—I want to know how many women came after me. *No pun intended.* Ugh! Just thinking about him with other women makes me feel so ... jealous! And I realize how ridiculous that is. I was *married,* for crying out loud! We've both lived our own lives for the past fourteen years!

Is this something I can ask him? I want to satisfy my morbid curiosity. However, I'm not sure what the protocol is for asking your boyfriend about his sexual partners. It's been years since I've dated. Scott and I had a limited past. Not only that, we shared our pasts with each other without a question. It was just a common thing to do at that age. I'm not so sure if that's okay *now*, though. Do adults discuss this, or do you just both assume you have a past and accept it with no questions asked?

I'm so out of the dating loop.

Mom comes downstairs about an hour later. Ellie is still playing away, and I'm half playing, half watching TV. "Good morning," I say to her as she walks in the room.

"Good morning," she says as she sits on the couch. "Did you have fun last night?"

"Yes, I did. How about you?"

"Well"—Mom chuckles—"we had a good night, for the most part. However, Ellie definitely missed her mommy at bedtime."

Crap. I should've known she'd have a hard time with this. I'm the only person who has put her to bed since she was born. Even when Scott and I were still together, I was the one who always did that.

"Oh no," I reply. "How long did it take her to go down?"

"About an hour," Mom says.

"An hour?!" Jeez, that's a long time. She usually goes down in no time at all. *Poor Mom!*

"It's okay, though. Don't feel bad. It'll get easier."

"I hope it does, but at the same time, I don't want you to go through that again. I'm the only person who's ever put her to bed before, so I'm not surprised it was rough for her. I just didn't expect her to have *that* hard of a time. Sorry about that."

"No need to apologize," Mom says. "So tell me what you and Ryan did last night."

I smile. Just thinking about Ryan and our date makes me happy. "He took me to dinner, then we saw a movie, and then we hung out at his place for a while. I met his brother's family."

"That's good. It sounds like you enjoyed yourselves."

"We did," I reply.

"When are you going to see him again?"

"I don't know. Maybe today. He has the day off, and he offered to come over just to hang out with Ellie and me, if I want him to."

Mom smiles. "I can tell he hasn't changed much since high school. He was always so thoughtful and kind to you. Do you want him to come over?"

My smile spreads a fraction more. I can't help it. Just thinking of spending more time with Ryan makes me happy. "Yes, I do. That is, if you don't mind?" I have to remember this is my parents' house. Maybe they have plans today that would interfere with me having Ryan over?

"Of course, I don't mind. Your dad and I were thinking of going out for the day anyway."

"Oh," I reply, happy to hear Ryan coming over won't cause any conflict. Not only that, but we'll also be alone. Well, except for Ellie, but that's okay. I'm actually looking forward to seeing how they interact. He was sweet when he picked me up last night, but he was only here for a few minutes. "Have you made coffee yet?" I ask, changing the subject. "I could use the caffeine."

"I turned the pot on right before I walked down here, so it should be done by now."

"Great. I'm going to get some." I stand and start to move toward Ellie to take her with me, but Mom stops me and says, "Go ahead, I'll watch her."

I go upstairs to the kitchen and find Dad pouring himself some coffee. "Good morning," he says to me.

"Hi. How are you this morning?"

"Good. How are you? How was your date?"

I tell him exactly what I told Mom. He seems happy that I went out with Ryan. It's funny because usually dads are overprotective of their teenage daughters when they date, but Ryan won my dad over when we were in high school. My dad actually *liked* my boyfriend. He knew how well Ryan treated me, so Ryan earned his respect. However, if my parents knew about him sneaking over in the middle of the night and all the things we did in my bedroom back then, I'm sure my dad's opinion of him would be different. Luckily, that's not the case.

When Dad met Scott, he also liked him. Scott treated me well, too. There really wasn't anything *not* to like about him. However, my dad lost all respect for him when he found out about his gambling habits.

I pour my coffee and add some creamer, then I go back downstairs. Mom is playing with Ellie. "Dad's awake," I tell her.

She stands. "Oh good. I'll go drink my coffee with him." She kisses my forehead and then heads upstairs.

I decide to get my phone and check my texts as well as Facebook. I have a text from Sarah.

How was your date last night?

I text her back, telling her pretty much exactly what I told my parents. Of course, she has more follow-up questions than my parents did, so we start chatting back and forth.

Sarah: *What did you do at his place? ;-)*

Me: *We kissed. We showed each other our tattoos. I helped him set up his Facebook account.*

Sarah: *You showed each other your tattoos? Were you naked?*

Me: *Not exactly.*

.   .   .

I laugh at the fact that I'm teasing her. I like torturing her by not giving her all the information, and I know it's driving her crazy. A moment later, my phone buzzes with her response.

Sarah: *What does that mean?*

Me: *I don't kiss and tell.*

Sarah replies with a crying smiley face emoji. Then I send her the smiley face that's blowing a kiss, and that's the end of our conversation. I'm sure she'll probably have more questions for me at the gym tomorrow night.

I click on Facebook to see what's going on there. I had accepted Ryan's friend request right away last night, but so far, he hasn't posted anything else. It's still kind of early, though, at eight thirty. I wonder if he's even awake yet? I decide to text him just to say good morning.

It takes him a couple of minutes to reply.

Good morning. I like having you as my wake-up call.

Then my phone rings. He's calling me.

"Hi," I say when I answer.

"Hi," he replies. He sounds like he just woke up. His voice sounds tired and sexy. "How are you this morning?"

"I'm okay," I say. "I didn't get very much sleep. Ellie woke me up just before seven."

"Sorry about that. I won't keep you out late anymore."

I laugh. "That's not going to happen."

He laughs as well. "Yeah, you're right. In fact, I'm kind of hoping it will happen more often now."

"Oh?" I say, trying to sound casual. Inside, my heart is racing, and I want to jump for joy that he wants to see me *more often.* "You must think you impressed me last night or something."

"I didn't?" he asks, sounding slightly surprised.

I laugh again. "Of course, you did! I'm hoping we'll see each other more often now, too."

"Good," he replies. "How about today?"

I smile even though he can't see me. "Today is perfect."

"How about I come over and hang out with you and Ellie? If we think of something else to do, we'll just go with it."

"That would be great," I reply. "What time do you want to come over?"

"Well, I'm still in bed, so ..."

I picture him lying in his bed. I wonder what he sleeps in? A T-shirt? Pajamas? No shirt? Nothing? "Oh?" I say, my voice dripping with sexiness. *Jeez, what's wrong with me?* Picturing him in bed with no shirt on makes my mouth go dry.

"Uh-huh. I'm just lying here," he replies, his voice dropping a little lower and sounding even sexier, too.

"Well ... when do you think you'll get out of bed?"

"I don't know," he says. He sounds like he's smiling. "I'm really comfortable here."

"So you'd rather stay in your comfortable bed than come see me?"

"No, not at all," he replies. "I'd pick you over my bed any day."

I giggle at his choice of words. "That sounded a little bit dirty," I boldly whisper.

He laughs. "I didn't mean it that way! *You* made it dirty! I'm shocked!"

I laugh with him, and I feel myself blushing. Really, what is wrong with me? I

need to get my mind out of the gutter!

"I'm sorry," I apologize, still laughing. "Don't hold it against me."

"What if I want to hold it against you?" he asks, sounding sexy as sin again. *Oh fuck.*

I keep laughing. "Now who's being dirty?"

"Okay, okay, I'll stop. But you started it."

"Whatever," I reply, trying to gain control of myself again. I love that we can tease each other like this. "How about you come over at noon? I'll make you lunch."

"That sounds good," he says. "I'll drag my ass out of bed by then."

I laugh again. *He is too cute.*

And now I'm picturing his ass.

A few hours later, I'm cooking lunch. Ellie is hanging out in her jumper in the kitchen with me. I wasn't sure what to make for lunch, but I decided on homemade cheeseburgers and Caesar salad. My parents left a little while ago to spend the day in downtown Seattle, going to lunch and walking around Pike Place Market. They won't be home for several hours.

Just as I'm finishing our lunch, there's a knock on the door. I walk into the living room and open the front door to find Ryan, looking so sexy. He's wearing jeans and a black vintage Nirvana T-shirt along with a black baseball cap. He's holding a bouquet. Really, how did I get so lucky?

"Hi," I say as I let him in.

"Hi," he says, walking in and putting his free arm around my waist. He pulls me close and kisses me briefly. "These are for you."

I take the bouquet of chrysanthemums and peonies from him and breathe in their exquisite smell. "Thank you. They're beautiful. You know you didn't have to do this."

"I know," he replies, "but I wanted to."

I smile, close the front door, and start walking toward the kitchen. "Let me put them in water."

Ryan follows me. I'm surprised when he squats down next to Ellie and says hi, then starts playing with her. She's all smiles and babbles at him. I find a vase and arrange the flowers in it, then I put it in the center of the kitchen table. They really are beautiful.

I squat down next to Ryan, still being entertained by Ellie. She turns her attention to me as soon as I join them. "Mamamama," she says.

"This is Ryan," I say to her. She looks back at him and smiles.

Ryan turns to look at me. "She's so cute."

"Yes, she is," I reply. I stand and so does he. Ellie jumps up and down, happy as can be.

"It smells good in here. What's for lunch?" Ryan asks.

I walk to the counter and pick up the two plates I had just finished placing our burgers and salad on, then hold them out for him to see. "Cheeseburgers and Caesar salad."

He smiles and walks closer to me, taking both plates from me. "You made this? It looks delicious!" He sets the plates on the kitchen table, and we sit down to eat.

"I did," I reply. "I wasn't sure what to make, but I know you like burgers, so I went with that."

"Thank you," he says. "I was expecting peanut butter and jelly sandwiches or something."

I quirk an eyebrow at him. "What? You think I can't cook?" I try to act offended.

He chuckles and shakes his head. "Not at all. But you never cooked like this in high school."

I smile at him. "Well, I've learned a lot since then."

We eat lunch together with Ellie next to us, playing happily.

"Can she eat food yet?" he asks, motioning toward Ellie.

"She eats some baby food, but no burgers yet," I say, jokingly.

"I know nothing about babies. I'm in awe when I see someone I know with a baby of their own. I feel so far behind and out of the loop."

"Well, if you want to hang around me, you'll have to learn how to be around a baby," I say, smirking at him before taking a bite of my salad. Maybe this would be a good time to ask him if he wants kids of his own someday? Part of me is afraid to ask so soon, though.

"Are you willing to teach me?" he asks, cocking an eyebrow and pulling me out of my thoughts. He looks adorable. And the fact he's asking makes my stomach do a little flip flop. *He wants to learn how to be around Ellie.* Surely, this is a good sign.

"Of course," I reply, surprised and grateful for his interest in my daughter. We come as a package deal, so if he isn't willing to have Ellie in his life, I know I'd have to end this.

"What's my first lesson going to be?"

I think for a moment before I tell him, "I think changing a diaper is pretty important to know."

He laughs. "Of course, you'd say that," he says. "That's probably the one lesson I'd like to avoid!"

I laugh and shake my head. "You can't avoid changing a baby's diaper. You might *have* to do it someday, and you need to know how."

He shakes his head. "At least let me finish my lunch first."

I laugh at his reaction. "You're funny."

Ellie makes noise, demanding our attention. We turn and talk to her. It dawns on me that this is what I always pictured in my mind when I was pregnant, only my picture then had Scott with me. I always imagined us having this type of family time together with our baby. I suddenly have mixed emotions; I'm a little sad that I lost this with Scott, but I'm also incredibly happy to be here with Ryan right now. I try to push the feelings about Scott aside. I don't want to ruin my afternoon with Ryan by feeling emotional about the ending of my marriage.

Ryan doesn't seem to notice a change in me at all, so that's a relief. I try to forget about my range of emotions by concentrating on being with him. Then he seals the deal for me.

Ellie is babbling at him nonstop. She puts her arms out

toward him as though she wants to be picked up, and without missing a beat, Ryan puts his burger down, bends over, and picks her up. He sets her on his lap, facing toward me. "Is that better?" he asks her. I'm just staring at him in awe, and I think at that moment I fall in love with him all over again. He's won me over with the care he's showing my daughter. He looks at me, and I realize I'm staring at him. "What? Is this okay?" he asks. "She seemed like she wanted out of that thing."

I smile at him, trying to rein in my emotions. He has no idea how he has just touched my heart. "Of course, it is," I stammer. "Do you want me to take her?"

"No, she's fine here." He smiles at me, and Ellie seems content. He continues eating his lunch one-handed while holding her with his other arm.

After we finish eating, Ryan hands Ellie to me and then proceeds to take our dishes to the sink. He cleans them off, then asks if he can put them in the dishwasher. *Have I died and gone to heaven? What man does this kind of shit?*

"Sure. But you don't have to," I tell him as I stand with Ellie in my arms. I fed her right before I made lunch, and she's starting to look a little tired. It's close to her nap time.

"You cooked lunch, so I'll do the dishes," Ryan says as he opens the dishwasher.

I stop and just stare at him. He has totally shocked me this afternoon.

"What is it?" he asks, looking confused.

I shake my head. "Okay, you're just going to have to stop right now."

"Why?" He looks even more confused.

"Because you're just too good to be true!"

"Why? Because I'm doing the dishes?"

"Yes!"

"Isn't that fair?"

I move closer to him and put my free hand on his stomach.

I'm momentarily distracted when I feel his tight abs through the thin material. I look him in the eye so he knows I'm being serious. "No one has ever done this for me before."

"Really?" he asks, looking surprised.

"Really."

We just look at one another for a moment. His beautiful chocolate brown eyes look into mine with so much care and affection, and I know I need to put Ellie down for a nap *now* so Ryan and I can have some *alone* time together.

I lean up on my toes and give him a peck on the lips. "I'm going to put Ellie down for her nap. I'll be back in a few minutes."

Ryan loads the dishwasher while I take Ellie downstairs to her room. As I change her diaper, I contemplate having Ryan come down so I can teach him how to do it, but then I realize I don't want to interrupt him from doing the dishes. I can't believe he actually volunteered to clean. Scott *never* did the dishes when we were married. Even when I was at work and he was left to make his own dinner, he *always* left the mess for me to clean up. Of course, it sort of annoyed me at the time, but it's just the way we were. I like that Ryan is willing to help.

I get Ellie changed and lay her down in her crib. I turn on her mobile and kiss her. "Take a nap, sweetie," I whisper to her.

I grab the baby monitor to take upstairs with me so I can hear her if she wakes up. I find Ryan still loading the dishwasher. I'm shocked to find he's done *all* the dishes for me, including a few left in the sink from breakfast. "Wow, you didn't have to do this," I say to him.

"I don't mind. Lunch was delicious. Thanks for cooking."

It's sexy seeing him so domestic. I can't help but sit down at the table and watch him continue to wipe down the counters. Pure mommy porn in the making.

"It's kind of weird being back here in your parents' house again," he says as he puts one last bowl on the top rack.

"It's weird *living* here again," I reply with a chuckle.

"I like the updates they've done to the place. It looks nice."

"Yeah, they've done a good job taking care of it." Over the past few years, my parents have remodeled the kitchen, replaced the living room carpet, and updated some of the furniture.

"My parents' house looks pretty much the same," he says. "They haven't done very much to it. It still looks nice, but it's just a little outdated now." He opens the cabinet under the sink and finds the dishwasher detergent. He fills the detergent holder, closes the dishwasher, turns it on, and even puts the detergent back under the sink where it belongs. I think I've died and gone to heaven. Not only is he the sexiest man alive, but he actually knows how to clean properly, too … and I get to just sit here and watch? I think I've entered an alternate universe I never want to return from.

"Wow, thank you," I manage to say as he washes his hands in the sink.

"You're welcome. You need to stop thanking me, though." He dries his hands and walks over to me. Putting his hands on the arms of the chair I'm sitting on, he bends down, and it makes my heart race. His face is so close to mine, and I hold my breath as I want nothing more than to be kissed. My wish is granted when he moves closer and presses his lips to mine, ever so gently. He pulls away much too soon, though, leaving me wanting more. I open my eyes to find him looking at me, his hands still on the chair, and his face still only a couple of inches away from mine. He has a sexy little grin on his face, and I can't help but smile back at him.

"Would you like to go sit downstairs in the family room?" I ask.

He nods his head and kisses me again. It's another quick kiss, then he stands and offers me his hand. I take it as I stand, and we walk hand in hand downstairs to the family room.

Ryan and I sit on the couch, each of us at opposite ends. Why we sit so far apart, I don't know, but I hope we end up closer to each other soon. I place the baby monitor on the coffee table, then bend my knee so I'm turned toward Ryan.

"You can watch her on that thing?" he asks, surprised, as he sees the monitor and notices the screen showing a live video of her.

I giggle at him. This is a typical baby monitor, but he really is out of the loop with baby stuff. Not that he would have any reason to be *in* the loop, but I still find him funny and cute.

"Yes," I reply.

"We're living in the future!"

I laugh at his reaction. He shrugs and smirks at me. God, he's adorable.

"So how long does she usually nap for?" he asks.

"At least an hour. Sometimes a little longer," I reply. "She's a good napper. I'm lucky."

"Does she just take one nap per day?"

"Now, yes. *Sometimes,* if she's had a really busy day, she might take another nap around dinnertime, but that's rare anymore."

"So we have an hour?" he asks me, giving me his crooked smile and waggling his eyebrows. My heart skips a beat.

"Yes, why?" I ask him, trying to sound like I don't know what he could possibly be thinking.

He moves a little closer to me, stretching both his arms out along the back of the couch. There's still quite a bit of space between us, though. "Oh, I don't know," he replies.

"What do you want to do?"

He smiles at me. "Talk?"

"Really? That's not what I thought you were going to say."

He moves a little bit closer to me. "What did you think I was going to say?"

He's such a flirt. "I don't know," I reply, trying to flirt back.

Again, he moves a little closer, but there's still a few inches between us. "We could reminisce about old times," he suggests.

"What would you like to reminisce about?"

He moves closer again. Now he's so close, his leg is touching mine. "I don't know. Is there anything you'd like to reminisce about?"

I can tell he wants me to make the first move, but I'm waiting on him. "We could discuss all the football games you won." I used to love watching him play sports, but football was my favorite.

He gives me his crooked smile. It takes all my strength not to kiss him right then and there. "We could," he replies.

"Maybe some of the school dances we went to?" I suggest, hoping he'll give in and just kiss me.

"Which dance should we reminisce about?" he asks, raising an eyebrow.

"I don't know. There were a lot." I can't help but look at his lips. I want to kiss him so badly.

Ryan smirks. "How about the Valentine's dance our junior year?"

My heart starts racing. I can't help it, having him so close to me, flirting like this, and talking about our past. That Valentine's dance was the first dance we went to together. We went just as friends, but by the end of the night, we were a couple. That was the first night we kissed. "Yes," is all I can say.

"Or junior prom," he adds. I know what he's doing. He's trying to break me down so I make the first move. The night of our junior prom was the first night we did a lot more than just kissing.

I smirk at him. "That was fun, too." I'm not giving in.

He moves his hand and touches the ends of my hair. He twirls some strands around his finger, almost absentmindedly. "What about homecoming our junior year?"

I'm suddenly confused. I look at him like he's crazy. "That was a few months before we got together. We didn't go to that dance together."

He continues twirling my hair, unfazed by my comment. "I know," he says. "But I remember it well. You went with Luke

Thompson and wore that blue strapless dress. I took Gina Smith, but I don't have a clue what she wore. I couldn't take my eyes off you all night."

I swear my heart is going to leap out of my chest. He's never mentioned this before. I just look at him, perplexed.

He continues, "I spent all night at that dance trying to figure out how to get you in my arms. I started having feelings for you the summer before our junior year. Actually, it was way before then, but I was too afraid to act on them because we were friends. When I saw you at that dance with Luke, though, I'd never been more jealous in my life. I always thought you were pretty, but when you walked into the gym that night, I thought you were the most beautiful girl I'd ever seen. I was probably a terrible date to Gina, but I couldn't get you off my mind. I couldn't help myself."

I'm speechless. *I never knew this.*

Ryan continues, "Everyone went to Kim Simpson's party after the dance, and I thought maybe I could make my move there."

I try to remember the party at Kim's. I'm racking my brain, and then it hits me. Luke had kissed me there.

"But Luke wouldn't leave your side all night. I was getting frustrated, and Gina got pissed at me for ignoring her, so she left early. I felt bad, but you were all I cared about. When I saw him kiss you later, I got so upset, I gave up and started drinking."

Suddenly, it all comes back to me. The football coach found out, and he was benched for the next three games as punishment, which happened to be the last three of the season. Athletes weren't supposed to drink, and there were severe consequences if they did. I remember consoling him about this as his friend. He never drank that much, and he was upset about missing his last three games. But I never knew he did it because of *me.*

"You did that because you were jealous?" I say quietly, still shocked by his confession.

I now notice Ryan's face is getting closer to mine although I really don't know if I'm the one moving closer or if he is.

He nods his head. "After that night, I knew I wanted to be more than just friends with you. I'd had a crush on you for a long time, but until that night, I was just afraid to take it to the next level. I spent the next few months trying to win you over, and at the Valentine's dance, I finally decided to make my move."

Our mouths are only a couple of inches apart now. "Why didn't you ever tell me this before?" I whisper as I feel him exhale.

"I don't know," he replies with a shrug. "Are you going to kiss me now?"

Unable to control myself any longer, I give in. I need to feel his lips on mine. We wrap our arms around each other, pulling each other closer. This kiss feels urgent as though we need each other. I think that's because we do. I need him in my life. I really do. And I want him to know that.

We continue kissing, not letting up. Suddenly, he pulls away, but only to move us so we're lying down on the couch. He's so strong, and he moves me with ease. Then our lips find each other again.

This is how things started last night, which quickly escalated to us being half naked and me ending with an orgasm. I didn't want to go all the way last night, and I still don't today. I don't want to go too fast even though I feel as if we're meant to be together after all these years. I'm just not ready.

However, last night he just wanted to make me feel good. Well, today, after hearing his confession that he kept secret all these years, I want to turn the tables and make *him* feel good.

Today is different, though. We're *just* kissing. As he caresses my face, he says, "I can't get enough of you," then our lips crash together again.

I feel the same. I can't get enough of him, either. I decide to show him by making my move. I slide my hands around to the front of his pants. Just as I'm about to unbutton his jeans, he grabs my hand and stops me. I'm more than a little surprised. "What is it?" I ask him.

He leans up on his elbow so he can look at me. "Last night, you weren't ready to have sex yet. Do you still feel that way?"

"Yes, but we don't have to have sex," I reply. "I just want to make you feel good like you did for me last night."

He looks down as though he's conflicted, then he looks back at me. "Brooke, I don't want to rush into things with you. Honestly, I feel a little guilty for what we did last night. I wish I had more self-control with you."

"Don't feel guilty," I say to him, and I place my hand on his cheek.

"I feel the same way you do about waiting," he says. "I want to wait a little while longer before we have sex. We've only been together for a few days now."

"Not counting the year and a half before," I interject.

He smiles. "I know. But you're in the middle of a divorce, and I don't want to be a rebound relationship for you. You mean too much to me."

I smile and stroke my hand against his cheek. I can't help grinning when he's being so thoughtful. It truly makes me happy that he's so considerate and taking our relationship seriously. "You mean so much to me, too. You're not a rebound, Ryan."

He continues, "My point is, when we do finally have sex again, I want it to be special. Not in your parents' basement while Ellie naps in the next room. The next time you make me come, I want to be inside you."

Holy hell. My stomach muscles clench at his words. I've never had anyone say something so erotic to me before. "Then the same goes for me," I say to him, practically whispering. "I don't want to come again until you're inside me."

He kisses me briefly. "I just don't want us to make out like wild teenagers and have it mean less than it does," he explains when he pulls away from my lips. "Not that it didn't mean anything when we were teenagers because it always did with you."

"I know it did. And it doesn't mean less to me now either, but I understand what you're saying," I reply. "And I appreciate that this means so much to you because it does to me, too."

"You have no idea how difficult this is for me," he says, chuckling a bit. "I want to take you right now." He puts his forehead against mine.

"I'd like that," I say, "but I know we should wait." Looking deep into his eyes, I see a reflection of my feelings. I finally break our silence with a reassuring whisper, "It'll be worth it."

We lie on the couch, just holding one another. Ryan's head rests on my chest as I comb my fingers through his hair. I'm still shocked he stopped me from touching him, but I enjoy cuddling with him now that I know we're on the same page and are in this for more than just tonight.

As I cuddle the sexy man before me and get lost in all that is Ryan, an unwanted thought barrels through me. The more I want to dismiss it, the stronger it becomes. I'm afraid to ask, but I need to know. I'm not sure how he will take this, and I don't want to upset him, but I have to know. Since we seem to be so open with one another, this might be the right time to bring it up.

I decide to go for it. "Ryan, can I ask you something?" I bite my lip, hesitating to go further.

"Anything," he replies. I can feel his voice vibrate on my chest.

I take a deep breath. "Please don't take this the wrong way, but how many women have you been with?"

He sits up and rests on his elbow again. He just looks at me warily. "You really want to know?" he finally asks.

Maybe I don't. This can't be good. I nod my head anyway.

He lets out a breath and moves a hand up to his forehead, then moves it back through his hair. *Oh, this is not good.* I shouldn't have asked.

He looks chagrin as he begins to talk. "Honestly, I lost count."

Shit. I suddenly regret asking him.

"Let me explain," he starts. "A few months after you and I

broke up, I was going to be deployed for the first time. I was excited but also scared out of my mind. You were the one person I wanted to talk to, but we'd stopped talking, and you were so far away. I didn't want to bother you. I really thought it would've been selfish to get back in contact with you. I wanted you, but then what? I'd be deployed. If I died, you would've been alone. Hell, you would've been alone no matter what with me being so far away, and I didn't want that for you. So instead, I decided I had to get you out of my mind ... so I started sleeping around. I thought if I was with other women, it would help me forget you. I'd just go home with random girls I'd meet at bars. I didn't keep track of how many there were."

I'm surprised, but I understand his explanation. I had a hard time getting over him, too. I'm flattered he thought of my feelings and worried about me being alone while he was deployed. He was always doing what was best for me. Although I feel extremely guilty about this, too. Why were *my* feelings more important than his? I didn't feel they were, but he let me go just to see me be happy in the long run. *That goes to show how much he really cared about me.*

"So you were a player?" I ask him with a smirk, trying to lighten the mood.

He chuckles. "You could say that. After my deployment, I eventually met a girl who I dated for a while. When we broke up, I just had one-night stands again until my next deployment. It was kind of a cycle. I came back from that deployment and ended up meeting another woman who I dated for quite a while. We stayed together while I was deployed a third time although I later found out she was cheating on me while I was gone. When I came back, I ended it with her as soon as I found out. So I just hooked up with women at bars again. Eventually, I got tired of it because I didn't want that for my life. I focused on my job in the Marines. My last relationship was with a girl when I lived in

California. We broke up about a month before I moved back here."

"Oh," I say, surprised. His last relationship ended just a few months ago? Is he over her?

He places his hand under my chin and lifts my head to look me in the eye. "I want you to know something, and I want you to know that I'm being completely honest."

His seriousness gets my attention. I'm still trying to process the fact he's slept with a large, unknown number of women, but now he has my full attention for whatever he has to say.

"I've never stopped thinking about you," he confesses.

What? Did I hear him correctly?

Ryan continues, "All those years, I've always wondered how you were doing. Each time I was deployed and stuck in some serious situations, thinking I could actually die, my mind always wandered back to you. Thinking of you helped me get through so much." He closes his eyes briefly as if he's remembering something painful. It makes my heart hurt for him. I can't imagine what he has seen and been through during his deployments.

I also can't believe what he's saying to me right now. *Thoughts of me helped him for the past fourteen years?*

I touch his cheek with my hand. "Ryan," I whisper. I don't know what else to say. I'm at a loss for words.

He copies my action and touches my cheek with his hand. "Honestly, I never stopped loving you, Brooke. I had to fuck you out of my mind with all those women, when really all I wanted was to be with you again."

I can't contain the tears forming in my eyes. He's being so honest with me right now, and there's just so much to process. My marriage just ended because my husband chose gambling over Ellie and me, and Ryan's here telling me he hasn't stopped wanting me for the past fourteen years. The tears start falling, but I don't know what to say.

"Don't cry," he says, wiping away the tears.

"I just don't know what to say right now. I can't believe what you're telling me."

"Please believe it, Brooke. Each time I entered a relationship, I had to convince myself I was over you. As soon as those relationships ended, my mind was back on you again. I can't even begin to tell you how much I've thought about you. There were several times I came close to trying to contact you again, but I didn't want to mess with your life. I figured you had moved on and were happy."

The tears keep falling as I realize I need to confess something to him. Without another thought, I blurt it out. "I had to fuck you out of my mind, too."

Ryan's eyes widen at my words, and he shakes his head. "Brooke," he says, his voice cracking at the end, letting me know he's feeling as much sorrow over our breakup as I am.

We both sit up on the couch as I wipe my eyes. All my feelings from when we broke up fourteen years ago come flooding back. Ryan wraps his arm around me, holding me close, trying to soothe me.

Eventually, I get a grip and start to explain. "After we broke up, I couldn't stop thinking of you. It took months, and I was so depressed. My roommate finally convinced me to go out with this guy she knew. We hit it off well enough, and I ended up going home with him that night. My only desire was to forget about you. The entire time, I thought of you, but it was awful because he wasn't you." I feel my face blushing. Embarrassment washes over me as I admit all this to Ryan. He doesn't say anything but just holds my gaze as he listens and runs his fingers through my hair. I know I need to tell him the rest. "Afterward, I thought I just needed to give the guy another chance to get you out of my head, so I went out with him again. But that didn't work either."

I sigh as I shake my head. "Eventually, I did get over you and ended up dating that guy for almost a year. After we broke up, though, you were never far from my mind. I figured you were too far away and had moved on with your life by then, so I made myself forget you again. A few months later, I met my ex-husband."

Ryan doesn't say anything at first. He just holds me as he wipes my tears away. Then his seriousness turns playful as he smirks at me. "So you're telling me you've only been with two other guys?"

"Yes," I reply with a chuckle.

"I feel like a whore," he says, trying to lighten the mood. I burst out laughing, and he joins me.

"I don't care what you did in the past. I'm just so happy to have you back in my life," I tell him. And it's true. Why should I care about his past? He's with me now, and that's all that matters.

He smiles. "Me too, Brooke," he says sincerely before lowering his lips to mine and kissing me sweetly.

We kiss for a while but do nothing else. It feels amazing to just lay and *be* together. I'm so happy to have Ryan in my life again. We've been apart for fourteen years, and I still can't believe he's saying he thought about me all that time. Even though I eventually went on with my life and got married, it warms my heart to know he was thinking of me while he was away in the Marines, fighting in war zones.

Suddenly, I break our kiss when another thought barrels through my mind. "How many times were you deployed?"

"Four times. Each almost a year."

Oh, my God. The thought of him deployed unexpectedly pains my heart in a way I didn't think was possible. He could have been hurt. Or worse. Having not seen his body entirely yet, I really have no idea if he was ever injured or not. "Were you ever hurt?"

He sits up and lifts his shirt so I can see his side. I see scars going from just below his armpit all the way down to his hip. I didn't notice them last night when we were looking at his tattoos since I was sitting on his opposite side. "Shrapnel from an IED."

Oh, my fucking God.

"When did that happen?" I ask as I sit up to be next to him. He lowers his shirt, and I reach out to hold his hand. All I want to do is comfort him.

"During my last deployment. It was a fucked-up situation. I lost a lot of friends. I almost died."

Holy shit. I always hear about military deaths and injuries in the news, but I never knew anyone directly involved. Tears spring to my eyes as I think about Ryan being injured and almost losing his life.

"I'm so sorry." I say the first thing that comes to mind. A tear escapes, and I wipe it away. I'm so grateful he's alive to tell me this, and that there's no chance of him going to a war zone again.

"It's okay." He puts an arm around me and holds me tight when he notices more tears falling down my cheeks. With his other hand, he gently wipes my tears away with his thumb. "Don't cry. I'm fine now. I won't lie, though. It was a difficult time in my life. I'm still mentally trying to get over everything that happened. I finally saw a therapist when I moved home."

His comment surprises me. It makes me wonder if he has PTSD. I decide not to bring it up since I know it's a sensitive subject. Instead, I decide to share my own experience.

"I know about therapy," I tell him as I run my hands through my hair in an attempt to regain my composure. "I started seeing a therapist when my husband and I separated."

"I'm sorry," he says sincerely.

"It's okay. Things happen for a reason and talking to a therapist helped." I smile, and he responds by kissing me.

Then he pulls back again, and his face is more serious than I've ever seen. "Brooke, there's one more thing I need to tell you."

"What is it?" I ask, curious what else he could say.

"I have PTSD."

"Oh," I reply. I'm relieved that he offered the information so I didn't have to ask, but my heart sinks for him once again. I can't help but be sad when I think of all that he's been through.

"I don't want you to worry, though. I just want you to be aware of it," Ryan continues.

"So what do you mean, exactly?" I ask, needing to know what to expect with his diagnosis.

"Well, I take anti-anxiety meds each day," he explains. "It's a low dose, but it helps. My anxiety kicks in when there's a loud, explosive-type noise. I don't like balloons; they pop unexpectedly. I know that sounds weird, but that's the way it is for me. That's the reason I haven't pursued being a cop. I'm not sure if I can handle it, or if they'd even hire me."

I let out a breath I didn't know I was holding. "Thank you for telling me. Please, just tell me if there's anything I can do to help you. If we're ever together and you start to feel anxious about anything, tell me. Please."

Ryan brushes his hand through my hair. "Thank you for being so understanding," he says as he brushes a loose strand of hair from my face. "You always were," he whispers.

I lean in and kiss him again. This time, it escalates. We make out until we hear Ellie cry.

"That would be my baby." I chuckle as we pull away from each other.

"You'd better get her," he replies, sitting up on the couch.

"Sorry for the mood killer." I laugh, walking to her room. As I pick up Ellie out of her crib, I know her diaper needs changing. Remembering our conversation during lunch, I call out, "Ryan, come here!"

He walks in the room just as I'm pulling Ellie's pants off. "What?" Concern is etched across his face as he closes the distance between us.

"It's time to learn how to change a diaper."

RYAN

$\mathcal{I}$'m changing a baby's diaper. *What universe am I in right now?* If someone had told me a month ago that I'd be doing this today, I wouldn't have believed them. And the crazy thing is, I *want* to help Brooke with her daughter. I *want* to know how to do this. I *need* Brooke to be in my life again, and her daughter is an added perk. I've always wanted to be a father someday, anyway.

Whoa ... Thinking of myself as a father right now might be jumping the gun *just* a tad. Brooke and I have only been back together for a few days. But I know if I'm going to be with her, Ellie is part of the equation. I can't date a single mom without considering the possibility of being her kid's stepdad someday. That would be irresponsible ... *wouldn't it?*

Maybe I'm thinking about this because of my past with Brooke. We've been in love with each other once, and the flame never completely went out for either of us. This isn't a brand-new relationship. Things with Brooke seem right ... as if it's meant to be. I know that sounds corny and cliché, but it's true.

"Here you go," Brooke says, holding a clean diaper out to me. "You hold this and watch while I take off the dirty one."

I can't help but chuckle at the smirk on her face, and I shake my head. "Whatever you say," I reply as she gets to work.

And *oh, my God, what the hell is that smell?* What the fuck is that orange stuff? This has to be the *nastiest* diaper ever! How'd this little girl, who weighs no more than fifteen pounds, produce so much shit?! I cover my nose with my hand, and it's then that I notice Brooke laughing at me.

"Don't laugh at me," I say, chuckling. "It stinks!"

Brooke shakes her head, and laughter fills the room. Somehow, she manages to clean Ellie up without missing a beat. It's as if she's on autopilot while changing her diaper, which, I suppose, is probably true for her. From the amount of crap Ellie just produced, Brooke has a lot of experience doing this.

"Are you paying attention so you know what to do?" she asks with a serious face.

I clear my throat. "Of course, I am," I reply. Although I've been watching her clean Ellie's backside and apply some sort of cream, I've been distracted by Brooke. She's just gorgeous. I've always thought so, and at this moment, I realize how lucky I am to have her back in my life. Even if I'm learning how to change a shitty diaper, I'm still more attracted to her now than I've ever been.

"Okay then, it's time for you to put the new diaper on," Brooke says to me.

"This one?" I stupidly ask, holding up the diaper in my hand. *Of course, she means this one, dipshit!*

Brooke chuckles again. "Yes, that one. Let's trade places so you can put it on her."

We switch our positions so I'm able to reach Ellie. I open the diaper and look at it, still confused as to which end goes where. Brooke shows me and talks me through it, showing me what to do. Before I know it, I have successfully diapered Ellie.

"Nice job!" Brooke congratulates me and pats me on the back.

"That wasn't so hard," I reply, trying to sound cool about the situation.

"Well, next time, you can clean her up, too." Brooke winks at me, then scoops Ellie off the changing table.

We spend the next couple of hours just hanging out with Ellie and making up for lost time by getting acquainted. When I notice Ellie needs another diaper change, I attempt to impress Brooke by volunteering to change her all on my own. I mean, how hard can it really be?

"You're kidding, right?" Disbelief fills her face as I pick Ellie up.

"I need to learn to do this on my own," I assure her as I carry Ellie into her bedroom with Brooke in tow. I lay Ellie down on her changing table and proceed to change her diaper. I have to say I even impress myself. This isn't so hard. The only thing Brooke needs to help me with is finding the supplies.

When I finish, I hold Ellie with her back against me so she's facing Brooke. She coos, showing me I must have done something right.

"I can't believe you just did that," Brooke says with a bewildered look on her face.

"I can't believe I did it, either," I reply, bouncing Ellie in my arms.

"You do the dishes *and* change diapers. How did I get so lucky?"

I shrug, then move closer to Brooke and kiss her. Ellie grabs for her mom, so she takes her from me. I happen to glance at the dresser next to the crib and see a framed picture of who appears to be Brooke's ex. He's holding Ellie in his arms. So *that's* what he looks like.

"That's Scott," Brooke says, sheepishly. "I put it in here for Ellie."

"I figured," I tell her as I smile and move closer, putting my arms around her waist. "You don't have his picture next to your bed, too, do you?" I have to tease her.

Brooke laughs. "You're funny," she says, rolling her eyes. "No, of course I don't. Would you like to see?" Still holding Ellie, she takes my hand in her free one and leads me across the hall to the same room she grew up in. I spent a lot of time in here many years ago, and the memories rush through my mind.

We stand in the middle of her room, and she lets go of my hand. "See? No pictures of my ex in here," she says, waving her hand around for effect.

I look around the room and take in the changes she's made. "I remember this room well," I comment.

Brooke chuckles. "You spent a lot of time in here."

"Yes, I did. Those were some fun times." I step closer, wrapping my arms around her. Ellie babbles something and tugs on my shirt, so I take her from Brooke. My move surprises Brooke, but Ellie seems happy in my arms, and it warms my heart.

Just then, we hear the front door upstairs open, and footsteps enter the house. "My parents must be home," Brooke says.

"Let's go up and say hi," I suggest.

We walk upstairs and spend some time with her parents. They comment on how beautiful the flowers I brought Brooke are, and how nice it is to see us together again. I've always liked her parents.

A little later, I suggest going out for dinner. Brooke's parents decline joining us. Apparently, they ate a big lunch while in Seattle, so they aren't hungry. That leaves Brooke, Ellie, and me on our first outing, so we go to a kid-friendly restaurant nearby.

"What are you doing tomorrow?" I ask Brooke while we eat our dinner.

She scowls, a reaction I wasn't expecting. "I have to take Ellie to Olympia to see her dad."

Ah, that explains the scowl. "In Olympia?" I ask, wondering why she has to drive so far.

"Yes, it's about halfway for both of us to drive," she explains. "We're meeting at the children's museum there. It's a good place for Ellie to play, and I can sit in the cafe and avoid him."

I chuckle. "That's good, I guess. Would you like some company? I don't have to work tomorrow, so I could go with you."

Brooke smiles, telling me she likes that idea. "As much as I want to say yes, I don't think that would go over very well with my ex," she replies. "Maybe someday, though. It's just too soon, I think."

That isn't exactly the answer I was hoping for, but I understand. "I totally get it, Brooke, but I want you to know I'm serious. I'll go with you anytime you want."

Brooke's smile lights up her face. I love her smile. God, I'd do anything for this woman.

"What time will you get back?" I ask.

"Hopefully no later than three o'clock," she replies. "Why?"

"Because I'd like to see you again tomorrow, if I can," I answer honestly. I love spending time with her.

Brooke's lips curl up again. "I was hoping you'd say that."

"Why don't you and Ellie come to my place on your way home? We can hang out there."

"Okay," she agrees.

After dinner, we return to Brooke's house. We've been together all day, but I'm not ready to leave her yet. Luckily, she doesn't want me to leave either.

Once inside, we hang out with her parents upstairs. When they go to bed, Brooke and I go downstairs to the family room and watch TV. It's late, but we're still not ready to say goodbye to each other. Ellie's asleep in her room, so Brooke and I cuddle on the couch and find a crime show to watch. We always loved watching those together in high school.

"Do you still like watching reality shows?" I ask her.

"Of course, I do," she replies. "When I actually watch TV by myself, that is."

"What's that one you always made me watch with you?" I ask, trying to remember the name of the show.

She laughs. *"The Real World?"*

"Yes! You loved that show. I couldn't stand it," I admit, chuckling.

Brooke sits up and looks at me with a surprised look on her face. "You didn't like that show? But we watched it all the time! I really thought it was one of your favorite shows!"

I can't help myself when I run a hand through Brooke's hair. I'm so attracted to her it's hard not to touch her. "You're right. I watched it all the time with you, but that's only because *you* wanted to watch it. It just gave me an excuse to cuddle with you."

Brooke doesn't say anything. She just leans in and kisses me.

BROOKE

*W*hen I wake up, I'm not in my room. It takes a moment for me to realize I'm on the couch, which explains why I'm uncomfortable. Ryan is cuddled up against me, which also explains why I'm so hot. His body is like a heater. Glancing at the clock on the cable box, I see it's three thirty a.m. We fell asleep watching TV, which is still on, showing an infomercial for some sort of kitchen gadget. I reach for the remote on the coffee table to turn it off.

I look at Ryan and debate whether I should wake him. He looks absolutely adorable asleep with his lips slightly parted and his hair out of place. As peaceful as he looks, I realize I'd be more comfortable if he moved a bit, so I wake him up as gently as I can.

He opens his eyes and stares. It takes him a second to realize where he is, and then he says, "We fell asleep?"

"Yep."

He sits up, as do I. "I guess I'll go home then," he says, wiping his eyes.

"It's late. You can stay if you want." I glance at the clock again. "Or early, depending how you look at it. Let's move to my bed where it's more comfortable."

He just looks at me for a moment before replying. "Are you sure? What about your parents?"

I chuckle. "I'm thirty-two years old and have a baby. I think my boyfriend can spend the night if I want."

Ryan shakes his head. "I can sleep here on the couch."

I stand and take his hand. "No, come sleep with me."

He hesitates, but then follows me into my room. "Okay, but we're just going to sleep."

"Deal," I say as I shut my bedroom door. "What do you normally sleep in?" I ask.

"Just my underwear," he replies, giving me his crooked smile. "Sometimes a shirt, too. Why?"

"I want you to be comfortable while you sleep." Who am I kidding? I'm really just hoping he takes some of his clothes off. I mean, I might as well enjoy getting to sleep with him.

He shakes his head, then takes off his pants. He folds them neatly, placing them on the bench at the end of my bed. Then he removes his socks and places those on top of his pants. He's only wearing his T-shirt and boxer briefs, and he looks sexy as hell. "I'm comfortable now," he says. "What do you sleep in?"

I walk to my dresser, take out a pair of pajama pants and a T-shirt, then move past him to my bed and pull the covers back. For a moment, I consider stripping in front of him to put my pajamas on, but then decide against it. Things might go too far if I do that, and we're committed to waiting. I idly wonder exactly how long he's planning to wait. *I hope not too long.*

"I'll change in the bathroom and wash my face. Be back in a few minutes," I say to him.

I leave my room as Ryan climbs into my full-size bed. It's actually the same bed I had as a teenager that we spent many good times together in.

As I get ready for bed, I think about our day. It amazes me how quickly Ryan and Ellie have taken to each other. He's so sweet to her, and considering he has no experience with babies, he's doing really well. I love the way Ellie beams at Ryan and lets him hold her without fussing. It gives me hope for our future together.

Ryan lying in my bed right now is surreal. We're sleeping in the same bed tonight and will wake up together in the morning. I couldn't be happier.

After I change, wash my face, and brush my teeth, I return to my room only to find Ryan asleep under my covers. I turn off the light and crawl into bed. Ryan surprises me by pulling my body against his and kissing me. I almost squeal, but I manage to stay quiet. He pulls his lips away from mine to whisper, "I love you."

His words are totally unexpected, but I instantly smile. It's dark in the room, so he can't see my reaction. I know it's taboo for him to say those words to me so soon, but as surprised as I am, those three little words bring me so much joy. He had hinted at his feelings earlier when he said, *I never really stopped loving you,* but I wasn't sure exactly what he meant. Honestly, as I spend more time with him, I feel the same way.

Ryan's body tenses, and his hold tightens around me as if he just realized what he said. Throw in the fact that I've stayed silent, he's probably freaking out. "I mean ..." he says, backpedaling now. "Did I just say that out loud?"

He must feel strongly about me to let those words slip out of his mouth. It lights me up inside to know I'm not the only one feeling this. Our lips find each other again, and we kiss for a while before falling asleep in each other's arms for the second time tonight.

BROOKE

*E*llie's crying. I need to get up, but I can't move. I open my eyes to find Ryan asleep next to me. We're tangled up, cuddling, and I'm trapped. He's too heavy for me to move. *Crap.* I shake him as I say his name, and he finally wakes.

"Good morning," he says in his groggy state.

"Good morning. I need to get Ellie," I reply.

He moves so I can get out of bed. "Sorry," he apologizes.

I look back at him and smile as I open the bedroom door. "It's okay. You're kinda comfy." Then I go across the hall to get my girl.

After I change her diaper, I bring her into my room and lie back in bed. I put her between Ryan and me, hoping she will snuggle and fall back to sleep. It's only 7:03 a.m. My body craves sleep, but Ellie has other plans. She's fussy, and obviously wants her bottle. "Can you watch her while I get her bottle?" I ask Ryan.

He opens his eyes again. "Sure," he says.

"Are you really awake?"

"Yup, sure am." He sits up a bit, resting on his elbow. He says good morning to Ellie, and she smiles at him. My heart just about melts at how cute he is with her.

"I'll be right back," I say as I head out of the room.

I walk upstairs to the kitchen and find Mom there, packing her lunch. "Good morning," I say to her.

"Good morning," she replies. She continues getting her lunch ready.

I start making Ellie's formula. Just as I seal her bottle, Mom is at my side. I turn to look at her. She stands close to me and speaks quietly, looking concerned. "I see Ryan's truck is still parked outside."

Why do I suddenly feel guilty? I internally cringe, but realize it was an honest mistake. Hopefully, Mom will be understanding. "We just fell asleep watching TV. We woke up at three a.m., but I told him to stay since it was so late."

Mom surprises me with a small smile, then says, "Honey, you're an adult, so it's really none of my business what you do. I just don't want you to move too fast with Ryan."

I look down at the bottle in my hands. I appreciate her concern. She's right; we *are* moving kind of fast. However, it's only like this because we've already been in a relationship.

I look back at my mom and smile. "Mom, I'm fine. Things are great, better than they have been in a very long time." I place a hand on her arm to reassure her. "Please, don't worry. Ryan and I are taking things slow. We really just fell asleep on the couch last night, honest."

She throws her arms around me in a hug. "I've worried so much about you over the past several months," she says. "I can see that he's already made a big difference in your life these past few days. You seem so much happier and back to your old self again."

"I am much happier," I assure her.

She releases her tight grip and smiles with assurance. "Well, I need to finish getting ready for work, and you have a baby to feed. I'll see you later tonight. Are you working out with Sarah?"

"Yes, it's Monday. Is that okay?"

"Of course, it is," Mom replies, then finishes getting ready for work.

I walk back downstairs. When I walk into my room, I find Ellie and Ryan still lying on the bed, facing one another. She babbles at him, and he talks to her like they're having a conversation. It's adorable. Ryan notices me watching and says to her, "Look, your mommy's back with your bottle!"

She squeals and kicks her arms and legs around. I laugh because she's so cute. I sit next to her on the bed to give her the bottle. "It sounds like you two were having a heart to heart," I say to Ryan.

He chuckles. "Something like that. She likes to talk. I just wish I knew what she was saying."

"Me, too," I knowingly state.

"What time do you have to meet Scott today?" Ryan asks.

"Eleven o'clock. I'll leave here at around ten."

"What time is it now?"

I look at the clock. "7:15."

Ryan groans. "It's so early," he whines as he pulls the pillow over his head.

I laugh. "It's normal for me."

He puts the pillow behind his head again and looks at me. "I slept really well in your bed."

I smirk at him. "So did I."

"Can we have more sleepovers?" He raises one eyebrow.

I laugh a little and reply, "I suppose so …"

"I'll remember you said that," he says. Then he gets out of bed and puts his pants on.

"Are you leaving already?"

"No, I just have to use the bathroom. I don't want to scare your parents if they happen to walk downstairs." He winks at me, then leaves the room.

I look down at Ellie, who takes the last couple of sucks on her bottle. She finishes her formula, so I take it from her to set on the bedside table next to me. I burp her as I walk into the family room so she can play with her toys. Ryan joins us, sitting next to me on the floor.

"I meant what I said last night," he says out of the blue.

"What?" *What is he talking about?*

"When I said that I love you."

My eyes dart to his.

"I know we haven't been together for very long," he explains nervously as he rubs his hands together, fidgeting, "but we have a history, so it's like we've been together longer. I also meant it when I told you I've never stopped loving you. I'm so happy we found each other again."

I don't know what to say. I love him too, though it does feel weird that we're admitting our feelings already. *It's day four.* Our first date was three days ago. I'm not even divorced yet. Yes, this feels right, but are we going so fast that we're going to crash and burn?

Ryan looks incredibly unsure now. Just like last night, I realize I haven't said anything yet. I need to speak, but he beats me to it.

"It's okay if you can't say it back," he says. "I understand it's too soon. I just wanted you to know that I meant what I said. I wasn't just in a sleepy daze."

"I love you, too," I tell him, realizing it doesn't matter that we're moving fast. I *do* love him, and I shouldn't have to hide my feelings just because I'm afraid of the timing. Ryan's mouth turns up in a grin as relief washes over him. "I feel the same way you do. As corny as it sounds, I feel like we're meant to be together."

Ryan closes the distance between us to kiss me sweetly on the lips. Before I know it, Ellie interrupts us by banging her toy on my leg. I break our kiss and turn to my demanding little girl. She babbles at me as though she wants to join in on our conversation, causing us to laugh. She's so cute. My heart is full.

RYAN

*A*s Brooke takes a shower and gets ready to go to Olympia, I watch Ellie. She's seriously the easiest baby to watch, happily playing with her toys. She only wants my attention once in a while, which I'm happy to give her. Otherwise, she entertains herself.

I still can't believe I'm here at Brooke's parents' house, watching her daughter for her. I never thought I'd be in this house again, and I definitely never thought Brooke and I would reconcile. I guess life has a funny way of working things out.

I can't believe I bared my soul by telling her I've never stopped loving her. Shit. It's such a relief to know she loves me, too. I know it's only been three days since our first date, and in any other relationship, having these feelings would be crazy. But Brooke and I go way back, so it's not like we just *met* three days ago. We're just playing catch-up.

Then there's Ellie. She's the first baby I've ever babysat in my life. Thanks to her, I know how to change a fuckin' diaper. What's crazy is that I don't mind doing any of it. Babysitting, changing diapers, and hanging out with these two are honestly more exciting than anything I've done since moving back to Seattle. Spending all day with them yesterday was one of the best days I've had in a long time, and we didn't even do anything special. I can totally see myself with Brooke long term. I don't want to get ahead of myself here, but I've wanted this since I was a teenager. Now, it could possibly become a reality. In the future, of course. I may have admitted my feelings to her, but I'm not ready to propose yet.

Yet. Fuck, I've got it bad if I'm already thinking about marrying her and being a parent to Ellie. Shit, I need to get a grip on my feelings and reel them in before I make an ass of myself. What the fuck is happening to me? Less than a year ago, I was a badass Marine, and now I'm thinking about marriage and babies? My friends would laugh if they could see me now.

Brooke walks out of the bathroom, dressed and ready to go. She looks beautiful. "You look way too pretty to be meeting your ex-husband," comes out before I can think.

She strides over to me with a smirk on her face to sit on the floor with Ellie and me. "Well, considering I'm going to your house after I'm done meeting him, maybe I'm trying to look pretty for you." She leans closer to me and plants a kiss on my lips.

"You don't have to *try* to be pretty. You *are* pretty," I say before kissing her again.

As much as I don't want to let her leave, I help Brooke load Ellie in the car along with her stroller and diaper bag. We say goodbye, giving each other another hug and kiss while standing in her driveway, then we both leave. She goes to see her ex, and I go back to my place.

To pass the time until she returns, I go for a run and do some exercises. Afterward, I just sit around the house, watching TV. Dan's at work and the boys are at school. Cari's at home, but I leave her alone to do her own thing.

Speaking of Cari, what a coincidence that Brooke used to be an ER nurse, just like her. As if everything else between us doesn't seem perfect enough, she even has that in common with my sister-in-law.

God, I can't stop thinking about Brooke. It's ridiculous how much I miss her even though we just spent the past twenty-four hours together. What's wrong with me?

Just before three thirty, there's a knock on my private entrance door. I know it's Brooke because she texted me before leaving the museum in Olympia almost an hour ago. I open the door to find Brooke standing there, a car seat in one arm and a diaper bag hooked over her shoulder.

"Come on in," I say as I step aside so she can enter.

She walks in and sets everything down on the floor next to my bed. I can see that Ellie is asleep in her car seat. I wrap my arms around Brooke and hug her, loving the feeling of her body in my arms again. "How was your day?" I ask her.

"Annoying," she replies with a sigh.

I continue to hold her as I plant a kiss on the top of her head. "How was it annoying?" I'm curious if something happened with her ex.

She doesn't release me. In fact, her grip tightens around my waist, prompting me to do the same to her. I kiss her head again as I wait for her explanation.

"Well, for starters, Ellie wouldn't go to Scott, so I had to spend the day with them. Every time he tried to hold her, she cried unless she could see me. She's never done this before, so I don't know why she did it today."

"I'm sorry," I say. I don't know what else to say. "What can I do?"

"Nothing," she replies, "except kiss me."

"I can do that." I lean down and kiss her as though I haven't kissed her in days.

Ellie interrupts us with a loud squeal. We break apart from each other, laughing, and look down at her in her car seat. "Yes?" Brooke says as she bends down to take her out of the seat.

I decide to be helpful by rummaging around the diaper bag to get some of her toys out. Then the three of us sit on the floor so Ellie can play.

Brooke and Ellie stay for a while, but around five o'clock, she starts packing their things up to go.

"I'm meeting Sarah to work out tonight," she reminds me. "Plus, I want to cook dinner for my parents. I haven't been able to in a couple of days, and since they've helped me so much with Ellie, I want to."

I'd rather have Brooke and Ellie stay with me the rest of the night, but I understand her reasons for leaving. Plus, haven't we seen enough of each other lately? If we keep spending this much time together, won't we get sick of each other? *I hope that doesn't happen.*

I help Brooke carry everything out to her car. After Ellie's car seat is securely in place and I place her diaper bag on the floor of the back seat, I hug and kiss Brooke goodbye.

BROOKE

*a*fter making dinner for my parents, who appreciate my gesture, I meet Sarah at the gym. "You have a lot of talking to do," she says as we start our workout.

I tell her about my weekend with Ryan. Well, the edited version. I don't tell her everything because some of the things Ryan and I have discussed should stay just between us.

"I'm so happy for you," Sarah says. "I can't believe you two found each other again. I'm telling you, it's fate!"

"It really does just feel right," I tell her.

"So … how long do you think you two are going to wait to do more than just kiss?" Leave it to Sarah to ask me this.

"I don't know," I reply. "I honestly don't know how long I *can* wait. I'm so attracted to him."

"Well, good luck with that," she says. "I predict it'll be sooner rather than later." She winks at me.

After I put Ellie to bed that night, I text Ryan.

Me: *Are you awake?*

. . .

165

Ryan: *Yes. What are you doing?*

Me: *I just put Ellie to bed. What are you doing?*

Ryan: *Watching TV. I miss you.*

I can't help but smile. I miss him, too.

Me: *You could come over.*

Ryan: *What would your parents think?*

I laugh. I love that he's concerned about what my parents think of him even though we're not teenagers anymore.

My phone rings, and I can't contain my smile. "Hi," I answer.

"Hi there," he says. "Do you really want me to come over?"

"Of course, I do."

"I want to."

"Then come over."

"I just don't want to disrespect your parents. You're living in their house."

I smile. He's so thoughtful. "I really don't think they'll mind."

"How do you know?"

"I talked to my mom this morning. She asked about your truck being outside, and I informed her we just slept. She said it's none of her business, we're adults, but she's concerned about us moving too fast."

"What did you say?" he asks.

"I told her we're taking things slow. She hugged me and said she wants me to be happy. She can tell I've been happier since we got back together."

"I'm glad to hear that," he says. "I want you to be happy."

"And I want you to be happy. So why don't you come over here, and we can be happy together?"

He chuckles. "How about his," he continues. "What if we wait to have another sleepover until this weekend? I have an idea."

I'm intrigued. "What's your idea?"

"Well, what do you think about spending the night at the Salish Lodge Saturday night? Do you think your parents can watch Ellie?"

Wow. I've always wanted to stay at the Salish Lodge. It's so beautiful, nestled right next to Snoqualmie Falls. The fact he wants to take me makes me a little more than excited. "I can ask them. They'll probably be okay with it."

"I hope so. I want some one-on-one time with you when we can really be alone and won't be interrupted." The way he says that, I know he means more than just talking or cuddling together.

"So you're saying you don't want to see me at all until Saturday?" I ask, sarcastically.

He laughs. "Hell, no! I can't go that long without seeing you! I just meant we should refrain from sleeping together again until then."

"Okay, good. I couldn't stay away from you that long, either." My cheeks are starting to hurt from all the smiling I've been doing lately. "So if you're not coming over tonight, when do I get to see you? I'm going to Sarah's house for lunch tomorrow."

"I'll come over for breakfast," he says.

"Really? That early?"

"I can't promise I'll be there by the time Ellie wakes up"—he chuckles—"but I'll be there by nine. I'll even bring breakfast with me."

"What are you bringing?"

"I'll get coffee and donuts. What kind of coffee do you want?" he asks me.

"I like caramel macchiatos." I can't believe he's actually bringing breakfast to my house.

After getting off the phone, I walk upstairs to see if my parents are still awake. They're getting ready for bed but still up. Their bedroom door is ajar, so I knock on it. "Come in," Dad says.

I walk into their room and explain Ryan's weekend plans, then ask if they can watch Ellie for me. Mom's eyebrows shoot up in surprise, but then her features soften. "Of course, we'll watch her."

I hug her, thanking both her and my dad. I rush downstairs to text Ryan, letting him know that we're free to go on Saturday. He replies with a smiley face.

When I go to bed, I lie there, thinking of Ryan and how excited I am for this weekend. The Salish Lodge is such a romantic hotel. I've never stayed there, but I've seen pictures and heard good things about the place. It's a well-known hotel because of its beautiful location.

I know this will be our chance to connect, and if things go well, have sex again. I'm both nervous and excited just thinking about it. My mind wanders to when we lost our virginity together in high school. We had been together for almost a year at the time, and even though we had done lots of other sexual things together, I made him wait to go *all the way*.

I remember he snuck over that night. We started out doing what we usually did, just kissing, undressing each other, touching each other in all the right places, and enjoying oral sex—not that we had oral sex very many times before that night. It was something still new for us then. He went down on me first, making me come, and then I pleasured him. Usually, he would finish, and that was it. However, this time, I wanted more. I stopped sucking him, moved back up his body, and whispered in his ear, "Do you have a condom?"

I'll never forget the surprised look on his face. We had talked about having sex before, but I wanted to wait until the moment felt right. I didn't want to plan a date for us to do it, like some people we knew did. Some of our friends actually planned when they were going to lose their virginity, like, "My parents are going to be gone Friday night, so he's coming over and we're finally going to have sex." No. That's not what I wanted at all. I wanted it to be special and spontaneous, not something I added to my schedule.

Ryan asked if I was sure about this, and I assured him that I was. He said he had a condom in his wallet, so he got it out of his pants pocket. I laid back on my bed as he put it on. Then he hovered over me, asking me again if I was sure. I told him yes, that I loved him, and then we kissed.

Of course, the first time hurt a little, but I'd never felt closer to him. Our bodies seemed to fit together perfectly, and we were so in tune with each other. Even though we were both virgins, we moved together as though we had done this a hundred times before.

Afterward, he stayed and cuddled for a while before sneaking home. I remember being a little afraid we were going to fall asleep and get caught the next morning, but luckily, that didn't happen.

Soon, my mind wanders to the *last* time we had sex; the night before I left for college. Again, he snuck into my room late that night. Even now, the memory evokes bittersweet emotions. At the time, we knew it would be a long time before we'd be together again. Little did we know, it would be fourteen years. We didn't hold back with each other at all. Honestly, as I think back on it now, I realize it might have been the best sex I've ever had in my life. We didn't get any sleep that night because he stayed until the sun started to rise. It was so hard for us to say goodbye. He came back later that morning to say bye again before I left with my parents to take me to college.

I wonder about what it'll be like now that we're older. He's been with a lot of women in his life. I've only been with two other guys. I hope I'm not a disappointment to him. I think about how good things felt the other night at his house, and it squashes any doubts I have. I know it will be amazing with Ryan, just as it used to be.

RYAN

$\mathcal{M}$y alarm wakes me at eight a.m. I usually enjoy sleeping in, but not today. Brooke is expecting me with breakfast, and the last thing I want to do is disappoint her. I stop at Starbucks and Krispy Kreme on the way to her house. I arrive right on time with donuts and coffee in hand.

We eat together, play with Ellie, and just enjoy each other's company. I also help her by watching Ellie again so she can shower and get ready for the day. Ellie and I just hang out on the floor with her toys. She crawls around and brings toys to me and babbles. I talk to her as if we're having an actual conversation, and she laughs at me. A full-on belly laugh. She has got to be the cutest baby I've ever met.

When Brooke comes out of the bathroom, hair and makeup all done, she finds me reading a book to Ellie, who is sitting on my lap.

"Wow," she says, looking surprised to find us like this. "It's nice of you to read to her."

Ellie babbles a few things to her, then tugs on the book in front of her, prompting me to keep reading.

I chuckle. "If you don't mind, I need to finish reading this book." Brooke smiles, looking at me as if I've just made her whole day. I like that look on her.

I continue reading the princess book to Ellie. Brooke sits next to us and listens to me read. I suddenly feel silly. All the funny voices I was doing for the characters before now seem ridiculous, but Ellie is totally into it. I can't stop even if I do hear Brooke giggling.

When I finish the book, Brooke pipes up. "Well, that was certainly a treat, wasn't it, Ellie?" She picks Ellie up off my lap and holds her.

"I've never read a kid's book before except when I was a kid," I admit, rubbing my forehead and setting the book on the coffee table. I can't believe I just read it out loud like that.

"Really?" Brooke sounds surprised. "You sounded like a natural!"

I chuckle. "I just remember how my parents used to read to me when I was younger, I guess."

Brooke leans over and kisses me on the cheek. "Thank you for doing that for her."

"It was no problem."

Brooke stands and sets Ellie on the floor with some toys, then starts packing things in the diaper bag. *Fuck, she's beautiful.* I can't help but admire her.

"Will I see you tonight? Or not until tomorrow?" she asks me.

"I don't know," I tell her. "I don't get off work until ten."

"Well, then how about tomorrow? I like having breakfast together." She smiles at me as she zips the diaper bag closed.

"I like it, too," I tell her, and it's the truth. It's been nice spending the past couple of mornings together.

She walks over to me and puts her arms around my neck. My hands instantly go to her hips, wanting to touch her. "I'll make breakfast tomorrow, if you want," she says, before kissing me on the lips.

I pull her down so she's sitting across my lap, her legs

outstretched on the couch. It takes her by surprise, and she squeals. "Oh, really?" I ask.

She giggles. "Yes. Do you like pancakes?"

I kiss her again, then reply, "Who doesn't like pancakes? Do you want me to bring anything?"

She puts a finger to her chin as she thinks. "How about coffee? I like my caramel macchiatos."

I smile. "Okay, deal."

* * *

The next morning, I show up at Brooke's house at nine o'clock again. She happily lets me in and thanks me for her coffee drink with a kiss.

"I'm just starting to make breakfast," she says as we walk into the kitchen.

Ellie sits in her high chair, playing with a toy. I give Brooke a hand and help her cook the pancakes. Cooking together is actually fun as well as an easy way to flirt with her. I touch her whenever I can or tickle her side as I move past her for something. She seems to enjoy the help, or maybe she just enjoys me touching her.

Our morning is spent pretty much the same as the day before. After breakfast, we play with Ellie, then I watch her while Brooke takes a shower. I honestly don't know what Brooke would do if I wasn't here to help her out. Maybe take Ellie in the bathroom with her? Not take a shower at all? Whatever it is, I'm glad I can help.

Later that evening, I'm at work when Brooke and Sarah come to the gym. I'm all too happy to see her again, which is really quite ridiculous since we've only been apart for a few hours. I can't wait for this weekend to get here so I can take Brooke away for some alone time.

* * *

The rest of the week flies by. I show up at Brooke's house every morning for breakfast, spend the morning and afternoon with them, then go to work. It's becoming our daily routine. Even Ellie is adjusting to it. She actually gets excited when I walk in the door, which melts my heart a little.

Saturday morning finally arrives. Tonight's the night I'm taking Brooke to the Salish Lodge, so I hope my work shift this morning doesn't drag by. I can't wait to get off and pick her up.

Of course, my morning starts out pretty great when Brooke and Sarah show up for their workout. I greet her with a kiss, and when they're finished working out, they stop at the front desk to talk to me.

"Have fun tonight," Sarah says to us with a wink before she walks out, leaving Brooke and me alone.

I lean on the counter, and Brooke leans toward me on the other side.

"I can't wait to get off work," I tell her. "I'm all packed and ready to go, so I'll come pick you up right away."

"I'll be ready. I can't wait, either." Her eyes dance with excitement, and I can tell she's looking forward to this as much as I am.

I lean in closer to her, and whisper, "I can't wait to be alone with you." Then I give her a quick peck on the lips.

She smiles. "Neither can I." Brooke kisses me again, and it takes everything in me not to say *fuck it* and leave right now.

Damn. Two o'clock can't get here soon enough.

BROOKE

*a*fter I get home from my workout, I spend the rest of the morning with Ellie. I feel a little nervous about leaving her. Even though she'll be with my parents, and I know she'll be fine, I've never been away from her for this long before. What if my mom has a hard time putting her to bed again? I hope this isn't difficult for them.

Shortly after two o'clock, Ryan arrives to pick me up. I'm both nervous and excited. He comes inside the house to say hi to my parents and Ellie. We don't leave right away. We spend a few minutes talking with Mom and Dad and saying goodbye to my baby girl until Mom finally convinces me everything will be fine.

We're quiet in the truck on the way to Snoqualmie. The music on the stereo is turned up, making it difficult to talk, which helps because I also feel a little nervous. I wonder if Ryan is quiet because he's nervous, too? I realize it's ridiculous to feel this way; I know I have nothing to be nervous about. It's just the idea that Ryan and I are finally getting some time alone together, and he's taking me to one of the most romantic getaway spots in the northwest.

About a half an hour into our drive, he turns the music down and asks if I want to take a hike to the waterfall when we get there. It's such a beautiful day outside, so I agree that's a great idea. Although part of me doesn't want to do anything that doesn't involve Ryan and a bed, I know we'll have plenty of time for that later.

We talk off and on during the rest of the way to the lodge. The view is so serene on the edge of the Cascade Mountains with the evergreen trees all around and a clear blue sky above. We've had a streak of sunny weather lately, rather than the rainy spring weather we often have in April.

When we arrive at the Salish Lodge, I'm in awe of its beauty. The rustic hotel is secluded and surrounded by trees. We can't see it yet, but the Snoqualmie River is just on the other side of the building. I can't believe Ryan brought me here. To say it's romantic would be an understatement.

"Let's check into our room and get settled before we hike to the falls," Ryan says as we get out of his truck.

"Sounds good," I reply. He puts the strap of his duffel bag around his shoulder and takes my suitcase before taking my hand in his.

After checking in, we make our way to our room. I'm surprised at how fancy it is. I don't think I've ever stayed at such a nice hotel before. Ryan must have spent a lot of money to bring me here, making me feel both special and guilty. He doesn't need to spend money to impress me.

Our room has one king-size bed, a gas fireplace, and a beautiful view. He must have really splurged because we have a view of the river and the falls. *Holy shit!* We don't even need to take a hike to see Snoqualmie Falls because we can see it right from our room! It's gorgeous, and I'm momentarily mesmerized by the view in front of me.

As I'm admiring the view, I feel Ryan come up behind me and snake his arms around my waist. "It's beautiful, isn't it?" His deep voice vibrates against my neck as he kisses me, sending tingles down my body.

I squirm, but he holds me in place, continuing to kiss me. "Ryan," I whisper. His lips on my skin are making me melt, but all too soon, he pulls away. He moves and stands in front of me, leaning against the window. I'm feel dazed, wanting to feel his body against mine again.

He smirks. He knows he's driving me crazy. *The bastard.*

"It's not even four o'clock yet, Brooke. We have plenty of time. Let's take the hike to the waterfall before it gets too dark."

"How long is the hike, anyway?" I ask, thinking it can't be *that* far if the falls are right outside our window.

"It's not far. It's super easy to walk. Come on, let's go," he says as he starts walking toward the door.

I follow him, and he holds the door open for me. Then he takes my hand and leads us in the direction we need to go.

The hike is not long at all, but the view is amazing. We take in the view of the falls with a few other tourists. Since the weather is so nice, a lot of people are out here today.

Ryan pulls his phone out and takes a selfie of us with the falls in the background. It turns out to be a great picture of us. It's the first picture we've taken together since we met again, and it makes me happy to have this memento.

We enjoy the view for a few more minutes, then we begin our hike back. "It's almost dinnertime," Ryan says. "Should we go eat?"

Part of me is frustrated we're not going back to the room yet, but the nervous part of me is a little relieved. His comment earlier, when he said we have plenty of time, repeats in my head. It's true. We should enjoy a nice dinner together, then go back to the hotel for some *quality* time.

"Sure," I reply as he takes my hand in his, and we begin walking back to the lodge.

We decide to drive into the town of Snoqualmie for dinner rather than eating at our hotel. The restaurant at the hotel is definitely a fancier place than what we're dressed for. We find a restaurant with several good reviews online, and we aren't disappointed.

Throughout dinner, Ryan and I talk as we usually do, but the magnetic pulse between us has intensified. I want nothing more than to return to our hotel room and be with him. This delayed gratification thing is driving me crazy, and I think he's feeling the same way. Every chance he gets, he reaches across the table and touches my hand. He just *looks* at me differently, more lovingly. I can't explain what it is ... maybe sexual tension? I've never felt this way before, even with Scott. If I wasn't afraid of being arrested, I'd crawl across the table and mount Ryan right here in the crowded restaurant.

Luckily, I'm able to control myself and act as normal as I possibly can.

As Ryan drives us back to the lodge, he holds my hand the entire time. I'm mentally preparing myself for what will happen when we get there. I'm not *nervous* to be with Ryan, but I am starting to worry I won't live up to his standards. What if I'm not as good as some of the women he's been with over the years?

He parks the truck in the lodge's parking lot and turns it off. He immediately turns to me, leans in closer, and takes me by surprise by kissing me. I open my mouth to his, and our tongues crash together. Our kiss lingers for seconds, maybe minutes. I lose track of time. All I can concentrate on is how good his hands feel in my hair, and how good his lips feel against mine. When he pulls his lips away, he rests his forehead against mine and boldly states, "I want you to know I have been looking forward to this night, not just for the past week, but for the past fourteen years."

My heart skips a beat, and my mouth goes dry. He moves his head back a bit so we're looking into each other's eyes. All I see is love and trust looking back at me.

Then he continues as if he were reading my mind. "I also want you to know that you're the best I ever had. That last night we had together before you left for college was amazing, and I've replayed it in my mind countless times over the years. I can't wait to make love to you again."

The muscles low in my belly clench, and my heart pounds faster. His words mean everything to me. Just like that, my worries from moments ago vanish.

Ryan leans in, and I moan as our lips make contact. I can't get enough of his kisses, but I'm ready to go up to our room and do more.

Eventually, we get out of the truck and walk hand in hand inside. My heart races, and it seems as if the walk to our room takes forever. I just can't wait. When we do finally get to our door, Ryan unlocks it and lets me in first. I turn on the lights, and he follows me into the room.

"I'll build you a fire," he says playfully as he flips the switch on the wall, turning the gas fireplace on. I smile at him, then watch as he walks past me to the other switches on the wall. The room suddenly has a romantic glow from the fire once the other lights are off

When Ryan returns to me, I can't help but stare. The flames from the fire light his skin and reflect in his eyes. His face is intense but sexy as hell. As he leans in to kiss me, my eyes instantly close. He's gentle at first, and his hands glide up my arms, past my shoulders, and all the way up to my face. Our kiss becomes more heated, and I wrap my arms around his waist, pulling him closer to me as I do.

Ryan doesn't break our kiss as he starts walking. Moving with him, I walk backward. This is the Ryan I know, and I trust where he's leading me. When the back of my legs touch the bed, we stop. He pulls away and quickly shucks his shoes and socks. I rush to do the same.

"Do you know how sexy you are?" His voice is deep and gravelly, setting my nerves on fire. He gently guides me onto the bed and nips at my neck. I can only manage a moan in response.

His mouth crashes down on mine while his hands begin to roam my body. My fingers inch along his arms, shoulders, and then stroke the back of his neck. Before long, I'm even more needy, wanting to feel more of Ryan's body. Our kiss gets more intense, and I plunge one hand into his hair while the other moves down to grab his firm ass.

Ryan reads me like a book and knows what I need. Suddenly, his mouth leaves mine to trail kisses down my neck. The sensation sends shivers down my body, and I grind against him. I claw at his shirt, and he sits up to take it off. He takes my hands in his and sits me up, grabbing my shirt and pulling it over my head.

"God, you're beautiful," he growls as he lowers me down again, covering my body with his.

The weight and heat of his body over mine is exactly what I need. He grinds down on me, pressing his hard cock into my core. Spikes of pleasure course through me, which intensify when his hands wander to my chest. He pulls the cup of my bra down, my nipple pebbling for his eager mouth. His tongue flicks it before he takes it in his mouth. I moan again, unable to control myself from all the sensations I'm feeling. *It's been so long.* His hard length moves against my center, my swollen clit begging for release. Ryan's hand deftly pulls the other cup of my bra down and gives that breast the same attention. *I need more.*

I writhe on the bed as Ryan moves lower, peppering kisses across my stomach. I instantly miss his cock against my core, but he continues moving lower down my body, kissing me until his lips reach the waistband of my pants. I lean up on my elbows to watch what he's doing. His fingers undo my jeans, then he slides them all the way off.

He stands in front of the bed, looking down at me lying in my black lace underwear and bra, though my bra isn't covering anything anymore. He looks as if he wants to *devour* me, making me feel sexy. I boldly crook my pointer finger and give him the *come here* signal.

"Fuck," I hear him mutter before he undoes his own pants and takes them off. His boxer briefs are bulging at the front, and I want to touch him.

Ryan climbs up the bed to hover over me. I lie back against the pillows, waiting for his kiss, but he doesn't do anything. He simply looks at me.

"What?" I whisper, desperate for his touch.

He shakes his head. "I'm just so happy to be with you," he says before kissing me again.

His hands reach around my back to unhook my bra. He slides the straps down my arms, then tosses it to the floor. His body settles between my legs, and I feel his hardness against me. It's even more heavenly without our pants on. Ryan massages my breasts while my hands explore his body. I love touching him. He's so fit; it's fun to run my hands over all the dips and grooves of his muscular frame.

Ryan kisses my neck, making me squirm. Then I feel his mouth on my earlobe, his teeth biting it lightly, driving me crazy. "Do I need a condom?" he whispers in my ear.

His question momentarily catches me off guard. I had assumed we would use one, though I *am* on birth control. I went back on it as soon as I could after I had Ellie and just never stopped even though I haven't had *any* sex since before she was born.

"Are you … clean?" I quietly ask him. I don't want to offend him, but he *has* been with his fair share of women. He turns his head to look at me; although it's so dark in the room, I can barely see his face.

"I am. I wouldn't ask if I wasn't. I'd never put you at risk, Brooke." He lowers his lips to mine, brushing over them lightly, then he trails soft kisses down my neck, down, down, down to my breasts again.

"I'm on the pill," I say as I run my fingers through his hair.

Ryan stops and moves back up until his face is level with mine again. He kisses me briefly then says, "I love you." *Kiss.* "I want to feel you," *kiss,* "finally," *kiss,* "without a barrier," *another kiss,* "between us."

Then he kisses me hard and grinds himself against me again, making me moan. *I need him inside me now!* We never had sex without a condom in high school. I wasn't on birth control yet, and there was no way I was going to ask my mom to take me to the doctor to get it. I didn't know how to be resourceful and get it myself back then.

Ryan moves to my side, sliding his hand between my legs. *Finally.* "You're so wet," he whispers when his fingers brush over my underwear.

I trail my hand down and rub his cock on the outside of his boxer briefs. "You're so hard," I say.

He moans, then it's as if something switches inside him. He sits up on his knees, grabs my underwear with both hands, and drags them off before taking his own off as well. He moves back over the top of me again, lining his cock up with my center. He doesn't enter me, though. He teases me by sliding it up and down, from my clit to my entrance and back again. I'm so wet, he easily glides between my folds, setting my nerves on fire.

"Ryan," I whisper as I start moving my hips, grinding against him as he moves.

"We're going to go slow," Ryan says as he starts to slide into me. He moves achingly slow, letting me feel every inch of him as he fills me. I'm tight, and it actually hurts a little. Not only is Ryan bigger than what I've been used to for the past fourteen years, but it's almost been a year since I last had sex.

"Are you okay?" Ryan asks once he's fully seated. He brushes a hand through my hair, then kisses me softly.

"Yes," I practically pant, adjusting to him. "It's just been a long time."

Ryan doesn't say anything else; he just kisses me passionately, his tongue finding mine. I run my fingers through his hair, lightly tugging on it as he rears back and begins to move at a slow and delicious pace.

Memories flood my brain. *This is what Ryan feels like.* I love the way he fills me. His dick slides in deeper than anyone else ever has, hitting that special spot, making my body tingle with pleasure. *Fuck ... How did I forget how good this was?*

I honestly don't remember the last time I made love like this. He's so gentle, so loving. Scott and I never had sex like this in all the years we were together. I've only had this feeling of intimacy with Ryan. Somehow, I'd forgotten what it was like. *Now I remember.* I didn't know what a special connection we had as teenagers. I've never felt this sense of *wholeness* with anyone else as though I can't feel close enough to him no matter what we do. I want to get closer and closer, but in reality, we're already as close as we can be. Not only that, but it's like his body is made for mine. He hits every spot in me so perfectly.

Ryan rolls us over, so I'm on top, and I continue the slow, sensual pace he's set. His hands move to my breasts, massaging and pulling at my nipples in *just* the right way. Suddenly, he sits up so we're face to face. I continue moving my hips, and he counters my movements in a perfect rhythm. His mouth travels down to my breasts, licking and sucking them, driving me wild. I pull on his hair and drag my nails down his back. I still feel like I'm not close enough and need to be closer to him. I claw at his back, trying to get as close as possible. I've *never* had this animalistic feeling while having sex before, but I can't help myself.

I'm starting to feel the buildup of my orgasm, and I know it won't be too long before I come. Ryan trails kisses back up to my lips and then kisses me again. All of a sudden, Ryan stills my hips with his strong hands and stops me from moving. "I want to make this last as long as possible," he whispers. "This is a dream come true, and I don't want to come yet."

It lights me up inside, knowing he's enjoying this just as much as I am. *It's so good.* We sit here, just holding each other, his cock buried deep inside me, kissing one another with all the passion we're feeling. Before I know it, he flips us back around so I'm on my back. He's so strong; it's no effort for him to move us.

He starts moving again, but at a faster pace. I tilt my hips, and he hits me harder and deeper. Even though he's not being as gentle as before, it's still equally as intimate. It doesn't take much longer for me to moan into his mouth and come apart, and he follows shortly after.

He holds me tight for a few minutes. I can feel his heart beating so fast against my chest. Finally, he looks me in the eye and growls in a low voice, "You're incredible."

"So are you," I reply with a sated grin.

He stands and, like the gentleman he is, puts his hand out to help me up as well. I go into the bathroom to clean up. When I return, Ryan heads toward the bathroom door. He stops to wrap his arms around me and whispers in my ear, "That was just round one."

"Oh?" *Thank God.* I want him again. Once was nowhere near enough.

He nods his head as we just hold each other, standing there naked, in front of the bathroom. "I can't get enough of you, Brooke. I've wanted this for so long," Ryan says before kissing my neck.

I lightly stroke my hands up and down his back, a contrast to how I clawed at him before. I can't believe I did that. It doesn't feel like I've done any damage, so that's good.

We stand like this for a short while, then he lets go of me, and says, "Go lie down. I'll be back in a minute."

He gives me his crooked smile and heads into the bathroom. I find a shirt to put on. My legs feel like Jell-O. I may be in good shape, but I just used muscles I haven't used in a *very* long time.

RYAN

The way Brooke and I just made love was beyond all my expectations. I knew sex together in high school was good, even for teenagers. We knew how to pleasure one another and had good chemistry in the bedroom. The first time I slept with someone else, I quickly figured out how good Brooke and I had it. It just wasn't the same, and then the next time after that, and so forth. Eventually, I forgot how incredible our connection was.

What we just did was fucking amazing.

Now, more than ever, I'm sure Brooke and I belong together. We're not moving too fast in our relationship because we're meant to be.

When I walk back into the room, I find her lying in bed. I crawl in next to her, and she cuddles into my side. My arm wraps around her, holding her close.

"You okay?" I ask, not because I think something is wrong, but to strike up a conversation.

"Mmmhmm," she says, sounding completely sated as her arm tightens around my waist, and she pulls me closer to her.

I can't help the huge smile that spreads across my face. She can't see it, but I don't care. I'm so fucking happy right now.

"Are you okay?" she asks me.

"Better than okay," I say as I lightly stroke my hand up and down her arm. "I've never made love like that before," I admit to her. "Except with you."

She sits up to look me in the eye, almost as if she can't believe what I said. "Me neither," she whispers.

I gently grip the back of her neck and pull her down so she's close enough to kiss. "I've never felt so close to anyone before. Only you, Brooke," I say before crashing my lips to hers.

After thoroughly kissing her, I pull back and continue, "I want to make you come over and over again."

Her breath hitches before she says, "I won't stop you. You're pretty damn good at it."

"I love making you feel good and watching you come apart," I add as she settles down next to me once again.

We make love two more times before going to sleep. Bringing her to this romantic place where we could be alone and finally reconnect without any interruptions was the best idea I ever had.

The next morning, I wake before Brooke. Her back rests against my front, and I have my arm draped over her glorious, naked body. The morning wood I'm sporting leaves me little choice but to give Brooke a sexy wake-up call.

My hand finds her bare breast. Her nipple hardens almost instantly, begging for attention. I pinch it lightly between my thumb and forefinger, and Brooke starts to wake up.

I don't stop.

I continue giving special attention to her nipple until she rolls toward me onto her back, exposing her body to me.

"Good morning." She sighs. Her eyes are still closed, but she's clearly awake, enjoying my touch.

I don't say anything. I just take her nipple into my mouth, then move my hand down to her naked pussy. *Fuck. She's already wet.* My fingers easily glide between her slick folds, and I slide two fingers inside her. She lets out a sexy sound, a cross between a moan and a whimper. Her hips move against my hand, letting my fingers fuck her deep.

Before I know it, her inner muscles clamp around my fingers, and I feel a rush of heat over them. She moans loudly, so I cover my mouth with hers to drown out the sounds of her coming.

We lie in bed together for a while afterward, just holding each other and talking. After quite a while of us being lazy together, I decide to look at my phone, which is next to me on the bedside table. There's one thing I really want to do if she'll let me. I know it sounds silly, but I'm going to ask her anyway. "When will you let me claim you as mine?"

She turns her head to me, giving me a look like I'm crazy. "I think I've pretty much let you claim me this weekend," she says with a laugh.

I chuckle. "I mean, when can I make it Facebook official? I'm so happy, and I want people to know we're together."

She rolls her eyes. "You're funny. Facebook official? You can tell people in real life we're together, you know."

"I know," I say, "but I want people to know about us." She looks at me as she considers it. "I understand your reasoning for not sharing it yet, but I just haven't been this happy in a long time. Facebook is like the modern way of shouting it from a mountaintop."

She laughs at me. "You mean like Ron Burgundy?"

I'm totally confused now. "What?"

Brooke continues to laugh. "You know, the movie *Anchorman*? Will Ferrell played Ron Burgundy, and he had a line about wanting to shout something from the top of a mountain."

I look at her, dumbfounded. She's thinking about Will Ferrell at a time like this? Actually, it kind of cracks me up and makes me want to see that movie now.

She shakes her head, still chuckling. "I'm sorry, I didn't mean to change the subject."

I lean over and kiss her, taking her by surprise. I can't help myself; she just looks too cute laughing about a damn movie quote. When I pull away from her, she looks as if she wants to pounce on me.

"Go ahead and post that we're in a relationship. Shout it from a mountaintop if you'd like. But only if you make love to me again *right now.*"

Her answer shocks me, to say the least. "Are you sure? I *do* understand if you want to wait longer." *Why am I still talking and not making love to her?*

"I'm sure," she says as she moves her body closer to mine. "Why should I care what a few people might think? I'm separated and almost divorced. I want people to know we're together, too." She leans in and kisses me on the lips, but pulls away much too soon. "Are you going to get inside me now?"

She doesn't have to ask me twice. I toss my phone aside and get right to it.

* * *

A couple of hours later, we check out of the hotel. I don't want to leave, but we made the best of our time together. We're not going home right away, either. We're going to take another hike nearby after we eat breakfast. Or brunch since it's already almost noon.

We go into North Bend and eat at the famous Twede's Cafe. It's a well-known diner in town that's been there forever. Many people know it from the show *Twin Peaks.* I've never watched the show, but when it came out, my mom was obsessed. She made Dad drive us here for lunch one time, just so she could say she'd been there. I just remember the cool setting and good food, so I figured it would be a good place to bring Brooke. She seems to enjoy it, too.

When we finish eating, we go for a hike in the woods. It's so beautiful here. That's one thing I love about living in the Pacific Northwest that I missed while I was in the Marines. There's so much natural beauty and so many trees, mountains, rivers, waterfalls ... You name it, you can see it all within an hour's drive.

As Brooke and I stand at a clearing overlooking a gorgeous view of the valley below us with the Snoqualmie River flowing through, I realize how lucky I am. I'm living in my home state again, have a great job with my brother as the best business partner, and now I have the most wonderful woman by my side.

After our hike, we head home. It's nearly four o'clock already, and Brooke is anxious to get back to Ellie. She's never been away from her this long before. She hasn't heard from her mom and dad, so I'm sure Ellie is fine, but I'll do anything to make Brooke more at ease.

When we get back to Brooke's house, her parents are in the living room with Ellie. Her mom's on the recliner, correcting papers, and her dad's on the floor, playing with Ellie. When we walk in, Ellie squeals and crawls over to Brooke right away. She bends over to pick her up. "Hi Ellie Bell! I missed you so much," she gushes as she hugs and kisses her baby girl.

"Welcome back," her dad says to us.

"How was your getaway?" her mom asks.

"We had a great time," I reply. "The weather was perfect, so we were able to take a couple of hikes."

"It was beautiful there," Brooke adds, bouncing Ellie in her arms.

Ellie notices me and squeals. She reaches for me, taking me by surprise. Brooke smiles as I reach over and take her in my arms. "Hi, Ellie," I say, and she smiles and laughs at me. She's so dang cute.

"Well, she certainly missed you," Brooke's mom says to her. "Bedtime was a little rough last night."

I look at Brooke and can tell that upsets her a little even

though she tries to hide it. She scrunches her nose at her mom, and says, "I'm so sorry."

"It's okay. She just wanted her momma, not me," her mom says with a laugh.

Ellie rests her head against my shoulder, cuddling in my arms. It makes my heart melt. Brooke looks at me and smiles. She brushes Ellie's hair back, then leans in and kisses her forehead.

"Let's go downstairs," Brooke suggests, so the three of us head down together.

This feels so right.

BROOKE

$\mathcal{W}$hen I pull into the museum's parking lot the next day, I see Scott's car right away. I park next to it, and he sees us. This is the last thing I wanted to do today. I would have rather stayed home with Ryan. He took Ellie and me out to dinner last night, then he came back to my place and stayed the night.

And oh, what a nice sleepover we had. Thank goodness Ellie sleeps through the night, so we had no interruptions. I replayed the memories in my head as I drove today, causing me to have a perma-grin on my face. However, now that I see Scott here, the grin is quickly fading.

Scott gets out of his car, then walks around to mine and opens Ellie's door. "Hi, Ellie," he says to her. She doesn't cry this time, so that's good.

I get out of the car and go around to the back to get the stroller out. Ellie's still content with Scott, so it's starting out better than our last visit. We get her situated in the stroller, get her diaper bag, then walk toward the museum's front doors together.

"So you're coming in with us again, right?" Scott asks as we walk in.

"Do I have to?" I ask. The only reason I did last week was because Ellie refused to let me leave her.

"Yes," he replies. "We have a lot to discuss."

I dart my gaze to him, wondering what that could mean. Did he see my Facebook status saying I'm in a relationship with Ryan?

Scott pays for our admission to the museum, and we start walking toward the baby play area. Neither of us is talking yet. I'm trying to work out in my head what I want to say to him and what my potential comebacks could be if he's upset. He doesn't have a right to be upset anyway. We're separated because he fucked up.

Once we get to the play area and let Ellie out to crawl around and play, he starts talking right away. "So you're in a relationship?"

I knew it. He found out.

I look at him and simply reply, "Yes."

He doesn't say anything at first. He just nods his head, then looks back at Ellie. "Who is he?" he asks.

I take a deep breath and sigh. "My old high school boyfriend, Ryan. That's why we've hit it off so quickly."

Scott looks at me. "Is he around Ellie a lot?"

I'm not sure how to answer that. I don't want him to be mad about Ryan being around her, especially since Ellie wasn't so sure of Scott last week. He might get jealous. "Sometimes," I tell him.

"Is that why she's acting so weird around me now? She's always fussy when I see her. Even today, though she didn't cry, I could tell she's skeptical of me."

"I don't know," I tell him, shrugging my shoulders. "It's probably not because of Ryan. It's probably just because she doesn't see you very often. Even if Ryan wasn't around, she still wouldn't see you as much."

Scott shakes his head and looks down. "I can't keep doing this," he says.

I'm not sure what he means. He can't keep doing what? I'm so confused especially since he doesn't elaborate.

Finally, I ask him, "What do you mean, Scott?"

He looks at me, his face filled with pure sadness. It makes my heart hurt for him. I've never seen him look so sad. "I need to see Ellie more. This is terrible, Brooke. I miss her so much."

I look over at Ellie, playing happily. I get that he's sad, but at the same time, he was never around her much before. Even before I moved, he only saw her a few times a week for short amounts of time. Is he just feeling regret now?

We don't say anything for a few minutes because I really don't know what to say. I don't want to travel far all the time for him to see her, and I'm sure as hell not moving back to Portland. Finally, I break the silence. "What do you want to do about that?"

"I guess we can FaceTime, I can drive to Seattle more, and we can still meet in the middle sometimes."

I'm honestly wondering if this will ever happen. He's always too busy. When will he make time for this? And then it occurs to me: I hope he doesn't try to change our custody agreement. Suddenly, I'm very worried.

"We can try FaceTime this week. Just let me know when," I tell him. I figure I should concede to what he wants; maybe he'll be less likely to take me to court.

"How about tomorrow before I go to work at around three o'clock. Does that work?"

"Yes, that will be fine," I say to him.

"Great, I'll FaceTime you tomorrow at three."

I try to smile, but inside, I want to scream.

We don't talk much the rest of the time Ellie plays. Scott goes to play with her, and I just watch from a bench nearby. Luckily, she isn't fussy with him at all.

A few hours later, Ellie and I are at Ryan's house. Scott

stressed me out this afternoon, but now I feel relaxed and calm. Ryan insisted on cooking dinner tonight. I text Sarah, letting her know I won't be working out with her tonight. She understands when I tell her Ryan's cooking for us.

Ryan cooks lasagna, which is impressive. He cooks enough for his brother's family, too. While he cooks, Ellie and I play on the floor of the family room, which is attached to the kitchen. His nephews are upstairs in their rooms, and Dan and Cari are both still at work, but they should be home soon. I'm looking forward to spending time with them and getting to know them better.

Dan's the first to get home. He walks into the kitchen from the garage and spots Ryan cooking. "Oh, honey, you're cooking!" he jokes with his younger brother.

"You're gonna love my lasagna," Ryan replies to him. "Laugh now, but you'll be impressed."

"Whatever," Dan says with a chuckle. Then he notices Ellie and me in the family room. "Oh, hey!" He walks over and crouches down by Ellie.

"This is Ellie," I tell him. Ellie looks at him as he waves "hi" to her. She squeals and smiles with delight.

Ryan pipes up from the kitchen, "Hey, I thought she only gets excited when she sees me!"

Dan and I both laugh.

"Ah, you should be used to that by now. You know the ladies always preferred me over you," Dan razzes Ryan.

Ryan fires back, "Whatever. By the way, when's your *wife* due to be home?"

Before either can say more, the sound of Dan's boys coming downstairs fills the room, ending the teasing between Ryan and Dan. Mason and Alex walk into the room, and Alex asks, "Is dinner almost ready?"

"Your mom should be home in about five minutes. We'll eat then," Ryan answers them.

"You guys can set the table," Dan adds. "Set it for six people."

Mason and Alex go about setting the table while Dan plays with Ellie. I've always found it cute to watch grown men play with babies. It's so unlike their usual macho selves—especially Marines like Ryan and Dan.

A few minutes later, Cari walks into the kitchen from the garage. "Hi," she says in greeting to everyone. "Wow, this is nice to come home to," she says, referring to Ryan cooking dinner and her sons setting the table.

Dan looks over at his wife, and says, "Hi, honey. Come here and look at this cutie."

She walks over and sits down on the floor with us. "Hi, Brooke," she says. Her face lights up when she sees Ellie. "Oh, my goodness, she's adorable!"

"Her name is Ellie," I tell her.

"See? We can have another one," Dan says to her.

Cari reaches for Ellie and picks her up. "Oh, no. No, no, no." she says in a sweet voice, "Two kids are enough!" She smiles sweetly at Ellie, then turns to Dan and scowls at him.

Dan looks at me. "She's so mean."

"I'm mean?" Cari asks as she bounces Ellie up and down. "I just enjoy sleeping every night and not changing diapers."

"She's always denying me one more baby," Dan says. I can tell they're joking with each other, but something tells me they're both partly serious, too.

"Dinner is ready!" Ryan announces.

We all make our way to the kitchen table. I'm impressed by how well the boys have set it. Cari's still holding Ellie, and I realize I don't have a high chair to set her in. "I'll get her car seat to feed her easier," I offer

"I'll get it," Ryan replies. He runs upstairs to retrieve it from his room.

"Have a seat," Dan declares. I pick a chair and sit at the square table that has two chairs on each side. Dave and Cari sit on one side together, Mason and Alex sit on another side, and the other place setting for Ryan is next to me. One side of the table is left empty, but the chairs look sturdy enough to place Ellie's car seat on. I pull the chair closest to me out a bit just as Ryan gets back with her seat. He puts it on the chair, then Cari hands Ellie back over to me so I can get her settled.

Once everyone is seated, we start passing the food around the table. Ryan made garlic bread and salad to go with the lasagna. He also placed a bottle of red wine on the table and gave the boys each a small can of pop. They look very excited to get it, which tells me it's not what they usually get to drink.

"Ryan says you used to work in an ER," Cari says to me.

"Yes, I did," I reply. "I loved it. Maybe someday I'll go back to it, but it's just too complicated with Ellie right now."

"I totally understand," she says. "I took a few years off when the boys were babies. I didn't go back to work until they were both in school, so I've only been at the hospital for a few years now." Then she turns toward her boys. "By the way, how was school today?"

"Fine," they both say, almost in unison.

"What did you do?" she asks, prompting to hear more.

"Stuff," Mason replies.

"I had PE today," Alex says.

Dan pipes up, "So you did stuff and you had PE all day?"

All of us grown-ups chuckle.

"Pretty much," Mason replies with a proud grin on his face.

"Okay, so I also did math, reading, and science," Alex tells them.

"Ah, good to know," Cari says. Then she turns to me, and adds, "This is what we hear every day. They never go into much detail."

I smile at them, remembering being a kid myself and giving my parents similar responses. Then I think about Ellie growing up and being the same way, and I secretly hope that she beats the odds and is more eager to share things with me. *I can always hope.*

"How was your weekend away?" Cari asks me, changing the subject.

I smile shyly, remembering just how great it *really* was. "It was nice!" I tell her. "Ryan spoiled me by taking me to the Salish Lodge. It was beautiful!"

Ryan looks at me, and says, "You deserve it."

"Did you hike up to the falls?" Dan asks.

"Yes, and it was perfect weather," I reply.

"We also hiked yesterday before we left," Ryan adds. "I love it up there by Snoqualmie."

"I'd love to go there sometime," Cari says, obviously hinting to Dan. When he doesn't respond, she nudges him with her elbow.

"What?" he asks.

"Take your wife to Salish Lodge," Ryan chides.

"Thank you, Ryan," Cari says.

Dan rolls his eyes. "Yeah, yeah. I'll try to plan something."

Cari looks at him and cocks her eyebrow. "Don't just try," she says in a stern voice.

I try not to laugh. They're funny together. He likes to joke around, and she's sassy enough to feed it right back to him.

Throughout dinner, we make small talk about various things. I really like Dan, and Cari and I seem to have hit it off. We have a lot in common, just as Ryan predicted we would. Mason and Alex are nice boys. Their good manners don't really surprise me because I know that's how Dan and Ryan were raised. When they finish eating, they ask to be dismissed from the table, take their dishes to the sink to rinse them, then put the dishes in the dishwasher. After all that, they go back upstairs, leaving just us adults and Ellie at the table. Ellie starts to fuss, so I take her out of her car seat. She's hungry now.

"Does she need her bottle?" Ryan asks.

"Yeah, I'll get her stuff out of the diaper bag," I say as I stand.

"I'll hold her while you get it," he offers, reaching his hands out to take her.

I smile and hand Ellie over. Inside, I'm beaming. I can't believe how helpful Ryan is. He even understood Ellie's fussiness as her hungry fuss. How did I get so lucky?

I retrieve everything I need and go into the kitchen to make her a bottle. Meanwhile, Ryan bounces Ellie on his lap while Dan and Cari comment about how weird it is to see him with a baby. They also say how good he is with her. They're obviously surprised.

"Wait until you have to change a diaper," Dan says.

"I've already mastered that," Ryan replies, trying to sound overly confident.

"What?!" Cari exclaims, obviously not believing him. "Now *this* I've gotta see sometime!"

"You don't believe me?" Ryan asks, sounding offended.

"Brooke," Dan says to get my attention. "Is this true? Can Ryan really change a diaper?"

I look over at them and smile. "Yes, it is! He's actually very good at it."

Dan and Cari look surprised again.

"No way! Dude, you're hurtin' me here," Dan says.

"What do you mean?" Ryan asks.

"You're setting the bar a little high. You take your girlfriend to one of the nicest, most romantic hotels in the area, you cook an amazing dinner, and now I find out you change her baby's diapers?"

Cari leans in, and adds, "That's because Dan hardly ever changed diapers when the boys were babies."

I laugh a little as I screw the cap onto the bottle, returning to the table. I hand it to Ryan, and he proceeds to feed Ellie.

"Ryan, I'm amazed," Cari says. Then she looks at me. "Do *not* let him go. You have no idea how good you have it!"

I sit at the table and admire Ryan as he feeds Ellie. I really do have it good. How many guys would do this? Maybe a lot of guys are helpful with babies when they're their own, but Ellie isn't his, yet he treats her as if she is.

Ellie and I stay for a couple of more hours, hanging out downstairs with Dan and Cari. At one point, Dan wants to show Ryan something out in the garage, so Cari and I are left in the family room together.

"I have to tell you," she says once the guys are out of the room, "that I have *never* seen Ryan like this before. He's obviously head over heels."

I blush a little. "Thanks. So am I."

She continues, "I only met one of his former girlfriends. It was the last one he had in California." She rolls her eyes. "He was *nothing* like this with her, though. She was nothing like you, either." She leans in closer, and whispers, "I actually couldn't stand her."

I smile. "I feel lucky to have found Ryan again."

"He seems happier, too," she says. "Before you came back, he was just all about work. When he wasn't working, he was usually holed up in his room, watching TV or playing video games. I was actually starting to worry about him."

"Oh?" Her comment takes me by surprise. *Why was she worried?*

"I'm sure he's told you about his PTSD?" she asks, looking at me curiously. I nod my head, and she continues. "Well, I was concerned about him because he almost seemed depressed. He was seeing a therapist for a while and got anti-anxiety meds, which helped, but he still didn't seem to have much of a life outside of work. He's just happier now and more like his old self." She smiles. "Even though it hasn't been very much time since you two got together, Dan's noticed a difference in him, too. So thank you."

I'm not sure what to say. I look at Ellie playing on the floor, then I look back at Cari and decide to be brutally honest with her,

"Really, he's the one who has helped me. Since I found out my husband gambled all our money away and lost everything, I've suffered from anxiety attacks on a regular basis. Not to mention, I was stressed to the max, being a new mom and all. My life has gotten better since I moved back up here, but I didn't realize how unhappy I was until Ryan came back into my life. These past few days with him have been amazing, and I feel more like myself again."

Cari smiles at me kindly. "He's so good with Ellie, too. I've never seen him with a baby, but he's a natural with her. It's amazing. I can tell he not only cares for you, but for Ellie, too."

As the guys walk back into the kitchen, Cari reaches over to squeeze my hand and smiles at me. I smile back. It's a small gesture, but it tells me she likes me and appreciates our conversation.

Ellie begins fussing again, so Ryan picks her up as he comes back in the room. "Oh, she definitely needs a diaper change," he says, giving me a sour look.

I'm about to get up and take her when Dan says, "Well, let's see you, baby brother. Go change her diaper!"

Cari and I laugh, but Ryan shrugs and accepts the challenge. "Just watch," he says smugly. He grabs the things he needs out of the diaper bag and goes about changing Ellie's diaper right there on the family room floor. We all watch him, but he does everything perfectly. After he has Ellie dressed again, he holds her up with both arms like a trophy. "Ta-da!"

Dan and Cari clap, and I join in, laughing. Ryan hands Ellie over to me and cleans everything up. I look at Ellie in my arms and notice she's yawning. I glance at my watch and realize it's almost her bedtime.

"I should get Ellie home for bed," I say to everyone.

"Oh, well, it was great hanging out with you tonight," Cari says.

"Yeah, we'll have to do it again," Dan replies.

I stand, and they both stand, too. I walk over to the kitchen table to put Ellie in her car seat. I strap her in, then walk back toward the family room to say goodbye to everyone. Cari gives me a hug. Ryan carries the diaper bag for me and follows me out.

I put Ellie in the car, then Ryan hands me the diaper bag to put in. I shut the door and turn toward him. He wraps his arms around me and leans in for a kiss.

"Thanks for dinner," I say after our lips part.

"You're welcome," he says. "Do you really have to leave right now?"

"Yes, Ellie's tired. I need to put her to bed."

"She can sleep here," he says, giving me his crooked smile. "And so can you."

I smile at him. "How would that work out? She doesn't have a crib to sleep in."

Ryan looks like he's thinking. Then he says, "Okay, that's true. Maybe our sleepovers will have to be at your place for now."

He leans in and kisses me again. I really don't want to leave him. I love spending time with him. "You can come over," I offer.

Ryan kisses me behind my ear, and it sends a shiver down that side of my body. *Oh God, I hope he decides to come over.*

"I'll sneak over later," he whispers in my ear.

I smile. "Really? You're going to *sneak* over?"

He nods his head and smirks at me. He's so irresistible.

"Seriously? Like you did in high school?" I ask, looking at him as if he's crazy.

He just chuckles. "What time do your parents go to bed?"

I laugh. "You know you really don't have to wait for them to go to bed. You really don't have to *sneak* over, either."

Ryan shakes his head and continues to smile at me. He's too adorable for his own good. "I know, but sneaking over sounds more naughty." He wiggles his eyebrows at me, which makes me laugh. "What time do your parents go to bed? If they're still awake when I get there, they'll wonder why I'm sneaking into the basement and not just coming through the front door. It'll get weird." He chuckles.

"I guess so," I say, laughing at him again and shaking my head. "They usually go to bed around nine thirty or ten."

"I'll come over at ten thirty to be safe," he replies with a wink. Then he kisses me again.

* * *

After putting Ellie to bed in her crib, I watch TV for a while upstairs with my parents. At nine thirty, my parents go to bed, so I go downstairs. I have a whole hour before he comes over. I kill time by checking Facebook. I haven't been on since Ryan tagged me as his girlfriend. I'm sure there are a lot of comments about that.

I'm right. Several people from high school made comments about how they thought it was great we got back together, how they always thought we would end up together, and just offering their congratulations. Even Scott's sister, who I'm still friends with, "liked" it. It reminds me of how Scott wants to FaceTime with Ellie tomorrow. It also reminds me of how worried Scott was today when he was asking about Ryan being around Ellie. It brings all the stress I was feeling earlier back again.

At ten thirty on the dot, a tap on my bedroom window makes me smile. He's here. This is exactly what he would do in high school. I pull the curtain back and see him outside, then motion for him to go to the door in the laundry room. I leave my room, go around the corner to the laundry room, and open the door quietly. He walks in and whispers, "Hi."

"Hi," I whisper back. "This feels like Deja vu."

"Tell me about it," he says, smiling. "Except it's much easier than it used to be. I didn't have to sneak out of my own house first."

"Did you park your truck at the park down the street and walk over like you used to?"

"No, I just parked here," Ryan says with a chuckle.

I shut and lock the door, and he takes my hand, leading me into my bedroom. I shut the door behind us, then he kisses me. "I've missed you for the past two hours," he says.

"So have I." We keep kissing, and we move toward my bed. We pull at each other's clothes, tearing them off. After wanting each other all day, we can't wait anymore.

I undo his jeans and start pulling them down. He stops kissing me to help take them off entirely, so I take the opportunity to take my own pants off as well. Once we're standing in front of each other in just our underwear, he playfully pushes me onto the bed and crawls over me. His mouth lands on my left breast, sucking and licking my nipple, driving me crazy. Bolts of pleasure spread through my body, and I move beneath him. My hand moves along his back, and I rake my nails lightly over his skin. He moans and grinds his cock right against my clit, which, of course, makes me want more. *I need him, now.*

He kisses my body, moving lower over my stomach until he reaches my underwear. His strong hands grip my panties and slide them down my legs, tossing them onto the floor. Then, without any warning, Ryan's tongue is *there*, licking my pussy, making me squirm and moan. I put my hands on his head to lightly pull his hair. It feels so damn good. Once his tongue finds my clit, it doesn't take long. He sucks and flicks and sucks again until I explode. I moan, trying to stay quiet, not wanting to wake anyone else in the house.

Ryan stands to remove his underwear, then crawls back on the bed over my body. I spread my legs, the need for him out of control. I can't get enough of Ryan. He looks sexy as hell, his cock in his hand as he guides himself into me. When he pushes all the way in, filling me up, I move my head back against the pillow. My hands reach behind me to grab my wrought-iron headboard. Ryan's mouth comes down on mine, kissing me hard.

He pounds in and out of me, hitting me deep, rubbing my G-spot. My body is tingling, getting closer to release, but I want it to last longer. I move my arms down to his shoulders, but he grips one of my hands in his and places it back against the head-board. "Keep your hands here," his gravelly voice instructs.

Well, this is fucking hot!

I move my other hand back and hold the headboard as Ryan's mouth trails down my neck to my breasts. His skilled tongue lavishes one nipple, then the other. I'm breathing hard, trying not to moan too loudly, but it's becoming difficult to stay quiet. Not being able to touch him and having my body at his mercy makes everything so much more erotic.

His right hand glides up my left arm, starting at the side of my breast and stopping when he reaches my hand. Gently taking my hand in his, he links our fingers together, setting them down on the pillow just above my head. His lips find mine again, whispering against my mouth, "I fucking love you," before he kisses me hard. I moan into his mouth and enjoy the faster rhythm he sets, fucking me harder.

I want to touch him with my other hand, but I keep holding the metal bar of my headboard. I wrap my legs around Ryan's waist, and before I know it, I'm coming. I can't help myself and move my right arm down, holding Ryan's shoulder as I come undone. He follows soon after me, quietly grunting, our mouths still fused together, muting our sounds.

Once he stills his hips, he kisses my nose, then my cheeks, then my mouth again. He smiles down at me, and says, "You feel so good."

"So do you," I say, my voice sounding all breathy as I try to catch my breath.

He kisses me once more before getting up. He puts his boxer briefs on, then lies down with me again. I'm still basking in the afterglow of my orgasm as he wraps an arm around me and kisses my forehead.

"I'm so glad I went back on the pill when I did. Otherwise, we'd have to use condoms." As soon as I say it, I wish I could take it back. I don't need to say everything I'm thinking around him especially striking up a conversation about condom use! Obviously, the afterglow has caused my brain to be a little foggy.

Ryan chuckles. "There's nothing wrong with using condoms. But I agree, I like not using them with you."

"Sorry, that was really random," I say, hoping he doesn't think it was strange.

He chuckles again. "That's okay. It's true. I'm glad you went back on the pill, too. We finally get to experience being together without one, and I won't have to worry about knocking you up yet."

"Yet?" I ask, shocked by the word yet at the end of his sentence. Does this mean he's thought about knocking me–err, getting me pregnant? *He has thought about this?*

I turn my head to look at him. He looks embarrassed. "I mean …" I can tell he's not sure what to say. He can't even complete a whole sentence, and he's blushing. "I don't know why I said that," he finally says.

I try to lighten the mood by making a joke of it. "Have you thought about getting me pregnant? Is that your evil plan?"

He rolls his eyes. He's obviously embarrassed. I'm really curious what he has thought about, though. Then he looks at me more seriously, and says, "Well, honestly, I've had all kinds of thoughts about the future since we've gotten back together. Haven't you?"

My heart starts pounding. *He's thought about the future.* It makes me happy that he's considered a future with me, but at the same time, I'm freaking out a little. Sure, we're in love again, and everything is great between us, but *everything's happening so fast!* Our first date was just a little over a week ago! What's even weirder, though, is that I don't know *why* I'm freaking out about this! Everything's going so well between us. Not only that, but I can't really blame him for thinking about a future with me because *I've done it, too.*

I take a deep breath to calm my nerves. I decide to be honest with him. "Yes, I have," I admit. "You make me happy, Ryan, and I want us to be together."

His grin captures my heart as he kisses my forehead. "Me too, baby," his deep voice rasps out. He pauses for a moment as if he's debating whether to say the next thing, but then he does. "Seeing you as a mother to Ellie, I can picture us having one of our own someday. That is, if I'm lucky enough to keep you in my life. I hope that doesn't freak you out, though. I know we haven't been together very long."

I stroke his cheek with my hand. I love how honest he's being with me right now, and I want to be truthful with him. "If I'm being honest, it *does* freak me out a little bit." I notice a brief look of panic in Ryan's eyes, so I know I need to continue. "But then I realize it shouldn't. We have a history together, Ryan. It's not like we just met a couple of weeks ago. It's easy to imagine a future with you because I used to dream about it all the time in high school."

Ryan relaxes, and his arm squeezes me gently. "I love you, Brooke. I don't want to move too fast with you, but this all feels so right and natural. I fell in love with you in high school, but I've fallen in love with you all over again. I've also fallen for Ellie."

Hearing Ryan say he loves me is one thing, but hearing him say he has fallen for my daughter? Hands down, the *best* words I think I could hear him say. I lean up on my elbow so I can reach his lips and kiss him.

And then, the worst thought pops in my head for some reason. Scott. All the stress I felt earlier starts flooding back again. I pull away from Ryan, and he knows something is bothering me. "What's wrong?" he asks.

"Just everything with Scott. I'm really worried he's going to try to change our custody agreement so he can see Ellie more."

I had already told Ryan everything from earlier today. He nods his head, and says, "Try not to stress right now. Call your lawyer tomorrow and talk to him. Scott might not be able to change it, or he might have no intention in doing so anyway. You might be worrying for no reason."

"I know, but I can't help it. He's hardly been in her life since she was born. She's more comfortable around you than him."

"Really?" he asks, his voice sounding a bit hopeful. I can tell that makes him happy.

"I think so," I reply. I really don't want to think about Scott right now, though, so I lean in and kiss Ryan again.

BROOKE

he next morning, Ellie wakes me up at 7:15. She hasn't slept in this late in a while. I detangle myself from Ryan without waking him to get her.

After changing her diaper, I take her upstairs with me to make her bottle. Mom's in the kitchen, getting her coffee. "Good morning," she says to us.

"Good morning," I say as I put Ellie in her high chair.

"I see Ryan's truck outside. He must've come over late last night."

"Yeah, he just decided to come over," is all I can think to say. I'm a little embarrassed because I know my mom must know *why* he came over and what we were doing. I mean, why else would he come over so late at night and then sleep over?

She doesn't say anything else about it and just gives me a small smile. I fix Ellie's bottle, and then my mom is by my side with her arm around me. "I'm happy for you, honey," she says. She releases me, then walks over to Ellie, gives her a kiss, and walks out of the room.

I take Ellie back downstairs with her bottle. I sit in the rocking chair in the family room with her and feed her. As she drinks her formula, I think about my conversation from last night. Ryan's thought about us having a baby of our own some-day. I've always wanted more kids. Now, I can actually picture a future with Ryan. It makes me smile even if this *is* all happening at hyper speed.

* * *

Later that afternoon, Ellie and I are alone at home, waiting for Scott's FaceTime call. Ryan stayed with us all morning and didn't leave until after lunch to go home and get ready for work. This is the part of the day I've been dreading. I don't know how well this is going to go. I've never done a FaceTime call with a baby before, so who knows if Ellie will even be interested, and if she's not interested, then Scott will probably get upset.

As I wait for him to call, I realize I've had a pretty productive day. I called my divorce lawyer. He didn't exactly assure me Scott couldn't change our custody agreement. However, he *did* assure me he will do everything he can to help me if it comes to that.

Ellie's happily playing on the floor when my phone rings, signaling Scott's FaceTime call. I answer it and see Scott on the screen. "Hi," I say. I can't tell where he is, but it looks like he's sitting on a couch. He's been staying with his friend, Danner, from work.

"Hi, Brooke," he replies. "Is Ellie there?"

"She's playing on the floor. Let me grab her." I stand and walk over to her, sitting on the floor and placing her on my lap so I can hold the phone in front of her. When I look back at the screen, I see and hear Scott quietly talking to someone, but I can't see them on the screen. If I'm not mistaken, it sounds more like a female's voice, not Danner. Hmm ... I don't think I'll question him about it right now. I just want to get this call over with.

"Here she is," I say to get Scott's attention. He turns back to the screen and starts talking to Ellie immediately. She smiles and babbles at him. So far, so good. This isn't too terrible, I guess. Ellie seems to be intrigued with seeing and talking to him on the screen.

It doesn't last too long, though. A few minutes later, she's squirming to get down and play again. "She wants down," I say to Scott.

"Put her down and turn your phone so I can watch her for a couple of minutes," he says. I do what he asks. A few minutes later, he says, "Okay, Brooke, I have to go."

I turn my phone back toward me. "How was that?" I ask him.

"It was great to see her," he replies. "Can we do it again?"

"Sure. Just let me know when, and if the time works for us, we'll be here."

"I was thinking ..." he starts to say, "How would you feel if I drove up to visit with her, too? Maybe every other week? I can just take her for the day and do something."

"Where would you want to take her?" I ask, surprised that he actually wants to do this.

"The zoo, children's museums ... Wherever you take kids to have fun. I just feel like I'm missing out on her whole life. I never realized this would be so hard for me."

"We can probably work that out," I tell him. That sounds better than changing our custody agreement, and I really *do* want him to have a good relationship with Ellie.

"Okay. Thanks again, Brooke. Talk to you later," he says before ending the call.

I put my phone down and think about his request. Suddenly, I'm a bit hesitant.

He wants to drive up here to see Ellie every other week? He wants to take her for the day by himself?

I really don't want to keep Scott from his daughter. That's *not* why I'm hesitant. I'm concerned about how this will go. Ellie hardly goes to him now as it is, so how will she react to him taking her someplace without me? I've anticipated this happening a few years down the road as she got older, but not so soon. However, she *is* his daughter, and he has a right to see her. I guess I'll just have to wait and see if Scott even follows through with this idea of his.

* * *

Later that evening, I cook dinner for my parents, and the three of us eat together with Ellie.

"I can't believe she's going to be nine months old tomorrow," Mom says.

"I know. Time needs to slow down with her," I reply.

"It's been so nice to have you two living here," Dad adds. "It's great to be able to watch her grow up."

"Well, I'm very grateful you took us in," I tell them. "I don't know what I'd do without you."

* * *

Ryan "sneaks over" again when he gets off work. He spends the night again, too. I realize this will be our fourth night in a row sleeping together. We haven't spent a night apart since our getaway on Saturday, and I couldn't be happier.

RYAN

*E*verything's going better than I could've imagined with Brooke. We spend the majority of our time together when I'm not working. Basically, the only times we're *not* together are when I'm working, she has her weekly lunch date or works out with Sarah, and when she meets Scott for his visitation with Ellie. I spend nearly every night at her house, although sometimes I do go home to sleep in my own bed. Not often, though.

A few weeks into our relationship, my mom invites Brooke and me over for dinner. Of course, she insists we bring Ellie, too. Mom has been looking forward to seeing Brooke again ever since I told her we're back together. She always liked Brooke.

I'll never forget when I told my mom Brooke and I broke up. I thought she was actually going to cry. She didn't, but she gave me an earful, telling me that I was being stubborn by letting her go. She thought Brooke was the perfect girl for me, and I was letting her go for all the wrong reasons. She knew true love when she saw it, and what we had was more than just the average teenage relationship. She also told me my dad and her survived being apart when he was in the Marines, so it's not impossible. I knew my mom was right about everything, but what she didn't understand was that I was letting Brooke go *because* I loved her so much.

But that was then, and this is now. Fate seems to have stepped in and brought us back together, and my mom couldn't be happier about it. It's Saturday, so after work, I go to Brooke's house to pick her and Ellie up.

"Guess what?" Brooke says when she opens the front door. Her eyes are lit up with excitement.

"What?" I ask, curious what she has to say.

"My divorce is final!"

I smile and embrace her. Her arms fly around my neck as she says, "I'm just so happy it finally happened!"

I pull her back and look at her. "I'm happy for you."

This is good news, and I'm relieved for Brooke. I know it was stressful for her to wait for the paperwork to make it official.

"Should we celebrate?" I ask her.

She smirks, then leans in and whispers in my ear, "We can celebrate later tonight. You can finally sleep with a single woman."

I roll my eyes at her and shake my head. "I'll take you up on that ... Although I wouldn't say you're single."

She quirks an eyebrow up. "No?"

"No." I pull her closer and kiss her briefly. "Come on, let's go to my parents' now. We can kiss more later."

Brooke gets Ellie as I grab the diaper bag she packed, and we leave to go to my parents'.

My parents' house isn't that far away. Brooke filled the short ride by telling me what she and Ellie did today and how relieved she was to learn her divorce is final. She also shares that although she's really happy, it feels kind of strange at the same time. She never *wanted* to be divorced, but everything happens for a reason. I understand what she's saying, although I have to admit I'm just glad it finally happened.

I reach over and take her hand in mine. "If you weren't divorced, you and I wouldn't be together right now, so I have to be selfish and say I'm glad you had to go through that."

She laughs. "That's definitely true. That's the only good thing that came from this, I think."

When I pull into my parents' driveway, Brooke says, "It looks almost exactly the same."

I kill the engine before turning to look at her. "I told you they haven't done very much with the place. It's mostly the way it was when you were here last." I lean across the console and give her a quick kiss on the lips, then we get out of the truck.

I open the crew cab and take Ellie's car seat out of the back seat. It's hard for Brooke to reach her in the middle of the back seat of my truck, so I gladly do it for her. She grabs the diaper bag and then we walk hand in hand to the front door.

Mom steps out on the porch just as we reach the top step. She stands there with a wide grin on her face. "Brooke!" she exclaims as she opens her arms for a hug. Brooke drops my hand and hugs my mom.

"It's so good to see you again," Brooke says, still embracing her.

"The pleasure's all mine," Mom says, patting Brooke's back. When they pull apart from each other, Mom homes her eyes on the car seat I'm carrying. "Is Ellie awake?" she asks in a quieter voice, almost whispering.

I look down at Ellie and see that she's wide-awake. I turn the car seat around so Mom can see for herself. "She sure is."

Mom gushes over Ellie. "She's just the cutest!"

We eventually go inside the house after Mom finishes adoring Ellie and getting a few giggles out of her. The house is a split level, so we go up the small staircase to the main floor. The delicious aroma of dinner is wafting in from the kitchen. It smells of Mom's meatloaf. One of my favorites.

I set the car seat down in the living room, next to the couch, and go about unbuckling Ellie to take her out. Brooke sets the diaper bag down next to it, and Mom claps her hands together and asks to hold Ellie right away.

"Of course," Brooke says, smiling. I hand Ellie over to Mom.

"She's so precious," Mom says, bouncing Ellie on her hip. She loves babies, and she's only ever had boys. First Dan and me, then Dan's two boys. Ellie should be a nice change of pace for her.

Dad walks in from the kitchen, holding two full wine glasses. "Welcome!" he says as he walks over and hands the glasses to us. Then he gives Brooke a side hug. "It's great to see you again, Brooke." His attention lands on Ellie then. "And this must be your daughter!"

Brooke introduces Ellie, and now both of my parents are adoring her. A future with Brooke suddenly flashes before my eyes. I see us having more family dinners here with my parents gushing over an older Ellie, as well as another baby—*our* baby. God, I hope we can give Ellie at least one sibling someday.

We have a nice visit with my folks. Dinner is delicious, and I was right—Mom made meatloaf. She also made mashed potatoes, gravy, and a mixed vegetable side dish. Mom asks Brooke various things about her life, her move back here, and about Ellie. Although she doesn't get too nosy, she also asks a few questions about her divorce and Scott. Luckily, Brooke doesn't mind answering her. At first, I felt protective of Brooke and wanted to change the subject, but Brooke handled it all with ease.

Mom also made dessert, so we enjoy cherry pie with vanilla ice cream. After we finish eating and are thoroughly stuffed, Dad says he wants to show me something in the garage. Something tells me he wants to talk rather than show me something.

But I'm wrong. When we get to the garage, Dad actually has a new power drill he just purchased and is proud of. He shows it off, telling me all about its amazing features. When he sets it back on the shelf, though, I know that was only his excuse to get me alone to talk.

"So you and Brooke seem really happy," he starts, sounding casual as he leans back against a workbench.

I cross my arms in front of me and stand firm. Total Marine style. Not that I want to intimidate my dad for any reason, but I want to show him I'm serious about what I'm going to say about my relationship with her. Dad doesn't always show his emotions, but he's not afraid to tell you what he thinks. Even though he's been polite and kind to Brooke all night, I have a feeling he's concerned we're moving too fast. "I'm happier than I've been in years."

Dad nods his head. "I can understand that. You two were happy together in high school. She doesn't seem to have changed very much in regards to her personality."

"She's still the same sweet girl I knew, just older and wiser now."

"And she's a nurse, like Cari. That's interesting. Kind of a coincidence, I guess."

"Yeah, they get along really well, too."

Dad cracks a smile. "That's great. I like Brooke too; she seems like the right fit for you. She always has."

Relief washes over me, but it's short-lived when Dad's face turns more stoic as if he's going to lecture me. I recognize this look from the talks we had when I was growing up.

"There's just something I want you to understand, Ryan," he starts, looking me square in the eye. Even though I'm a thirty-two-year-old retired Marine, that look still makes the hairs on the back of my neck stand on end. *Oh fuck. Dad's going to lecture.*

Dad continues. "I know you love Brooke, but she's a mom. That baby upstairs is a serious investment in your relationship. Now, you seem to be taking on the role of dad right now, but I want you to understand how serious this role is."

I relax my stance a bit and put my arms down, shoving them into my jeans pockets.

"Ryan, being a dad—or stepdad—is a big job. It might seem

fun and easy right now since it's all new to you, but times will get harder. Trust me on this. I don't want you to abandon Brooke just because parenting gets too difficult. Because it *will* get difficult."

I understand his concern. Maybe I should be more offended that he thinks I'll leave Brooke because of Ellie, but I know he's just making sure I'm aware of how serious this is. I look my dad in the eye to let him know I'm speaking the truth. "I've actually already thought all of this through. Ellie and Brooke are a package deal, and I understand how important being a dad is. I had *you* as the best role model, so I know what it entails." My dad's eyes soften at my words, and his mouth lifts a fraction. "Also, I know parenting isn't easy. I mean, just think about how Dan and I were growing up!"

Dad chuckles. "Ain't that the damn truth," he mutters, shaking his head. Then he looks at me again and continues. "I just wanted to make sure you knew that this commitment is bigger than if Ellie wasn't involved. Don't commit to Brooke if you can't also commit to Ellie."

I nod my head. "I'm totally committed to them. And I know Brooke has been through a lot this year, so I'm trying to take things slow. I want her to know she can trust and depend on me."

Dad smiles as he steps forward, embracing me in a hug. "I'm happy for you, son. I'd say you're stacking the deck in your favor. Brooke seems happy, and she's lucky to have you." He pats my back a couple of times, then lets go. His words mean a lot to me.

When we get back upstairs, we find Mom, Brooke, and Ellie in the living room together. Ellie's on the floor, playing on a blanket surrounded by her toys while Mom and Brooke talk on the couch. They turn and look at us when we walk in the room.

"And speak of the devil," Mom says, making me wonder which one of us they were talking about. Brooke smiles as I sit down on the floor with Ellie to play with her. Dad sits on his recliner.

We visit with my parents for a while longer until Ellie starts to get tired, then we get ready to leave. Brooke uses the bathroom, and I remember I want to show her something before we leave, so I wait in the hall for her to come out. Mom and Dad are busy playing with Ellie in the living room.

I accidentally startle Brooke when she exits the bathroom, causing her to jump. "Sorry." I shrug in apology. "Come here." I take her arm and show her the plethora of pictures Mom has hanging in several collage frames on the wall. They're from various years, starting all the way back when she and Dad were just married up to the present with Dan and his family.

"I remember some of these were up when we were in high school," she says as she looks at them. She studies the frames until she gets to the ones I want her to notice. Her face changes when she sees it. Her eyes widen a fraction, and her hand flies up to her mouth. "Oh, my gosh!" she whispers. "She kept these up?" Her eyes dart to mine.

I nod. "Yeah, she did." I look back at the wall at the two small pictures of Brooke and me, still hanging on the wall over a decade later. One is a wallet from a school dance we went to, and the other is a four-by-six photo of us at our graduation. I don't know why Mom never took them out of the frames. I never asked why or if she'd remove them. Whenever I came home to visit, I *wanted* to see Brooke's picture on the wall. I wanted to see us still together.

"I can't believe she never took them down," she whispers, presumably so my mom doesn't hear. They're not very far away in the living room.

I shrug, then I lean in closer to her ear, and whisper, "I never asked why because I just wanted to keep you up there."

Brooke looks at me, her cheeks blushing. I take her hand, and say, "There's one more thing I want to show you." I walk a few steps down the hall and take her into the bedroom that used to be mine. It's now a spare room with no trace of me ever living in there.

"Oh my gosh," Brooke says. "It looks so different!" She looks around the room at the flowery bedspread, paintings on the wall, and candles on the dresser. "I remember this room, but it didn't look like this."

I chuckle. "Yeah, Dan's and my rooms are pretty much the only rooms she's redecorated." I slide my arms around her waist and pull her closer. She looks up at me, looking slightly nervous for some reason. Maybe she's afraid my parents will walk in and see us? I'm not worried, though. We're adults now. I don't mind reminiscing, however. I kiss her nose and whisper, "Do you remember what happened in this room?"

She blushes and tries not to smile. "I remember *a lot* that happened in this room."

I smirk. She's right; we spent a lot of time in here after school. Sometimes when Dad was at work and Mom was out running errands. "Well, one particular memory I have is when you gave me my first blow job."

She giggles and covers her mouth with her hand. "I remember that *very* well." She puts her hand back around my waist, and whispers, "I also remember you giving me my first orgasm in here."

I smile, remembering all the firsts we had together. *Fuck.* Just thinking about making her come and her mouth wrapped around my cock is making me horny. I need to take her back to her place.

We walk back to the living room to say goodbye to my parents. We gather Ellie's things, hug my parents, and thank them for having us over before leaving. I latch Ellie's car seat in the crew cab, then I drive us to Brooke's house. Once Ellie's asleep in her crib, we try to relive a lot of our *firsts* together again, and fuck if it's just as good, if not better, than the first time.

BROOKE

*T*he next few weeks go by, and I can't believe it's already the beginning of June. Things with Ryan are incredible. Ever since we went to his parents' house for dinner a few weeks ago, things have only gotten better and more serious between us. He sleeps over *every* night now. My parents don't say anything about it, but I know they don't mind. Since they work, the only days they're home when he gets up in the morning are on the weekend, and they just treat him like he belongs here.

Like part of the family. We haven't discussed our future again since that one night over a month ago, but I've thought about it a lot more. Honestly, Ryan and I act like a married couple. He acts like Ellie's dad. He's practically moved into the basement with us. We both know we want to be together, so it's really just a matter of making things official between us. I'm not going to rush him, though. The reality of the situation is that we've still only been together for less than two months.

It was a relief when my divorce was finalized, though I had a mix of emotions I wasn't expecting. As much as I wanted a divorce from Scott, I never *wanted* to be divorced, if that makes sense. I just never thought I'd have to go through this. Girls often imagine their weddings when they're growing up, but not their divorces. However, my divorce paved the way for Ryan and me to wind up together again, so there's that.

Scott and I agreed on a new schedule where he gets to see Ellie more often. He FaceTimes with her once a week, usually on Thursdays before going to work. We still meet in Olympia once a week, and now every other Tuesday, he drives all the way up here to spend time with Ellie, too. Sarah and I moved our weekly lunch playdate to Wednesdays. I decided not to fight Scott on this since I really don't have a good reason to do so. I don't have a job, so it's not like I *can't* fit it into our schedule, and I really do want Ellie to have a good relationship with her dad. So far, he has driven up here once to spend the day with her. He came over to our house, and I let him hang out with her there first so she could warm up to him. Then since the weather was nice that day, he took her to the park down the street. She did great with him, and Scott was thankful that I gave him the opportunity.

Ryan and Scott still have not met each other. I'm not sure when that time will come. Scott hasn't bothered me about him anymore especially since Ellie is not so fussy with him when she sees him now.

When I join Sarah at the gym on Wednesday night, I'm proud of myself for sticking to our routine. My muscle tone has really improved, and I finally feel like I'm getting back to my pre-pregnancy body.

As Sarah and I get on the elliptical, she invites me to go out Saturday night. "It's a girls' night out," she explains. "Do you remember Kelly Andrews?"

"Of course, I do," I reply. "We were only cheerleaders together for four years. I haven't seen her online at all, though. What's she up to now?"

"Well, she's not on Facebook," Sarah tells me. "She does Twitter, but she hasn't ventured into the Facebook world. Anyway, she's a party planner now and pretty successful at it. She's coordinating the night out. I think Jaime Pickett and Emily Johnson will be there, too."

"I'm friends with Jaime and Emily online. It would be nice to see them again. What are the plans?"

"First, we're meeting downtown for dinner and drinks at Wild Ginger. It's a delicious Asian restaurant. Then we're going dancing."

I haven't gone dancing in years, so it sounds like fun. I don't even remember the last time I had a girls' night out. Maybe my bachelorette party? No, I'm sure I had one since then, but I just really can't remember. "Sure, I'm in," I say.

Sarah smiles. "It'll be so fun! We can celebrate your divorce, too!"

After our workout, of course I stop at the front desk to talk to Ryan. Sarah says goodbye and leaves. "Are you coming over after work?" I don't know why I even ask him anymore. He always does.

"If you want me to," he replies, giving me his crooked smile that I can't resist.

"Of course, I do."

"Good, because I was already planning on it." He leans in and kisses me. "I'll see you later."

When I get home, I get Ellie ready for bed. Once she finishes her bedtime bottle, I put her in her crib. Once she's asleep, I take a shower. Ryan knocks on the laundry room door at about 10:30. It's not that he's sneaking over; he just uses this door since my parents are already in bed, and he knows I'm downstairs with Ellie. I let him in, and he greets me with a kiss.

"Hey there," he says after he pulls his lips away from mine. He keeps them close, though, and his hands wrap around my waist to pull me closer to him.

"Hey yourself," I reply. "How was work?"

"It was fine. I had a late training session, though, so I'm pretty tired." He brushes his lips against mine.

"Oh? Too tired for me?" I ask, looking into his brown eyes. I move my own hands down from his hips to his ass.

He smirks. "That depends. What did you have in mind?"

"Oh, I don't know ..." I kiss him behind his ear, then whisper, "Maybe we can go in my bedroom ..."

"Oh, yeah?" His hands cup my ass, pulling me even closer, grinding his cock against me. "What would we do in there?"

I kiss down his neck, then whisper in his ear, "I thought we could take our clothes off ..."

"And?"

"Lie down together on the bed ..."

"And?"

I move my hand between us and rub the outside of his pants over his cock. His breath hitches. "Kiss each other everywhere ..."

"And?"

He's wearing track pants, so I easily dip my hand inside and start stroking his length. "And then you can make love to me ..."

"That sounds nice," he says, his voice getting hoarse. He's moving with my hand now. I kiss him on the lips, and he deepens the kiss, moving his hands up to my face and into my hair.

All of a sudden, he pulls my hand out of his pants, then leads me into my bedroom. I shut the door behind me, and he backs me up against it, kissing me hard. His tongue sweeps into my mouth, and he kisses me like he needs me more than his next breath.

My hands grasp at his shirt, yanking it over his head, then he does the same to mine. I unhook my bra and toss it to the floor, then our mouths crash back together. My nipples graze against his chest, making me needy for more of him. Our hands grab for each other's pants, but then he pulls his mouth away from mine and kneels in front of me. He takes my pants and underwear off in one fluid motion, leaving me totally naked in front of him. His eyes rake me up and down, a slow smile forming on his lips.

"You're so fucking beautiful," he says as he stands and kisses me again, his hands framing my face.

His mouth doesn't leave mine as he pulls me toward the bed. We stand there, just kissing for several seconds before he pulls his lips away from mine. "Lie down," he says.

I pull the covers back and lie down. As I get situated, Ryan removes his own pants and boxer briefs. I watch as his naked body climbs onto the bed, and he crawls up to me like an animal stalking its prey. He looks fucking *hot* as I watch how his strong muscles flex and move with each advance he makes toward me. His hard cock sways under its own weight as he moves. Suddenly, I want to pleasure him first.

"You lie down," I say as he hovers over me. I try to push his body to the side so he lies next to me.

He doesn't budge, though. He's too heavy.

Ryan chuckles. "What are you trying to do?"

I smirk as I move my hand down and wrap it around his cock. He looks down at what I'm doing between his legs. "Lie down for me," I plead in a sexy, almost whiny voice.

He moans, then does what I ask and rolls over to his back next to me. I immediately sit up and move between his legs. I take his cock in my hand again and stroke it a couple of times before leaning in closer and licking it from root to tip.

"Shit, Brooke," Ryan rasps out. One of his hands moves to my head, and he holds it there.

I swirl my tongue around the tip, then I suck it into my mouth. I don't take it all in, though, just the tip before letting it go with an audible *pop!* Ryan moans, and I start again, licking him like a lollipop, sucking in just the tip, then repeat. I do it just a couple of more times before I take his full length in my mouth as deep as I can. I use my hand to stroke the base in rhythm with my mouth. Ryan's hand guides me up and down, and I hear his breathing becoming more labored.

"I'm going to come," he warns me, probably assuming I'll stop.

But I don't want to stop. "Brooke," he says, his gravelly voice telling me he's about to lose it.

Instead of letting up, I use my free hand to reach out and touch his stomach, then rake my nails down lightly all the way to his upper thigh next to my head. As soon as I stop, he comes in my mouth. Ryan moans, quietly, and his hand grips my hair so tight it's almost painful. I swallow all that he releases, then I sit up and look down at how sexy he looks now, all naked and satisfied and ready for more.

His cock is still semi-hard, but I know we'll have to wait before having sex. I crawl over him and kiss his neck and his hands wrap around my body.

"I love your hot little mouth," he growls, his skin vibrating beneath my lips from the deep timbre of his voice.

Before I know it, Ryan flips me over onto my back. We've traded positions, and he's settling between my legs.

"I also love your hot little pussy," he says as he lowers his mouth to my core and starts licking. Between his words and his tongue, my lower belly muscles clench, and I know it's not going to take very long for me to come.

I grab the bedsheets on either side of me, trying to hold something to steady myself. His tongue is working its magic, licking me from my entrance up to my clit and everywhere in between. He licks me fast, then slow, then fast again. I can't handle all the different sensations he's giving me. I'm hot; I'm cold; I'm writhing beneath him. Once he sucks my clit into his mouth, my orgasm shakes me, vibrations of pleasure racing through every nerve in my body. I somehow manage to stay quiet.

Ryan doesn't waste any time. He crawls back up over me, positioning himself and sliding into me without warning. It feels so incredible. It's the best feeling.

Ryan kisses my mouth as he fucks into me so deep and hard, I'm afraid I'm going to come again and not be able to hold myself together.

"Do you like that?" Ryan says, pulling his lips from mine. "Do you taste how sweet your pussy is?"

I moan. I can't seem to speak at the moment.

Ryan continues pounding into me at a delicious rhythm. He's rubbing my spot deep inside, and I know I won't be able to hold off much longer. Just as my orgasm is building, though, he buries himself deep and just stops. His mouth peppers kisses along my neck all the way to my breasts where he gives my nipples the attention they're begging for.

I need my release, though. I try to move my hips, but he holds them with his hands to keep me still. "Not yet. I'm going to come too soon. I want this to last."

He continues licking and sucking my nipples. It shoots streaks of pleasure right down to my core, and I realize I'm going to come from this alone. As soon as his teeth lightly nibble at one, that's it. I come apart, squirming beneath him. He moves his lips back up to mine to help stifle my moans. After I come down, he says, "That felt amazing. Your muscles clenched around my dick so hard."

I open my eyes and look at him. He has quite the mouth tonight. "Make me come again," I whisper to him, feeling bold with my words as well. "Start fucking me again."

Ryan starts moving, but unlike before, he's now going slow. He kisses me sweetly. *This* is making love.

"I don't want to fuck," he says against my mouth before kissing me again.

He continues to move at a slow pace, but it feels amazing nonetheless. He's so sweet and gentle with my body, and I try to do the same with him. Ryan rolls us over so I'm on top, and I ride him. He reaches up to massage my breasts, then I lean down and kiss him. I don't ever want this to stop. Sex with Ryan is, and always has been, sensational.

Ryan flips us over again, and we continue to move in sync together. He's hitting me in just the right spot, and I know I'm going to come. My orgasm hits me before his does, but he comes soon after me.

A little while later, we're dressed and ready for bed. I'm cuddled into his side, which is how we fall asleep every night.

* * *

The next day, Ellie wakes up a little after seven. I'm shocked when Ryan actually gets up to get her before I can. He's never done this before. "What are you doing?" I ask.

"I'll get her. You stay here," he says. Relieved for the help, I relax back into bed. I can get used to this. Ryan is really too good to be true sometimes.

I hear him talking to her in her room as he changes her diaper. It's adorable.

Ryan carries Ellie into my room and places her on the bed next to me. She's happy to see me. "Hi, baby girl," I say to her. Ryan goes into the bathroom, and when he's done, he goes upstairs. I look at Ellie. "Is he doing what I think he's doing?" She smiles and kicks her legs and arms around. I can tell she's getting hungry, though, so I really hope Ryan is making her bottle.

He comes back to my room a few minutes later with Ellie's bottle, ready to feed her. I'm so grateful. "Wow, thank you," I say as he lies back on the bed and gives Ellie her bottle.

"You're welcome," he replies.

"What made you decide to do all that?"

He shrugs. "I don't know. I just thought you deserved a break. You're always getting up early with her."

I smile. He's so thoughtful.

We lie on the bed and watch Ellie drink her formula. I'm still so tired; I wish I could go back to sleep, but I know I have to stay awake. Ellie is up, so I am up. Ryan usually stays asleep in bed this early in the morning and wakes up an hour or so after me, so today is different.

As we watch her, I tell Ryan about Sarah's plans for the girls' night out.

"Sounds fun. Who's all going?" he asks after I tell him.

"A few girls from high school, actually. Remember Jaime Pickett, Emily Johnson, and Kelly Andrews?"

Ryan's face is unreadable for a second before saying anything, which seems odd. "Yeah, sure," he replies. "Are they all going?"

I'm a little curious why he reacted in that sort of awkward way just now, but he was likely just trying to remember who they are. "Yeah. I don't know if there are more people, but they'll be there."

"Cool," Ryan says. "When was the last time you saw them?"

"I'm friends with Jaime and Emily on Facebook, but not Kelly. I haven't seen her since high school."

He nods, then turns his attention to Ellie to ask her, "Do you think Mommy should go out Saturday night?"

She doesn't say anything, of course. She just continues to suck down her formula.

"She doesn't seem to have an opinion," I say.

"If you go, I guess I'll have to sleep at my own house all alone," Ryan says with a dramatic sigh.

"I think you can handle it for one night," I reply.

"Where are you guys going?"

"Dinner at Wild Ginger, then dancing," I tell him.

"Have you been dancing in the past few years? It gets a little crazy in Seattle sometimes," he says.

"Whatever," I say, thinking he's just joking with me, but he looks serious.

"I'm not kidding. So many fights break out in the bars downtown."

I roll my eyes. "Fights? Really? Why does it sound like you don't want me to go?" I'm getting the feeling he really doesn't want me to go out, which bothers me. I haven't had a night out in forever, and I really want to go!

He shrugs. "It's not that," he says.

"It seems like it." I'm annoyed. I'm going no matter what, so he'll just have to get over it.

"Who's going to watch Ellie for you?" he asks.

"I'll ask my parents. Or you. Would you like to watch her? You can stay here with her, and then I'll come home to you." I wink at him. Maybe that will soften him up a bit.

He smiles a little. "I guess I can do that. But I'm serious, there can be some crazy people downtown on Saturday nights. I don't want anything bad happening to you."

I roll my eyes again. He's really being overprotective. "I'm going. Are you going to watch Ellie for me?"

He rolls his eyes, too. "Will your parents mind if I stay here with her?"

"Probably not. I can ask them, if it'll make you feel better. They might just volunteer to watch her themselves, so I'll let you know what they say."

* * *

Later, my parents offer to watch Ellie for me when I ask them, but they also tell me they wouldn't mind if Ryan watched her here, either. I leave the decision up to Ryan, and he volunteers to watch her. I am both surprised and flattered. He's so good to Ellie. It's nice he wants to spend time with her without me. Also, this way I get to come home to him after my night out.

On Friday night, Sarah and I go shopping together. When we realized we have nothing to wear, we hit the mall. My mom watches Ellie for me. I end up buying new jeans, a black strapless top, a silver necklace, and black boots. I also get a long-sleeve black crop jacket to wear since it's chilly at night. Sarah also gets new jeans, a flowy silver shirt, and some shoes.

* * *

On Saturday, Ryan comes over after work, so we hang out all afternoon before it's time for me to go. Sarah's husband drops her off at my house at seven o'clock, and we call an Uber to take us downtown.

The Uber arrives, and Sarah and I are ready to go. Ryan holds Ellie as I kiss my baby girl on the cheek to say goodbye. Then I give Ryan a quick kiss on the lips.

"You look amazing," he whispers to me. "Don't stay out too late." He gives me his crooked smile, telling me he wants me later.

"I'll wake you up if you're asleep," I whisper, then I kiss him again.

"Come on, you two," Sarah says, opening the front door. "Time to go, Brooke."

I say goodbye once more, then Sarah and I are out the door. It takes about twenty minutes to get to Wild Ginger. Our reservation's at seven thirty, so we get there just a little bit early. We're the first ones in our party to arrive, so we wait by the door.

"It's been a long time since I've gotten this dressed up," Sarah says. "Joe wanted to ravage me before I left. He told me to get home early."

"Same here," I reply. "Ryan wants me home early, too."

"Well, we do look hot," she says, motioning toward both of our new outfits. "Who can blame them? And I'll probably be drunk and horny by the time I get home, so Joe will get his wish." She laughs.

Kelly, Jaime, and Emily show up together. They all look incredible, in great shape, and like they're ready for a night of fun. We say hi and exchange hugs, then the waitress seats us.

We order drinks and begin catching up with each other. Jaime and Emily are both married, but Kelly is single. She owns a party planning business that, from the sound of it, is doing quite well. She's busy nearly every weekend. This is one Saturday night she's not working, so she organized a night out for fun. Jaime's a middle school teacher in north Seattle, and Emily's a dental assistant. I drink my martini and enjoy everyone's company. It's nice to have a night out where I can let my hair down and have fun.

Dinner is delicious. We order family style, so we can all try the various dishes. I make a mental note to bring Ryan here someday.

"So, tell us how things are with you now, Brooke. Are you doing all right since you've moved back?" Jaime asks.

"Actually, I've never been better," I reply.

Emily jumps in, and adds, "Of course you are! Jaime, didn't you see her relationship status on Facebook?"

Jaime shakes her head. "I'm not on Facebook enough. Who are you dating, Brooke?"

"Ryan," I tell her. I can't help but smile.

"Ryan Hall?!?" Jaime looks surprised.

I nod my head.

"That is so great! When did this happen?" she asks.

"A couple of months ago," I tell her. "Sarah and I started working out at the gym he owns, and we reconnected."

"That is so great!"

"I'm so happy for you," Emily says.

"They're still the perfect couple," Sarah adds.

Jaime and Emily continue to ask me questions about how Ryan and I got back together. Kelly's quiet, though. I glance at her, and she's taking a drink of her cocktail.

"He's even babysitting Ellie tonight," Sarah tells them. "Brooke has hit the jackpot with Ryan. *Again.*"

We all continue talking, and eventually, when the conversation takes a turn, and we're onto another topic, Kelly joins in again. I think it's weird she never said a word while we were talking about Ryan, though. Not that I expect her to say how happy she is for me, but she had been so vocal with all our previous conversations, so I just found it strange she became so quiet.

After we finish dinner and our second round of drinks (third for Kelly), we order an Uber and have it take us to Pioneer Square, where all the dance clubs are. It's not super busy yet because it's only ten o'clock, but the DJ is already playing music, and a few people are dancing at the club we go to. We head to the bar and order drinks first, then find a table to sit at in the corner. More and more people start to arrive as we sit and drink. Kelly disappears for a few minutes, then returns with a round of shots for us. We toast to friendship and take the shots, then we agree it's time to dance. When I stand, I realize I'm really starting to feel drunk now.

I check my phone, just to make sure Ryan isn't having any problems with Ellie and tried to call me. There's a text from him, but it's a picture of Ellie, sleeping soundly in her crib. I quickly reply.

Me: *Awwww, she's adorable. So are you. :-)*

Ryan: *Come home soon. :-)*

Sarah, who was also checking her phone, pulls my arm. "Okay, Momma. Time to dance!"

I text Ryan back with a heart, then head to the dance floor with Sarah. We join the others and all dance together. I haven't done this in so long, and I'm remembering now how much fun it can be!

After dancing for a while, we decide to get more drinks. The club has gotten busy, so we stand on the side of the dance floor while we drink. Kelly's the first one to go back on the dance floor, except she's not alone. She's dancing with a guy. I pull my phone out again and see that Ryan replied to my text earlier with

the smiley face blowing a kiss. I'm really feeling drunk now, so I
text him back again.

Me: *You better be ready when I get home.*

Ryan: *Are you drunk?*

Me: *Maybe*

Him: *Be careful. I'm serious. Stay with Sarah.*

Me: *I will. Don't worry. I'll text you when we leave and I'm on my
way home to attack you.*

Him: *Okay. Love you.*

Me: *Love you too.*

"How's Ryan doing?" Sarah says to me, practically having to
shout in my ear because the music is so loud.

"Great! He got Ellie to bed."

"That's good," she says. "Joe keeps texting me saying he wants
me to come home to have sex." She laughs.

"Ryan wants me to come home, too," I tell her.

"We're not leaving yet!" Sarah exclaims, and she pulls me back
out onto the dance floor.

We dance for quite a while, and it's so fun. Sarah, Jaime, Emily, and I are good at diverting grabby guys from each other who are trying to dance with us. Kelly's still dancing with the same guy. He's good looking, and I wonder if they're going to hook up tonight.

A little while later, Kelly's suddenly dancing beside me. I don't know where her guy went, but she seems to be back with our group for now. We're all having a great time together, dancing away. When my phone buzzes again, I look to see who it is. Of course, it's Ryan.

Coming home soon?

Kelly leans over and looks at my phone. She's obviously drunk. I lost count of how many drinks she's had tonight, but I know it's more than me, and I've had four plus a shot. "Ryan?" she asks, shouting because it's so loud.

I nod my head, then proceed to reply to him.

Soon. I'll text you.

Kelly leans close to my ear, and says, "He's so hot!"

I'm not sure who she's talking about at first. I look at her and shrug, trying to tell her I don't know who she means.

"Ryan!" she shouts.

Oh. Well, yes, he is. I nod my head and put my phone away.

Then she leans in to say something to me again. "You're so lucky. He's so fucking good in bed."

My head whips to look at her. *What the fuck did she just say?*

BROOKE

I stop dancing and just stare at Kelly. Everyone else we're with catches onto my body language and can tell I'm upset by the way I'm looking at her. "What did you just say?" I yell at her.

She laughs. She actually laughs.

Sarah moves in closer and asks what's wrong. I tell her what she said, and she looks at drunk Kelly. "What the hell do you mean?!" she yells at her.

Kelly looks at us and shakes her head. "It's not what you think!" Then she grabs both of our hands and leads us off the dance floor to the other side of the club where it's not as loud.

I'm so livid, I am shaking. How the hell does she know what Ryan's like in bed?

Kelly stumbles a bit, but catches her balance and looks at me. Then she says, slurring her words, "Ryan and I used to hook up. It's been a long time. I'm just telling you I know how lucky you are!" She smiles as if I should be happy with this news.

I know she's drunk as hell, so I try not to lose my shit with her, but I want more information. "When did you and Ryan hook up?"

"It's been a long time. Before Christmas."

Holy shit. He's been with her since he moved home?! How the hell did they start hooking up, and why didn't he tell me? He knew I was going out with her tonight!

"How?" Sarah asks. I'm glad she's able to form words right now. I'm speechless.

"Oh, it started years ago. We ran into each other at a bar when he was on leave. We'd hook up whenever he came home. Just casual. No strings. But God, he's good. You're a lucky girl, Brooke!"

What the fuck?!?

I can't even respond to her. I'm so shocked and beyond upset, I've actually sobered up. I look at how ridiculous Kelly looks. She can hardly stand straight. But she's beautiful. And her body is fit. And my boyfriend has fucked her. I want to scream!

I turn around and walk as fast as I possibly can to get out of the club. Once I'm outside, I keep walking up the street. "Brooke!" Sarah calls behind me. I know she's following me, but I can't stop. I just keep walking. I've been hit with a ton of bricks, and I want to get as far away as I can from the situation.

I finally stop a couple of blocks up the street. I turn around to Sarah, who's just a couple of steps behind me. "What the hell?!" I yell.

"Calm down," she says as she pulls her phone out. "I'm going to text Jaime and tell her we left and make sure Kelly gets home safely. She's too drunk."

Tears start to form in my eyes, and I can't control it. I start crying. "What the fuck, Sarah? She's slept with Ryan!"

She puts her phone away, placing her hands on both of my shoulders, looking me square in the eye. "Calm down, Brooke. She said it's been months, before Christmas. He hasn't cheated on you or anything."

I wipe my tears and nod my head. "I know," I start. "It's just shocking to hear. Ryan knew I was going out with her tonight.

Why didn't he just tell me about their history together?" Then I remember his strange reaction when I first mentioned who Sarah and I were going out with. He had tried to talk me out of going. Holy crap, he didn't want me to find out about them!

"What is it?" Sarah asks. I fill her in on how Ryan acted. Then she says, "You need to call him. Right now. Tell him you know and see what he says." She takes her hands off my shoulders, so I can call him.

I wipe my tears and take my phone out. I'm so nervous. What do I say to him? But I need to know now. I can't wait until I get home. I pull his name up and call. He answers on the second ring.

"Are you on your way home now?" he asks, his voice dripping with sexiness.

"No," I reply. My voice is shaky, so I know he can tell that I'm upset.

"What's wrong?" he asks, sounding panicked. "What happened, Brooke?"

"Nothing," I reply. "I just got some shocking news from our friend, Kelly."

He's silent for a moment, and then all he says is, "Oh." He doesn't say anything else.

"Is that all you can fucking say, Ryan?" I yell into the phone.

"Brooke," he says, sounding nervous. "I never cheated on you. It's been a long time since I was with her."

"When was the last time?" I want to hear his response. I'm hoping their stories match up.

"It's been months. I think the last time I saw her was in December. Definitely before Christmas. I haven't been with *anyone* since then. It's only been you, Brooke."

I wipe away more tears. "She said it started years ago, and you would hook up whenever you came home."

Ryan lets out a breath. "It's true," he says quietly. He takes a deep breath, then pleads, "Brooke, just come home so we can talk in person. Please."

I don't say anything. I just sniff, very unladylike, and wipe my nose and my eyes. I'm a mess.

"Brooke, I would never cheat on you. Please believe me. I don't want anything to do with her."

"Why didn't you just tell me then?" I ask. "When I told you I was going out with her tonight, why didn't you just tell me?"

"I don't know." I can hear the regret in his voice. "I guess I didn't want you to get upset."

"Brilliant!" I exclaim. "Because I'm not fucking upset at all!" My voice is full of sarcasm.

"Come home, Brooke," he replies. His voice is shaky now, and I wonder if he's actually about to cry.

"I'll be home soon," I say, then I end the call. I look at Sarah, and she hugs me.

"I'll get us an Uber," she says.

* * *

Sarah and I are quiet all the way home. The driver drops me off first. Sarah gives me a hug and wishes me luck, before I get out of the car and walk up to the front porch. I unlock the door and walk in quietly, not wanting to wake my parents. Then I go downstairs and find Ryan sitting on the couch in the family room, waiting for me.

He stands and walks to me, wrapping me in a hug. I don't hug him back. I can't bring myself to do it right now.

"Don't hate me," he says quietly, still embracing me. He nestles his head into my shoulder. He's begging for my forgiveness.

I don't say anything. All I can think about right now is him fucking Kelly. How his hands that are around me right now have also touched her.

He pulls away from me and takes my hands. He looks me straight in the eyes, and I can tell his eyes are red and bloodshot. He's been crying. "I should have told you myself," he says. "It was stupid of me, and I should have been honest. I want you to know that I've never lied to you or been dishonest about anything else. I told you that I used to hook up with a lot of women; you knew that. I never thought this would come back to bite me in the ass like this. Kelly was just another girl. She means nothing to me. She was just a distraction for me at the time."

I don't know what to say. I keep looking at him. Do I forgive him this easily? I can't stop thinking about the two of them together. It makes me sick. I know he has been with a lot of women, but before, none of those women had a face or a body that I could picture him with.

"I love you, Brooke. I've never loved anyone like I love you. No other woman in this world compares to you. I don't want my history—and my stupidity—to ruin what we have. Please, *please* forgive me."

I take a deep breath, trying to steady my nerves. "It was shocking to hear it from her," I say. "She told me I was lucky because you're so good in bed."

His facial expression changes from being concerned and loving to being extremely pissed off. "She said what?" he asks, trying not to raise his voice.

I nod. "I believe her exact words were, *you're so fucking good in bed.*"

He lets go of me and runs his hands through his hair. He's really upset. He lets out a deep breath, then turns back to me and takes my hands again. "I am so, so sorry, Brooke. I can't even imagine how mad you are right now. If some guy came up to me and told me that about you, I'd lose my fucking mind."

"She was really drunk," I say. *Why am I defending her?*

"I'm so sorry," he repeats. "What can I do to make you feel better?"

I don't know how to answer him. I'm so tired, mentally and physically. I thought I had experienced my fair share of drama this past year and was done with it.

Suddenly, I'm hit with the realization that if he was not completely honest with me about this, what else could he be hiding from me? I've dealt with enough lies in the recent past with Scott, and I don't want to deal with any more. I feel as if I was so naïve in my marriage, and I'm not the same person I was then. I'm not going to let another man fool me.

Ryan and I fell so hard for each other so quickly, reliving our teenage years. Have I been living in a fantasy, completely fooling myself? Fourteen years is a long time. There's a lot I probably don't know about him. There's a lot he really doesn't know about me, honestly. I'm not exactly the same person I was at eighteen years old.

Ryan tries to wrap me in a hug, but I pull away. I walk across the room to get my distance. "Just leave," I say, trying not to cry again. I keep my back to him because if I look at him, I'll break.

I sense his panic as he strides over to me and places his hands on my shoulders. "Brooke, please–"

"No. Just go." I wipe a tear from my eye, praying he just leaves so I don't have to face him again. I'm done with men keeping secrets from me. I need to end this with Ryan before I fall deeper with him and then learn more secrets from his past.

Ryan takes his hands off me, but I still sense his body there. I can't turn around and look at him. I'm afraid I'll give in and be weak. I have to be strong for myself and Ellie. She doesn't deserve to have another untrustworthy man in her life.

"I love you," Ryan says quietly.

I don't respond. As much as it's hurting me, I have to do this.

We continue to stand there for what feels like an eternity until I finally hear him turn around and leave. When I hear the laundry room door close and I know he left, I break down crying and fall to the floor with my head in my hands.

RYAN

*F*uck! I sit in my truck in front of Brooke's house, contemplating what the hell I should do. I want to go back inside and explain everything. Make her understand I was an ass for not being honest with her. She needs to know Kelly and I were *never* serious. What used to happen between us ended long before I saw Brooke at the gym. I have no desire to ever be with another woman again. *Just Brooke*. We're meant to be together. This can't be happening!

I can't go back inside, though. I don't have a key to let myself in, and I don't want to knock on the door. I might wake her parents or Ellie, and I don't want to do that. Brooke wanted me to leave, anyway. She needs space. I can give her a little time, but not a lot. I need to fix this.

When I get home, I pace around my room, not sure what the fuck to do. If Brooke won't talk to me in person, I can at least send her a text. I take my phone out of my pocket and see I have a few missed texts already. They're not from Brooke, though. They're from a number I don't have saved in my phone, but as soon as I read them, I know they're from Kelly. I had deleted her as a contact when Brooke and I got back together.

. . .

I'm so sorry for causing a problem with Brooke.

I don't have her number to apologize to her.

Will you let her know I'm sorry? I'm stupid drunk right now. I'm really sorry.

Shit. I'm not going to reply to her, though. I only care about talking to Brooke and figuring out how to get things back the way they were. I start typing.

Brooke, I can't apologize enough. Please let me explain everything to you. Nothing was ever serious between Kelly and me. I told you I slept around a lot. Well, she was who I hooked up with whenever I came to Seattle. I can't change the past, but I want you to know that she means nothing to me. You are the only woman I love and want to be with. I should have told you about her, but I was scared and embarrassed to admit it. I wasn't thinking straight, and I didn't want to upset you. Clearly, I made the wrong choice. I will always be honest with you. I have no other secrets. Ask me anything and I will tell you the truth. Always. I love you. Please call me. I want to come over and hold you in my arms again.

I send the text, then sit on my couch, waiting for a response. A minute goes by. *Nothing.* Two more minutes. *Nothing.* Five minutes. *Still nothing.* I wait and wait, but Brooke doesn't text back. I toss my phone onto the coffee table in front of me and get up. I pace around my room a bit more, hoping to hear my phone buzz with a text. *Nothing.*

It's so late, and I know I should just go to bed and get some sleep. I can talk to Brooke in the morning. She's probably asleep by now anyway. *She probably cried herself to sleep.* Fuck! I can't believe I was so stupid!

I strip down to my boxers and T-shirt, then crawl into bed. I can't relax, though. My mind races with all the possibilities of what could happen tomorrow. Brooke could forgive me, or she could decide she's done with me. I can't let my mind go there. I love her too much; we can't be over.

Anxiety takes over, though, and I can't fall asleep. My chest feels tight, and I know I'm in for a restless night of hell if I don't take a sleeping pill. My doctor prescribed them, but I haven't had to take one in a couple of months. Not since Brooke came back into my life.

I get out of bed and go into my bathroom, opening the medicine cabinet and finding the bottle of pills. I take one out, noticing my hands are shaking. Shit. I'm really stressing about this. I haven't felt this anxious in a long time, and I really hope I'm not riddled with nightmares tonight. Part of me doesn't want to fall asleep, afraid of where my unconscious brain might go. But I can't stay awake like this either, letting my mind wander to all the what-ifs.

Popping the pill in my mouth, I turn on the faucet and use my hand as a cup to take a drink. I feel the cold water go all the way down to my stomach. I say a silent prayer, hoping for a good night's sleep.

After checking my phone for a text or call from Brooke and seeing that she still hasn't responded, I crawl into bed and close my eyes.

* * *

The ground is shaking. Fuck, we must be having an earthquake! I jolt upright and find myself in bed. Confusion sweeps over my foggy brain. I'm in my room. It's dark, except for the light from the hallway, illuminating my room, meaning my door is open. I'm wet. Drenched with sweat. And my brother is sitting on my bed next to me.

What the fuck?

"Ryan, you're having a nightmare," Dan says gently. His hands are resting in his lap. He's wearing his pajamas. I look at the clock on my bedside table and see that it's almost four thirty a.m.

Shit.

I rake my hand through my hair and take a deep breath. I was afraid this would happen. I don't even remember the nightmare I was having. Those sleeping pills are crazy sometimes. "Sorry, man," I reply. "I hope I didn't wake up everyone in the house."

"The boys are still in their rooms with their doors shut, so I think they slept through it. Cari's awake, though."

"Fuck. Was I yelling?" Embarrassment washes over me even though I know it shouldn't. If anyone understands these nightmares, it's Dan. He used to suffer from them, too. He's been doing really well the past few years, though.

Dan shrugs his shoulders. "I heard you yelling like you were in distress. I couldn't make out what you were saying, though. When I came in here, you were tossing and turning."

I lay back against my pillow again and rub my face with my hands.

"What happened? Did you and Brooke have a fight?" Dan asks, sounding genuinely concerned.

I move my hands and look at my brother. I don't want to have a heart to heart with him and spill my guts, but I'll give him the basic version. "Yeah. She found out I used to hook up with someone we knew in high school."

Dan's face scrunches up. "Dude, how'd that happen?"

I lean up on my elbow. "Long story. She's fuckin' pissed at me, though. I should have just been honest with her."

Dan stands and looks down at me. "Are you all right? Can I get you anything?"

I shake my head. "No, but thanks. Go back to bed. Sorry to wake you and Cari."

Dan nods his head and walks about of my room, shutting the door behind him. My room is pitch black. I reach over to the bedside table and grab my phone. Still no reply from Brooke. *Fuck.*

I set my phone down and lie in the darkness. I guess it's good that I don't remember the nightmare I was having, but it also leaves me on edge. I haven't had one in so long, and I feel guilty for waking Dan and Cari.

Sleep seems impossible now, but there's no way I'm taking another sleeping pill. I just keep replaying all the events from tonight in my head. Everything that happened from the time Brooke called me at the club in a panic about Kelly to when I left her house. *I shouldn't have left.*

I lie here, my heart pounding from all the worry and anxiety I'm feeling again for what feels like at least an hour. When I look back at the clock, though, I see that only twenty minutes have passed. I need to do something. I can't just lie here, obsessing over what happened and worrying about what could happen tomorrow.

Without really thinking it through, I pick up my phone again and call Brooke. As it starts to ring, I realize what an ass I'm being. It's a quarter to five in the morning. She's probably asleep, and if her phone is by her bed, I'm waking her up now. *Great. Another reason for her to hate me.*

She doesn't answer, so I leave her a voicemail. There's nothing else I can fucking do right now, and I feel so helpless. I'll have to face this all in the morning. Hopefully, Brooke will talk to me, and we can work things out. Otherwise ... I can't even think about that right now.

BROOKE

*E*llie wakes up early the next morning, and I feel like I've been hit by a truck. I fell asleep on the couch for a little while, but I cried most of the night. I also started questioning whether I overreacted with Ryan. I mean, it's not like he cheated on me at all; he really didn't do anything *wrong*. However, he wasn't exactly honest with me, either. Why didn't he just tell me about him and Kelly before? I have been lied to enough in the past by my ex. I don't want to deal with another dishonest man.

My mom notices something is wrong the moment I see her upstairs. "What happened? Where's Ryan? I noticed his truck is gone," she asks, concerned.

I put Ellie in her high chair and go about making her bottle. "I sent him home last night."

"Why? Are you hungover? What's wrong?" Mom is by my side at the counter, obviously very concerned.

I screw the top of the bottle on and turn to her as I start shaking the formula up. "I'm fine. I found out Ryan wasn't exactly honest with me about something, so I made him leave. I don't want to discuss it right now."

I move away from my mom because I really don't want any

sympathy right now. Nor do I even want to talk about all this with *anyone* at the moment. I sit next to Ellie and give her the bottle.

"Well, if you want to discuss it, I'm here," Mom says as she stands

there, looking at me. I can tell she's not sure what to do or say. She knows what I've been through with Scott. I'm sure my mom can tell I don't want to talk right now, and she *gets* me. She knows I just want to be left alone right now.

"Thanks," I say, although I can't bring myself to look at her. I keep my eyes on Ellie. If I look at my mom, I know I'll see her concern and sympathy, and then I'll break down again.

I hear her start to walk out of the kitchen, but then she stops, and says, "I'll watch Ellie for you if you need a break. Just let me know." Then she leaves the room.

I lean my elbows on the kitchen table and put my head in my hands. I really don't know what to do. Do I want my mom to watch Ellie, or do I just want to be alone with Ellie today? Or should I run away for the day and be by myself to think? Maybe I should call Sarah and go see her? I feel at a complete loss.

"Mamamama!" Ellie demands my attention and bangs her bottle against her high chair tray.

I look up at her and smile. Only she can make me smile right now. She's truly adorable, and she's perfect. She's all I need. "What can I do for you, Ellie Bell?"

She shakes her bottle at me and smiles.

"Do you want some Cheerios?"

Ellie smiles big and moves her arms up and down, indicating that's what she wants. I stand and get her the cereal, pouring the little round pieces out onto her tray. She immediately starts eating them, happy as can be. She has no worries in this world. I'm suddenly jealous of her for that.

After showering and getting myself ready for the day, I decide I need to get out of the house and think. I take my mom up on her offer to watch Ellie so I can be alone. I have no idea where I'm going to go or what I'm going to do, but some time to myself sounds like just what I need.

I grab my purse and look for my keys inside. I notice my phone, which I haven't looked at since I got home last night, and I decide to check it. Sure enough, I have several texts. A couple of them are from Sarah.

Call me tomorrow. I hope everything turns out okay. Love you!

Kelly is asking me for your number...

Kelly was asking for my number? Ugh. I don't want to think about her, let alone *talk* to her.

The other text I have is from Ryan. I can't bring myself to read it right now, though. I look to see who called me instead.

Of course, it's from the same two people. I don't want to listen to Ryan's voicemail right now, but I listen to Sarah's. "Hey, Brooke. You didn't text me back. I know you're probably busy talking to Ryan, but Kelly keeps bugging me for your number. I won't give it to her without your permission, though. She keeps calling me, saying she wants to explain everything and apologize to you. She says she didn't mean to cause any harm. She and Ryan were never a couple, and they've been over for a while. Call me tomorrow, okay? Love you!"

I take a deep breath. I don't feel like talking to anyone right now. I can't bring myself to listen to Ryan's voice or read his text. I need to get out of this house and drive somewhere alone.

I hand Ellie over to my mom and leave. I still don't know where I'm going, but I'll figure it out. Heading to I-5 and deciding to go north, I blast the radio. Music usually helps clear my mind.

I turn on a country station because that's one type of music Ryan never listens to, so none of those songs will remind me of him.

A couple of miles down the interstate, Zac Brown Band's "Toes" comes on the radio. At first, the cheeriness of the song makes me want to change the station. I'm not in the mood for it. But then the "tropical vibe" of the song and thinking about the beach makes me realize where I need to go. Alki is not a tropical beach, but it's one of my favorite places in Seattle.

It's an overcast day—typical of Seattle this time of year—but it's not raining. The gray sky mimics my mood. I feel so let down by Ryan. Why did he have to hide this from me?

Maybe his text or voicemail have an answer.

My subconscious needs to shut up. I can't bring myself to read his text or listen to his voice yet.

When I arrive at Alki, I'm pleased to see it isn't terribly crowded. On a sunny day, this place would be crawling with people, but today, I find a place to park right away and hardly anyone is on the beach. *Perfect.*

I grab my crossbody purse and put it around one shoulder, get out of my car, lock my door, and start walking. I love this part of the city. The Olympic Mountains are to the west, and the Seattle skyline is to the east. Ferry boats carry cars and passengers across Puget Sound between Seattle and Bainbridge Island. I love it here even when the weather isn't perfect.

Walking along, I try to come to a conclusion. Should I just forgive Ryan? My biggest fear is that there's more he hasn't told me. I can't be in a relationship with someone who isn't completely truthful and open with me. I thought we had that. I thought Ryan was my dream come true. Now I'm afraid I was wrong.

There's an abandoned fire pit ahead of me. Someone must have had a bonfire last night, which is common here. There's a large piece of driftwood, like a makeshift bench, next to the pit, and I decide to sit down. It reminds me of when I was a kid, and my parents would bring my sister and me here sometimes. Dad would build a fire, and we'd make s'mores. Those were good times.

That's what I need. My sister's advice. Becca always knows the right thing to say, and she knows me better than anyone. I pull my phone out of my purse and call her. It's Sunday, so she shouldn't be at work today.

"Brooke!" Becca exclaims happily when she answers the phone.

"Hey!" I try not to sound as depressed as I feel.

"What's up?"

"Oh, nothing. I just wanted to talk to you!"

"What's wrong?" Becca asks, noticing the edge in my voice even though I tried to mask it. Even from the other side of the country, she can always tell when I'm upset.

I groan in frustration. "Why do men have to be so stupid?"

"Oh crap," she says. "What did Ryan do?"

I tell her everything that happened last night. I'm anxious to hear her reaction to it all. I value Becca's opinion. I always have.

After I finish explaining, there's just silence on the other end of the line. "Well?" I ask her, waiting for her to say something.

Becca lets out an audible breath before she speaks. "Well, I think that the first thing you need to do is read his text and listen to his voicemail."

I roll my eyes.

"Then," she continues, "I think you should get back in your car and drive over to Ryan's house and have a nice, long grown-up conversation with him. Then take him back."

"What?" *Did she really just say that?*

"You heard me," she says. "I think you're making a huge mistake if you let Ryan go over this. Talk to him. Clear the air. Make him promise he's not keeping anything else from you, then take him back."

This isn't exactly what I was expecting to hear. "Just like that? Take him back *just like that?*"

"Yes!" I can hear the frustration in my sister's voice. Am I really being that ridiculous? "Listen, Brooke, I know you and Ryan were meant for each other. I could have told you that in high school. He didn't cheat on you. He just made a stupid mistake by not telling you something, but he didn't *lie.* Talk to him. As long as he's not hiding anything else from you, and as long as you feel like you can trust him, *take him back!*"

I groan in frustration. "But that's the thing," I reply. "How do I *know* he's being truthful with me and not hiding anything else? How do I just take his word for it?"

"Oh dear," Becca says with a sigh. "Scott really did a number on you, didn't he?"

"What do you mean? Of course, he did! He fucking lied to me, and we lost everything!"

"Listen to me," she continues before I can get another word in. "Scott was an asshole. Screw him! But Ryan is *not* Scott! I know I haven't seen Ryan since high school, but from everything I've heard from you and Mom and Dad over the past few weeks, Ryan is the perfect guy for you! You need to trust him."

I don't know what to say. Is she right? I do value her opinion, but I didn't expect her to be so *Team Ryan* right away. Honestly, I thought I'd have a little backup on my side. Now my mind is all jumbled again.

Suddenly, I hear another voice on Becca's end of the line. It's a male voice. *That* gets my attention. "Who's that?" I ask her. As far as I know, she's not dating anyone.

"Oh," Becca says, sounding guilty, "that's my friend, Jack."

"Your *friend?*"

"Yes."

"Are you at home?"

"Yes."

"And Jack is there just … hanging out?"

"Yes."

"Why are your answers so short all of a sudden?"

"Okay, look," Becca replies, but this time it sounds like she's talking with her hand over her mouth. "It's nothing really, just a friends-with-benefits thing."

"Oh, *really?*" Something tells me it's more than that. Friends with benefits in the middle of a Sunday afternoon?

"Yes. Kind of. I'll talk to you later. Promise."

"Oh, you bet we will," I say to her, laughing a little. My mood is lifted a bit.

"Okay," Becca says in her normal voice again. "I'll talk to you later then."

"Love you. Thanks for your advice, by the way."

"No problem," Becca replies. "Love you, too. Talk to you later!"

I hang up and look out toward the water. There's a small break in the clouds, and I see some blue sky. I think about what my sister said, and I decide she might be right. I look down at my phone again and open Ryan's text.

Tears form in my eyes as I read it. I know he really loves me, and I really love him. How did everything get so messed up so quickly?

I open my voicemail and listen to the one he left me at a quarter to five this morning. *Why the hell was he up at that hour?*

"Hi, Brooke," he starts. His voice sounds so sad. "I can't sleep. I don't know why I called you this early because I wasn't really expecting you to answer. I just hoped to hear your voice and maybe get to talk to you, but I understand why you're not answering. Fuck, you're probably asleep. Anyway, I can't say I'm sorry enough. I want you to know how much I love you. Of all the things I've done in my life, I only have two real regrets that I wish I could take back. The first one was breaking up with you fourteen years ago. I've regretted that every day since it happened. Seriously, Brooke, if I could go back in time and change things, I would've insisted we find a way to make our relationship work because our relationship *does* work. We're meant to be together, and I don't want to lose you again."

Now I'm really crying. I wipe the tears from my eyes as I continue to listen to the rest of his message.

"The second regret I have is not being honest with you about Kelly. I should have told you before you went out last night. Actually, no, I should have told you back when I was telling you about the relationships I had and the women I slept with. There's no excuse for it. I'm a dumbass. And now that I'm thinking about regrets, I have a third. I regret ever sleeping with anyone other than you. I'm serious. You're the love of my life, Brooke. It makes me sad to think of all the time we missed with each other, and I'm sorry that I can't say I've only ever been with you. Please don't leave me now. I want to love you for the rest of our lives. We belong together. Call me back, please."

I'm speechless. He really does love me, and I really do love him. I need to see him, *now*. I wipe my eyes again and put my phone back in my purse. Then I head back to my car.

When I arrive at Ryan's house, Cari is in the front yard pulling weeds out of the flowerbed. She waves when she sees me pull into the driveway. I get out of the car and walk to say hi to her. She stands up and smiles at me.

"It's good to see you," she says as she wipes her forehead with her arm. She has gardening gloves on that are covered in dirt. "Ryan's upstairs in his room. I haven't seen him all day."

"Okay," I say. I'm not sure if she knows what happened.

"By the way," she starts again. "It's none of my business, but I know something must have happened between you two because I heard him come home late last night. Plus, I think he had a nightmare. He hasn't come out of his room all day, which isn't like him, either."

Suddenly, I'm concerned. "How do you know he had a nightmare?" I ask. That's one of his PTSD symptoms, although he hasn't had one since we've been together. I've never witnessed him having a nightmare.

"He was yelling," she replies, looking concerned. "It woke Dan up, too. He went into Ryan's room and woke him up. They talked for a while."

I look down at the ground. I feel awful. I love him so much, and it hurts me to know that he was going through this because of our fight.

"Hey, things happen," Cari says, trying to make me feel better. "It's not your fault. Dan used to have nightmares. They weren't always triggered by us having an argument, but I could count on him having one whenever we had a fight. It was scary, and I always felt so guilty. They're triggered by stress, so whenever we had a disagreement or he thought he might lose me, it stressed him out enough to cause a nightmare."

Her words help me feel a little better. She's been through this, too. "Thanks," I tell her. "I'm going to head up to Ryan's room and see how he's doing."

She smiles and nods her head, then goes back to her flower garden.

I decide to use his private entrance from the back porch. When I reach the door, the curtains are closed, so I can't see inside. I knock on the door and wait. No one answers, so I knock again. Still nothing. I pound a little harder, and he finally opens the door. He looks relieved the second he sees me. And he looks disheveled as though he just got out of bed. He's squinting from the outside light.

"Hi," he says.

"Hi. Can I come in?"

He steps aside so I can walk in. I put my purse down and turn to look at him.

"I was hoping I'd hear from you today," he says, moving closer to me.

"Did you just get out of bed?"

He stops about a foot in front of me and looks down at himself. He's wearing sweats and a white T-shirt. His hair is a mess. "Yeah, I couldn't sleep last night."

"I had a hard time sleeping, too," I admit.

If I'm being honest with myself, he actually looks sexy as hell right now. It's taking all my strength not to jump on him and kiss him. If I'm going to get through a serious conversation with him, I need to keep my distance, so I decide to go sit on his couch.

"Can I get you something to drink?" he asks as I sit down.

"No, I'm fine. But thanks."

"Did you get my messages?" he asks as he sits on the couch as well. We're at opposite ends away from each other. We're both sitting with one knee bent, facing one another.

"Yes, I read your text," I reply.

"What about my voicemail?"

"Did you have a nightmare this morning?" I ask him, changing the subject. I'm really concerned about him, and I want to get things out in the open.

He looks taken aback. "Why do you ask?"

"I saw Cari outside, and she said you did."

Ryan looks down at his hands. Then he runs them through his hair and leans back against the couch. "I get them when I'm stressed. I'm so worried about us."

"I'm sorry." I scoot next to him, wanting to be closer to him now.

Ryan looks at me, confused. "You're sorry? For what? I'm the one who's sorry."

I reach out and put my hand on his arm. "I'm sorry that I kicked you out of my house last night and caused you stress. I'm sorry you had a nightmare."

He takes a deep breath and takes my hand off his arm, linking my fingers with his. "Did you listen to my voicemail?" he asks again.

I nod my head and look down at our joined hands.

"I'm sorry, Brooke." He reaches out and places a finger on my chin, lifting my head up to look at him. "I love you so much. Don't ever doubt that. And don't ever apologize for stressing me out. You didn't cause my nightmare. It just happened. I don't want you to ever feel like it's your fault when I have one."

"But—"

"But nothing," he cuts me off. "I love you, Brooke. Do you still love me?"

I melt at his words and the love I see in his eyes. Before I can answer him, though, I need to know everything is out in the open. No more secrets.

"Ryan, I need to know I can trust you. Always. I need to know you're not hiding anything else from me. I've been lied to enough."

"I know. I understand now why you were so upset with me," he says. "You've been through enough with your ex, and I want you to know that I will *never* lie to you. I will *always* be honest with you."

"I didn't realize how hard it would be for me to really trust people after what Scott did. It's a real issue for me." I look down again, holding back tears.

Ryan kisses the top of my head. "I'm so sorry."

I look into his eyes and see his love for me. I see the sadness he's feeling. I see the boy I fell in love with in high school, who has become a hardworking, respectable man. A man I still love. I can't imagine my life without him now. I lean in and press my lips to his.

My phone starts to ring. I ignore it and keep kissing Ryan. My phone finally stops, but just a couple of seconds later, it starts ringing again. "You should get that," Ryan says to me as he pulls away so I can go get my phone out of my purse.

I don't recognize the number on the screen, but it has a Portland area code. I answer it.

"Brooke?" I don't recognize the man's voice, but he sounds panicked.

"Yes. Who is this?"

"It's Brady Danner. Listen, something's happened to Scott."

My stomach flip flops, and I sit on Ryan's couch again. Brady is Scott's good buddy from work. They went through the academy together years ago, and he's the one Scott has been living with. If he's calling me, it must not be good. Panic starts to set in.

"What happened?" I ask him, my voice shaky.

"He was shot."

BROOKE

hree hours later, Ryan and I are crossing over the Columbia River into Oregon. We'll be at the hospital soon. After I got off the phone with Brady, Ryan got dressed and we left immediately. I called my parents to let them know what happened, and they said they'd watch Ellie for me as long as I needed. I also called Becca and Sarah to let them know what happened. I needed something to keep me occupied in the car as Ryan drove. Calling and talking to them somehow made me feel calmer than when I was just sitting in the truck watching the scenery go by.

I feel totally helpless.

We've been quiet during the drive. If I'm not on the phone with someone telling them what happened, Ryan and I don't talk much. There's not much to say anyway. My ex-husband has been shot, and I don't know his condition. My mind is spinning. I may not be married to him anymore, but we had over a decade together that was full of love and happy times. We have a daughter together. *He has to be okay.*

I wish he was in the hospital where I used to work. If that

were the case, I could call Amber and try to get more information on his condition. But he's at another hospital, one that specializes in traumas like this, and I don't know anyone who works there.

When we get to the emergency room, we see news reporters waiting outside. It's weird to think they're here because of Scott and the other officers. Of course, police officers being shot on the job make for a big news story. I feel like I've entered an alternate universe. None of this can really be happening.

Scott and his fellow officers were ambushed. They responded to a 911 call for a domestic dispute, and when they arrived, the man inside the house opened fire. One officer died at the scene. Scott and two others were hospitalized. Scott's in critical condition.

Ryan and I walk into the hospital and immediately see several police officers there. They all look distraught, and it makes me feel sick. Brady walks over to greet us. His eyes are bloodshot. This is not good.

"How is he?" I ask him.

Brady pinches the bridge of his nose with two fingers and closes his eyes. When he opens them again, he looks me in the eye and places his hands on my shoulders. "We haven't heard anything in a while. All we know is that he's still in surgery right now."

I suck in a breath. Brady sets his arms back down, and Ryan puts an arm around my shoulder for comfort.

Brady motions toward some empty chairs nearby, and Ryan leads me over to them. The three of us sit down. Brady is on my left, and Ryan is on my right.

Brady continues, "All I know is that he was shot more than once. He's a fighter. He'll pull through."

This can't be real.

Tears start to run down my face. Being here with all these uniformed officers, as well as others in plain clothes, reality sets in. How could this happen? Scott has a daughter. Ellie needs to grow up and know her dad. Even though our relationship fell apart, he *was* my husband. I *did* love him for over ten years. This was one of my biggest fears when we were together, but I never really thought it would happen. Even with his dangerous job, I took for granted that he would always be here.

We sit in silence for a few minutes. I'm silently praying that Scott pulls through. Ryan's arm is still around me, holding me close. I lean my head on his shoulder. I'm so relieved to have him in my life. What happened last night doesn't matter anymore.

Just then, I look across the room and see a strawberry blonde woman sitting in a chair, hunched over with her elbows on her knees, hands covering her face, crying uncontrollably. A couple of cops are trying to soothe her. Her husband must have been one of the other officers who was shot. Maybe even the one who was killed. I wonder who she is? She looks to be about my age, maybe even younger.

I just watch her as she is starting to make more noise with her sobbing and drawing a lot of attention. She must have just gotten here? I didn't notice her before although there are *a lot* of people in this room. It would have been easy to miss her.

I turn to Brady. "Who is that?" I ask, pointing toward the woman.

"Oh," Brady says, sounding unsure. He shifts in his seat. I turn to look at him, wondering why he's hesitating to answer my question.

"Who is she?" I ask him again.

His gaze darts from her to me. "That's Lisa …" He just lets her name hang in the air as if I should know who she is.

I look at him, confused. "Lisa who?"

Brady looks down at his hands and rubs them together. Then he looks back up at me, and replies, "I hate to tell you this, but, um … Scott has been dating her."

What? Scott has a girlfriend?

I turn toward Brady, shrugging out of Ryan's grasp on my shoulder. "What? Since when?"

Brady looks hesitant before answering. "Since January."

What the actual fuck?!

"What?" My voice comes out as a whisper, and the tears continue to fall.

Brady continues, "He moved out of my apartment in March. They've been living together since then."

My head is spinning. Why didn't Scott tell me about this? He's been dating her since January? That's before I even moved to Seattle! And he's been living with her for the past three months? I'm finding it hard to control my emotions now. I was sad and worried before, but now I'm feeling enraged! He gave me the third degree when I started dating Ryan, and all along, he's had a girlfriend?!? I was so worried about starting things up with Ryan because I felt it was too soon for me to move on, yet Scott moved on just a couple of months after we separated?!?

I look back at Lisa. She's still crying uncontrollably with several people trying to comfort her. Does she know about me? If she does, does she know I'm here? *Did Scott keep Ellie and me a secret from her, just as he kept her a secret from me?*

I turn back to Brady for answers. "Why didn't Scott tell me about her?"

Brady shrugs. "I have no idea. I'm so sorry, Brooke."

"Does she know about me? That he has an ex-wife?"

"She knows about you and Ellie. I know he told her."

I look back in her direction. I still can't believe this. Lisa must sense that I'm looking at her because suddenly she looks up at me. We make eye contact and just stare at each other for a few moments. Then she stands, and I'm instantly thrown for *another* loop.

She's pregnant.

"Um, yeah," Brady continues, sounding sympathetic. "There's that, too."

I turn to Brady again, the look of shock not leaving my face. *What the fuck is happening?*

"That's why Scott moved in with her," he explains, looking sheepish.

To my surprise, I hear a female voice say my name then. I turn and see Lisa standing right in front of me. I look at her, and she puts her hands on her belly. I can't tear my eyes from her stomach, and she doesn't miss a beat.

"I wanted him to tell you," she says, still sobbing.

I just stare at her, unsure of what to do or say. Ryan squeezes my shoulder, and I take that as a sign that he's here for my support.

My mind is racing.

What do I say to her?

Surprisingly, I'm not really *angry*. How can I be angry with her at a time like this? Scott is in critical condition, fighting for his life right now! She must be hurting as much as I am, if not more. Yet she had the courage to walk over to me just now.

I decide to do the only rational thing I can think of. I stand and hug her. It takes her by surprise, but then she wraps her arms around me and hugs me in return. We stand there together and just cry for several minutes before we finally pull apart and sit down together.

Brady lets Lisa have his seat, so she and I can talk.

"I'm sorry we had to meet like this," she says, wiping the tears from her eyes. "You probably have a lot of questions."

"You could say that," I say, chuckling. "How did you and Scott meet?"

"We met on New Year's Eve. At a casino." She looks at me as if she knows mentioning him being at a casino will sting.

She's right. His gambling addiction ended our marriage.

"He got help, you know," she adds.

I knit my eyebrows together, not sure what she means by that. "He got help with what?"

"His gambling addiction. He hasn't gambled in months. He went to counseling."

To say I'm shocked would be an understatement. I think I've had my fair share of surprises to last the rest of my life. "When? How?" I ask her. I had no idea Scott finally admitted he had a problem and got help.

"I discovered he had an addiction shortly after we started seeing each other. I told him we couldn't continue dating unless he got help. I guess he was finally ready to admit he had a problem, and he agreed to go to Gamblers Anonymous."

I don't think my eyebrows can go up any higher than they are. *She convinced him to get help?* He wouldn't listen to me, his wife of nine years, but a woman he had just started dating was able to get through to him? I'd be lying if I said I wasn't upset about that. This hurts! Weren't Ellie and I good enough for him to want to quit?

Lisa continues, "I think he just realized that if he already lost his wife and daughter over gambling, and now I was calling him out on it as well, then he must really have a problem and needed help."

I take a deep breath, trying to process all this new information. Scott has had a girlfriend for over five months now. She convinced him to get help. He no longer gambles. She's pregnant.

Not to mention the awful news that brought me here in the first place. Scott is still fighting for his life in the operating room right now.

But what Lisa just said to me makes sense. Maybe it wasn't that Ellie and I weren't enough for him to want to quit. Maybe it was the fact that he already lost us and was about to lose the new woman he liked if he didn't get help.

I look down at my hands. I try to focus on what all this means. I'm in love with Ryan now. I really have no reason to be upset with Scott. I should be relieved and happy for him, actually. He stopped gambling, he has a new girlfriend who obviously cares about him, and he's expecting a new baby.

Fuck.

I should be happy, but why did he keep all this a secret from me?

I look back at Lisa. "Why didn't he tell me any of this?"

She shakes her head. "I don't know. I kept telling him to, but he kept putting it off. I think he was afraid of your reaction, honestly. He didn't want you to be upset."

I shake my head. "I can't believe all of this."

"I'm truly sorry, Brooke."

Ryan has been quiet all this time until now. "How far along are you?" he asks Lisa.

Lisa looks down and rubs her belly with one of her hands. "Four months. I'm due in November," she says, looking back at Ryan and me.

I quickly do the math in my head. That means she got pregnant in February? They weren't together very long before that happened.

Lisa continues, "I know things have happened quickly between us. We obviously didn't plan the pregnancy, but I feel as if it's a blessing. I think it's another reason he agreed to get help."

I nod, still trying to process all this newfound information.

We stay in the waiting room for quite a while along with all the other officers, waiting for answers about Scott's condition. It seems to take forever. We get an update on the other two officers first, who aren't in as bad of shape as Scott and are expected to make a full recovery. But we continue to wait for news on Scott.

Ryan takes me to the cafeteria to eat. We don't talk much while we're there. I'm just so overwhelmed. I call my parents to let them know what's going on, and I also fill my mom in on Lisa. She's as shocked as I am.

Ryan and I go straight back to the waiting room again after we eat. Everyone is still waiting for a doctor to give us news. I notice Lisa has some friends, or maybe family members, there to support her now. I also see that Scott's sister is here, and she's sitting with Lisa. *So his family is aware of his new relationship.*

His sister comes over to give me a hug and talk. I've always liked her. She's obviously stressed and worried about her brother. Their parents are on their way here from Florida, but their flights take a lot longer than her flight from Idaho did. They should be here by tonight.

Finally, hours after we arrived, a doctor comes in with news. He speaks to Scott's sister, Lisa, and some police officers while the rest of us wait. Then they share the news with everyone else.

He's expected to make a full recovery!

He has a long road ahead of him, but he's going to be okay. He's not going to be paralyzed, and he didn't suffer any brain damage.

I hug Lisa. I'm relieved for her. She won't have to go through the rest of her pregnancy or raise their baby alone.

Ellie pops in my head. She won't have to live in a world without her father.

I feel for the family of the officer who didn't make it. This attack was a huge loss for the community. It's making national headlines, too. There are news crews all around the exterior of the hospital.

Ryan and I decide to stay in Portland for the night, so he makes a hotel reservation. Since we didn't bring anything with us, we find a Target and buy pajamas, toothbrushes, and other necessities. I don't know how long we're going to stay down here, but hopefully, we can head home tomorrow. Now that we know Scott is going to be okay, I really don't *need* to be here.

My parents agree to watch Ellie for me, and Mom takes tomorrow off to stay home with her. I feel bad that she has to do that, but she insists it isn't a problem.

When Ryan and I go to bed that night, he instantly pulls me against his body. I love the comfort he brings me, making me feel secure and loved. He kisses my forehead. "I'm so sorry about everything that happened, Brooke."

"It's okay," I reply as I wrap my arm around him and lay my head on his chest. This is all I need right now. Just him. This is the first time we've really been alone since we arrived in Portland, and I've craved this closeness. The past twenty-four hours have been beyond stressful, but now I'm starting to feel at peace.

We lie together in silence. The lights are off in our room except for the lamp beside our bed. I can hear his heart beating, and it calms me. I run through all the events of the day in my mind. First, having to deal with the fallout Ryan and I had last night.

God, was that just last night? It feels like a lifetime ago.

Then, immediately after we made up, I got the phone call about Scott, so we rushed down here. Finding out about Lisa, as well as the fact she's pregnant, just added to the overload of emotions I felt. Did all this really happen in just *one* day?

Then it occurs to me; I never answered Ryan's question when we were at his house. He asked me if I still loved him, and I never told him before Brady's phone call interrupted our talk. Now that I think about it, I haven't told him I love him at all today. I need to tell him *now*. If there's anything I've learned today, it's that life can change in a heartbeat.

"Ryan?" I hope he's still awake. I sit up and look down at him. He looks at me, lovingly, and reaches up to tuck some of my hair back behind my ear.

"Yeah?" He sounds tired.

"I love you," I say to him.

"I know that, baby," he replies as he strokes my cheek with the back of his hand.

"I never told you today, though." I brush my hand through his short hair.

He leans up on his elbow so we're face to face. "Brooke, you've had a hell of a day. It's okay. I understand. I know you love me, and I love you."

"You asked me at your house, and I never answered you. I never want you to doubt how I feel."

He reaches out and pulls my head down to meet his. His lips brush against mine but don't lock in a kiss. "I love you," he says before his mouth claims mine. Our tongues tangle together sensually. I'm overcome with emotions and pouring them all into this kiss.

Ryan pulls my body on top of his. We keep kissing, and our hands are roaming, groping, and caressing each other's bodies. After all the sadness, brokenness, guilt, and anger I have felt today, this is the release I need. This is *exactly* what I need. Ryan's love.

I sit up and tug on Ryan's shirt. I try to take it off, but he doesn't move to help me. He gently grabs my arms and stops me instead. "We don't have to, Brooke," he whispers. "It's been an emotional day."

"I don't care." He might be trying to be a gentleman, but I *need* him! "You're right, it *has* been an emotional day. But this is the only emotion I want to feel right now. We're alone, and I just need to feel you. I need to know we're okay, and I want to show you how much I love you. Please, Ryan."

I don't have to say anything else to convince him. Ryan loosens his grip on my arms, sits up, and drags his shirt off. Then he pulls my shirt off and drops it to the floor along with his. He stays sitting, with me straddling his lap. Reaching up, he puts his hands on either side of my face, pulling me in for another kiss. He holds me there, kissing me hard, and again, I'm letting go of every emotion I felt today.

My hands find his chest and caress him slowly. His skin warms my fingertips as I trace every dip between his muscles. Ryan's hands skim down my sides, tickling me and making me squirm on his lap. I grind against his hard-on, and I moan at the contact. His hands move to my front, kneading my breasts and pulling on my nipples enticingly. God, he knows how to make me feel good.

I lower my hands to try to pull down his boxer briefs. It's hard to get them off while I'm sitting on him, but I manage to get them down far enough. I wrap my hand around his dick and stroke him, causing Ryan's head to fall back. A moan escapes his mouth. I lean forward and kiss his neck.

"Fuck, that feels good," he says as I taste his skin and work his cock with my hand.

Ryan's hands continue to touch me as well, working me into a sexual frenzy. The need I have for him to fill me right now has never been greater. I know it's because of everything that happened last night and today, and this is the only way to make me feel like everything is all right again.

"I need you," I whisper to him.

He looks at me, a sated look on his face. I'm still stroking his cock, and his fingers are still twisting my nipples. We just look at one another with hooded eyes, enjoying each other's touch.

Finally, he replies to me. "I fucking love you, baby. God, I need you."

His hands trail down my stomach until he reaches my underwear. Thank God I decided not to buy pajama pants to sleep in. I settled on a long T-shirt-style nightgown when we were at Target. Since I'm straddling him, though, there's no way to pull my underwear off unless I get off him, and I'm not willing to do that right now.

"Just pull them to the side," I say to him, desperate to have him inside me already.

Ryan doesn't do that, though. He uses both hands to grip one side of my underwear and rips them in half. Then he does the same to the other side as well. Hell if this isn't one of the hottest things I've ever had a guy do to me! Then he slides my ripped panties out from under me.

I don't waste any time. I know I'm wet enough and ready, so I grip his cock and slide right onto him, both of us moaning into each other's mouths as I kiss him again. I ride him hard and fast. My breasts rub against his chest, and his hands grip my ass.

Ryan's mouth trails down my neck, licking and sucking all the way to one of my nipples. I arch my back, shoving my breasts closer to his mouth. He gives both breasts equal attention, sending waves of pleasure throughout my body.

"Fuck me," I whisper to him. "Harder."

Ryan stops and looks me in the eye. He stills my hips from moving.

"Brooke, I don't want to fuck you," he whispers to me, then he kisses me. "Not after everything that happened last night and today," he says before kissing me again.

We stay like this, not moving our bodies, just sweetly kissing for a few moments. It's such a contrast from how we were just having sex. He's still inside me, but he's gripping my hips, not allowing me to move.

When he pulls his lips away from me, he rests his forehead against mine, and says, "I want you to know that I'm here for you, Brooke. I want you to know that I love you, and that I love making love to you. But I need you to know that even when we're fucking, I'm still loving you. And I never want to hurt you during sex or any other time. But if you need me to fuck you hard right now to help you deal with today's events, I'll do whatever you want. Because I'll do anything to make you feel better."

I'm breathing hard, and his words only make me want him more.

Tears threaten my eyes. I can't help it. I am feeling so much right now, and I *need* him to understand where I'm coming from. "I love you so much it doesn't matter if we're making love or fucking. It's all the same to me. I just need to feel your body as close to mine as possible. That's how I know I'll be okay, when you're loving me."

Ryan doesn't waste another second. He kisses me again and carefully flips me over so he's on top. Then he makes sweet love to me.

"I love you," he says to me between kisses. He's moving at a slower pace than we were before, being gentle and taking his time with me. "I'll still fuck you if you want, but I think this is really what you need right now."

How does he know exactly what I need better than I know myself? My emotions are still on overload, and tears roll down my cheeks.

Ryan kisses every inch of my body he can as he slides in and out of me at a slow, delicious pace. He wipes away my tears, lightly strokes my hair, and continues to whisper, "I love you," to me between his sensual kisses.

My first orgasm comes out of nowhere. He keeps the same, slow pace, and eventually, I come again at the same time Ryan pours himself into me.

I thought Ryan and I had made love before, but this ... This is beyond words. I can't even explain the emotions I felt; it was so intense.

* * *

The next day, Scott's sister texts me, asking me to meet them at the hospital. *Them* being Scott's parents, Lisa, and herself. Ryan and I check out of the hotel first. We already decided that we'll drive home tonight so my mom can return to work tomorrow.

I haven't seen Scott's parents since Ellie was born. They came to town right after I delivered her, but that was obviously before our plans to divorce. Of course, I'm friends with his sister on Facebook, but I haven't had any contact with his mom and dad since we split. I was a little worried about how they would treat me at first, but they were just as warm and loving toward me as they always were.

His parents are also just as nice to Lisa. This was the first time for them to meet although they knew about her already. *Unlike me.* I suppose it's a good thing they get along since Lisa is pregnant with their grandbaby.

Apparently, everyone in Scott's family knows about Lisa being pregnant. Not only that, but everyone's also aware of their plans to get married around Christmas. That's one piece of information Lisa failed to tell me yesterday. So not only does Scott have a girlfriend, but she's also pregnant with their child and they're engaged to be married.

As we spend time in the hospital with Scott's family and Lisa, I realize that I really like Lisa. If we'd met under different circumstances, we'd probably be friends. This is important to me, considering she's going to be Ellie's stepmom once they tie the knot.

When Ryan and I finally get back to Seattle, he drives to my house. It's almost nine o'clock when he pulls in the driveway. We go inside and find my parents in the living room with Ellie. I'm so happy to see my baby girl that I sit down on the carpet and scoop her into my arms. She has no idea how drastically her life could have changed yesterday. Luckily, her dad will be around to see her grow up.

Ryan and I visit with my parents for a while, filling them in on Scott's condition. I also tell them all about Lisa. My parents are surprised with all the news, to say the least. They're also relieved Scott's going to be okay.

After my parents excuse themselves to go to bed, Ryan and I take Ellie downstairs. I change into my pajamas, then I get Ellie ready for bed. After I tuck her in her crib, I find Ryan in my room. We cuddle together on my bed.

"Thank you," I say to him.

"For what?" he asks.

"For taking care of me."

He kisses the side of my head. "That's what I'm here for."

"I love you," I tell him.

"I love you, too."

We sit in silence for a while then, just holding each other. I almost fall asleep, but then Ryan speaks again.

"You know we can give Ellie siblings someday, too."

His statement takes me by surprise. It's completely out of the blue.

I sit up and look at him. "What made you think of that?"

He shrugs. "I don't know. I had a feeling it was bothering you a little."

I had never told him this, but he knows me so well. He's right that I was sad I wasn't giving Ellie a sibling myself. I never mentioned it because I thought it made me sound selfish.

"We should get married first, though," he continues. "I like to be traditional." He closes his eyes like he's resting. As if he didn't just discuss marriage and babies with me!

I just look at him. I don't know what to say. Of course, it makes me happy to hear him talk about our future together, but I'm speechless.

He opens one eye, and adds, "That's not my proposal, though." He opens his other eye and smirks. "Trust me, when I propose to you, it'll be more special than us sitting in your bedroom on a Monday night."

I lean down and kiss him. It's the only logical thing I can think to do. I love him so much, but words have escaped me.

We kiss for a bit before I pull away and find the words to continue our conversation. "I don't want to have another baby until Ellie is two or three years old."

"I think that's a good idea," he agrees with a smile on his face. Then he kisses me again.

"You're so good to me," I say against his lips.

"That's because you're good to me," he replies.

"I mean it," I tell him, pulling back a bit. "The past couple of days were beyond stressful, and you've been here for me the entire time. Not only that, but you also treat Ellie like she's your own daughter. I love you."

"I love you, too," he says as he leans in and kisses me.

I realize then that I've never been happier in my life. I have everything I need. Ryan and I found our way back to each other. Everything feels as if it's clicking into place, just the way it was always meant to be.

EPILOGUE

*E*llie's first birthday party is a complete success. With the help of Sarah and my mom, I pulled it off without a hitch. Ellie seems to have a good time, too. Sarah's kids and Dan's boys were the only other kids there, but there were several adults. Becca is visiting from New York, and Scott and Lisa came, too.

Ryan's parents came over as well. It was a little strange to have them in the same room with my ex and his fiancée, but everyone was cordial with one another.

Scott is still recovering from the shooting, but he's doing all right. He can walk, but he needs to use a cane for now. He's expected to make a full recovery and be able to go back to work within a few months; although he'll be assigned to light duty until his body is strong enough to go back on the street again.

Of course, everyone spoils Ellie today. She receives a ton of cute clothes and toys for presents. She's in seventh heaven playing with them all. Now that she's walking, it's hard to keep her in one place. Her toys are spread all over the family room. It looks like a toy bomb went off.

Lisa and Scott play with her on the floor. She has started

accompanying Scott on his visits since his accident. Lisa is good to her, and Ellie's warmed up to her quite easily.

After all the presents have been opened and the cake has been eaten, Scott and Lisa say goodbye and leave. They have a long drive back to Portland. Scott's pain meds also tend to make him drowsy.

Everyone else is still here, hanging out in the basement with us as Ellie and the other kids play on the floor. It's crowded, but everyone is talking and enjoying themselves. We could have had the party upstairs, but I didn't want to make a mess in Mom and Dad's living room. Since Ellie started walking, we spend more time with her down here, where things are more babyproof.

"It looks like you need more space," Ryan casually says as he's sitting on the floor in front of me on the couch.

I sigh. "I wish. All these toys make our living space seem smaller and smaller."

"It's only going to get worse. Trust me," Sarah, who's sitting next to me, chimes in.

I shake my head at her. "That's because you have three kids. I still only have one."

"For now ..." Sarah says, wiggling her eyebrows.

I pick up the throw pillow I'm leaning against and hit her with it. She laughs at me.

Ryan starts talking again as he turns around and rests his arms on my legs. "Well, I think I have a solution for your space issue," he says. He's kneeling on the ground in front of me and moves closer, wrapping his arms around my waist.

"Oh, yeah? What's that?" I ask, smiling and wrapping my own arms around his neck.

"We can move in together. Get a bigger house."

The only noise in the room is coming from all the kids playing. All the adults are now silent and looking at Ryan and me. Did he really just suggest we move in together?

I'm speechless. We've talked about this before, but as something we'd do in the future. We both wanted to save money first.

My heart is racing, and I can't help the huge smile that spreads across my face. I lean closer to him, and say, "I love that idea." Then, in front of our family and friends, I kiss him.

Everyone claps, hoots, and hollers for us. My cheeks flush, but I don't care.

Dan exclaims, "Get a room!"

Everyone laughs, including us, causing us to end our kiss. Once he pulls himself together, Ryan continues. "I'm glad you've agreed to live with me, but that's actually not going to be good enough." He pulls away from me, leaving me totally confused. I watch as he reaches into his cargo shorts pocket. All the while, I'm trying to figure out what he meant by what he just said.

Suddenly, Ryan adjusts the way he's kneeling in front of me by lifting one knee off the floor.

Holy shit.

He holds out a ring, which is what he must have pulled from his pocket. My hands fly to my face, covering my mouth. I'm stunned. *This is happening!*

"Brooke, I've loved you since we were teenagers," Ryan starts, looking at me with so much sincerity that I feel tears forming in my eyes. "I believe fate brought us back together after being apart for so long. I can't imagine living my life without you and Ellie in it. Will you do me the honor of being my wife?"

I'm aware that we're surrounded by our closest friends and family, but I tune all them out. Focusing only on Ryan, I process everything he's just said to me. I move closer and wrap my arms around him. "Of course, I will," I say before I kiss him again.

Everyone else in the room claps and cheers for us once more. When we finally pull away, he puts the ring on my finger. It's a beautiful, large round solitaire diamond on a gold band. It's perfect.

Ellie makes her way over to us and tugs on my leg. I pick her up and set her on my lap. "Look, Ellie Bell," I say as I show her my ring. "Ryan's officially going to be your stepdad."

Ryan kisses Ellie on the cheek. She smiles and squeals loudly. Then she squirms for me to set her down again, going back to playing with her toys. Immediately, all our friends and family offer their congratulations.

Surrounded by our family and friends, I realize life is better than I ever imagined it could be. Everything happens for a reason. The years Ryan and I spent apart were meant to be that way. He served our country while I married the man who gave me Ellie. Life's circumstances led us both back to Seattle and to each other. Fate. Destiny. Kismet. Whatever you want to call it, I know that the cards weren't stacked for Scott and me while Ryan and I *were* meant to reconnect again.

It's as if life is one giant puzzle. Each major event that's happened, and every important person who has come into my life laid their pieces into place, adding to my big picture. Ryan just never set his piece down when we were eighteen. He held it, keeping it close to his heart all these years. Now I finally have that missing piece I always needed. I can't wait to see what the future holds for us and to lay the rest of the pieces into place with Ryan by my side.

The End

ALSO BY C.L. COLLIER

Discovering Us Series

Finding Our Rhythm

Worthy of Love

Meant to Be

Discovering Love - A Discovering Us Series Collection

The Vagabond Series

Passion in Paris - this book also has connections to Stacking the Deck!

Belize Bliss

Cancun Crush

What I Never Knew Series

What I Never Knew

What I Never Knew I Wanted

What I Never Knew I Needed

Summers in Seaside Series

Summer Magic

Summer Craving

Summer Break

Harbor

Seasons of Love Series

Holly

Summer Love (A Summers in Seaside and Seasons of Love Crossover)

Autumn

April

Hot Vegas Nights Series

Playing Vegas

Visit C.L. Collier's web site

ACKNOWLEDGMENTS

I have so many people I'd like to acknowledge for their endless support. Thank you to my beta readers for always reading my unedited versions, giving your honest feedback, and putting up with me. 😜

Thank you to my kids who tolerate me writing and working on "author stuff" all the time. You're both great writers yourselves, and I hope you continue to enjoy it. 🩶

Thank you, again, to Amy Queau of Q Designs for designing another beautiful book cover! And Jenny Sims of Editing for Indies – you always make my words sound better so my stories don't suck! 😆

Finally, I'd like to acknowledge all my readers. Thank you for reading my books! I truly appreciate your support and hope that you enjoyed Stacking the Deck! 😊

ABOUT THE AUTHOR

C.L. Collier is a USA Today Bestselling Author who lives in the beautiful Pacific Northwest. She was raised in the Seattle area, and although she lives closer to Portland, Oregon now, she frequently visits the hometown she loves. When she's not writing, you can find her reading, watching her favorite sports teams, spending time with her family, or going to concerts. She likes her music loud, wine and coffee sweet, and her books steamy.